[the]
money
shot

Glenn Deir

BREAKWATER
P.O. Box 2188 | St. John's | NL | Canada | A1C 6E6
www.breakwaterbooks.com

LIBRARY AND ARCHIVES CANADA CATALOGUING IN PUBLICATION
Deir, Glenn, 1958-, author
The money shot / Glenn Deir.
ISBN 978-1-55081-657-0 (paperback)
I. Title.
PS8607.E4824M66 2016   C813'.6   C2016-905776-3
Copyright ©2016 Glenn Deir
Cover Photo ©Shutterstock | Vlad_Nikon

We acknowledge the support of the Canada Council for the Arts, which last year invested $153 million to bring the arts to Canadians throughout the country. We acknowledge the financial support of the Government of Canada and the Government of Newfoundland and Labrador through the Department of Business, Tourism, Culture and Rural Development for our publishing activities. PRINTED AND BOUND IN CANADA.

Canada Council   Conseil des Arts
for the Arts   du Canada   Canadä   Newfoundland Labrador

MIX
Paper from
responsible sources
FSC   FSC® C016245

Breakwater Books is committed to choosing papers and materials for our books that help to protect our environment. To this end, this book is printed on a recycled paper that is certified by the Forest Stewardship Council®.

For Bryan Hamilton
A fine shooter and an even better friend

money shot

noun

1:    the scene in a pornographic movie in which a male actor ejaculates
2:    a very important, impressive, or memorable picture or scene

Merriam-Webster Dictionary

[one]

Sebastian Hunter needed God to reach down from the heavens, tap the house, and finish the job. Just his index finger would be fine, the one Michelangelo painted on the ceiling of the Sistine Chapel, the same one that created Adam. The house refused to topple. It defied the law of gravity. The situation called for divine intervention.

"What's holding it up?" asked Sebastian.

Bruce rocked back from the viewfinder of his Sony high-definition camcorder. The camera stared forward, motionless, locked on the tripod.

"Stubbornness?" suggested Bruce.

"Doesn't it know I have a deadline?"

Police Line—Do Not Cross fluttered between Sebastian and the slanting house. He stood at the end of the driveway. Red bricks with splashes of grey led up to the danger zone.

It had been the Andersons' "dream home." A two-storey colonial with cedar shakes, nestled in old-growth forest atop a steep headland that offered panoramic sunsets over Paradise Point.

That was before the storm.

On the map it was called Loon Bluff. The less-charitable locals had turned that into Loony Bluff. The Andersons had been warned not to build there. Sebastian heard the I-told-them-so chorus all day.

The bluff always had a reputation for tumbling rocks, but the Andersons couldn't resist the view. They built twenty metres from the bank, a sensible and safe distance they thought. Neither they nor their architect had counted on Tropical Storm Fran.

Fran had blown through only yesterday and she made quite the impression. Gale force winds whipped up the bay. Waves as big as buses pounded the bluff, chewing their way inland. Torrential rain soaked the ground and turned the soil into soup. Landslides lopped off the Andersons' front lawn, dragging a slate patio and matching Adirondack chairs to their demise. The storm gnawed at the earth underneath the basement, tearing off chunks.

Word quickly spread around town that something bad was happening to the Anderson house. Dozens of gawkers gathered for the deathwatch, smart phones at the ready. Their tweets and posts acted like chum to the sharks of the CBC newsroom. Sebastian could smell blood.

He and Bruce had hit the road before sunrise. They arrived in time to capture the house tipping forward. Boards snapped viciously enough to make children cover their ears. It should have slipped over the edge, the way a sinking ship slips beneath the waves. A smooth descent into the abyss, but the house would have none of it. It stopped sliding and teetered on the rim.

"A million-dollar home is on the verge of being swallowed up by a million-dollar view," said Sebastian.

●

Monotony deserved to die. Sebastian juggled words, looking for just the right combination to amuse himself. He didn't notice three men in hard hats and safety vests walking down the road.

"Don't get any closer," barked one of them.

Sebastian glanced back only to discover the rebuke was directed at a teenage girl posing for selfies while leaning backwards over the police tape. A posse of paparazzi couldn't have generated as many camera clicks.

"Kids today," said Sebastian, shaking his head with mock disapproval. "Such narcissists."

"Are you the same Sebastian Hunter who said, 'Vanity, thy name is TV reporter.'?" asked Bruce.

"Yes, but does Instagram really need more *I'm Awesome* pictures?"

Sebastian watched the hardhat trio drift away. Each had a reflective yellow X on his back. XXX. Side by side they walked up the hill, superimposing themselves against the dawn sky. XXX over crimson.

"Amsterdam's red-light district," exclaimed Sebastian. "Inspiration at last."

Sebastian needed an audience; even an audience of one would do in a pinch. You can't waste a good line on just yourself. Bruce's face was jammed against the viewfinder. Sebastian whispered, "Do you know what porn and TV news have in common?"

Bruce's closed eye popped open. He pulled back from the viewfinder and shook his head. There was no turning back to the camera until Sebastian uttered his quote of the day. A quote that would delight Bruce's black humour. A quote you would never say into a microphone.

"Someone's going to get fucked and you'd better get the climax on camera."

Bruce covered his mouth to stifle his laughter. The camera's microphone might hear. Such a sound at such a time would not do. Better to leave it for the sanctuary of the cameramen's room.

"How much longer?" Bruce asked quietly. Sebastian shrugged. Bruce checked the record light for the umpteenth time. It blinked on. His picture was sharp. No need to adjust the focus. The audio metre bounced with the wind. What he needed was a climax. And until it happened, the camera would roll.

Sebastian could tolerate surliness, disinterest, timidity, boredom, even the occasional episode of sloth, but missing the money shot— never. There'd be hell to pay. A full-blown rant in front of the entire newsroom about how he had been sabotaged by incompetence. Sebastian always got the video he demanded. It wasn't worth the grief to do otherwise.

The impending calamity electrified Twitter. Sebastian's hashtag #HouseOfCards was trending. Re-tweets burst with OMG and WTF hysteria. He had the Twitterites hooked. Now he had to deliver the goods.

Sebastian extended his index finger, lining up the tip with the lopsided roof. He pushed down.

Come on, just let go.

●

Sebastian hit End Call with panache. "Thank you, God, thank you, Jesus," he said, lifting his eyes to the heavens.

Bruce stopped inserting fresh batteries into the wireless microphone. "What's up?"

"The premier and that house have a lot in common. Both are hanging on by their fingernails and both will fall."

"What have you got?" Bruce mimicked Sebastian's eagerness.

"Too early to say. It's just a tip, but a good one. I could be calling sources right now if not for bloody radio."

CBC Radio demanded to be fed. The beast had a voracious appetite; it devoured news every hour. No matter how many baskets of stories reporters dumped into its gaping maw, it could never be sated.

Sebastian compared radio to a fruit fly—a nuisance and impossible to swat. What a waste of time to describe what pictures could easily show. His future father-in-law called radio the senior service. Sebastian called it the senior-citizen service. News for the horse and buggy crowd. Despite his best attempts at ridicule, The Desk still insisted on a live report during *Radio Noon*.

Notwithstanding his disregard for the visually reluctant, Sebastian would not have anyone say he mailed it in. He had professional pride. If grandpa and grandma needed a picture painted he would paint a masterpiece.

The space between the basement and the floor joists looked like a V lying on its side. Sebastian held up a protractor borrowed from a retired geometry teacher down the road, lining up the cavity with the degrees.

"Unbelievable. Thirty degrees. Bruce, that house is tilted thirty degrees."

Sebastian had an angle of inclination but who besides math geeks would understand. Certainly not the boss's mother. Evan Forbes often demanded rewrites with the admonition, "Mom won't get it." A seventy-year-old woman, whose comprehension faltered after knit one purl one, was an unseen guardian of clarity for Canada's public broadcaster.

Still, Mrs. Forbes was a useful yardstick. If she could grasp a concept, anyone could. Sebastian needed a common item to illustrate the angle. Something simple for listeners to imagine.

Nothing popped into his head. Perhaps Warren Zevon could bring out an idea. Sebastian opened the music icon on his iPhone. Zevon was a favourite. Sebastian admired his bizarre lyrics, his dark humour wrapped up in rock and roll. Zevon wrote about an excitable boy.

Well, he went down to dinner in his Sunday best.
Excitable boy, they all said.

Sebastian hit pause. "He went down to dinner…stairs."

A quick Internet search on his iPhone told him the typical staircase was thirty degrees. Even Evan's doltish mother could picture a house sliding down a staircase.

Sebastian felt like an excitable boy.

●

If anyone could make soil erosion sexy, it was Sebastian Hunter. The trick was to ignore soil erosion, more specifically the geotechnical analysis. Sebastian interviewed a geologist prattling on about a silt-clay matrix, glacial sediment, and wave action; an explanation only the U.S. Army Corps of Engineers could possibly understand, or care about. Normal eyes glazed over. Sebastian could at least fake interest. He opened his laptop and scanned the ten-minute interview with the jargon-riddled geologist before homing in on the ten seconds he could actually use.

"Nothing but a miracle can save that house," said the geologist, his voice trailing off. "It's just a matter of time before it topples over. I wish I could do something, but I can't."

Sebastian had a reputation for getting good clip, and that was good clip. No need to ask another question. Thank the guest. Down tools.

Compassion from an expert was a small coup, but Sebastian knew he needed more than that to make the victory bells peal. The house in peril had owners. Getting the distraught couple on camera would put a lump in the province's throat. Sebastian had them in his crosshairs.

"Get 'em while they're in shock," he muttered to himself.

The Reporter's Creed guided all of Sebastian's actions. The longer upset people think about a request, the less likely they will agree to it. So make the approach early, be empathetic, and push gently. The technique rarely failed him. Battered women, grieving parents, scammed investors. Sebastian had convinced them all to expose their wounds on TV.

John Anderson stared at his listing house, his arms wrapped around his wife, her face buried in his chest. He rubbed her back with soothing, almost indiscernible movement. All filmed at a shrewd distance, a zoom lens catching every tear running down Beth Anderson's cheek. Sebastian waited until they broke apart to sidle over.

"Mr. and Mrs. Anderson, I'm Sebastian Hunter with CBC News. I'm terribly sorry for all that's happened."

"Please," Mr. Anderson said, holding up his hand to signal stop. "We just want to be left alone."

"I understand that. I don't want to make your lives more difficult than they already are, but your house is news across the country. Millions of people, millions of home owners, are worried about you. They want to know if they can help."

"We have all the help we need," said Mrs. Anderson. "The police, the fire department, government officials, our neighbours—they've been wonderful. We can't thank them enough."

"You can thank everyone through us," said Sebastian. "I've seen dozens of people in hardhats around here today. I can't imagine you've met all of them. Use us to send a message. Let them know how much you appreciate what they're doing."

Mrs. Anderson dabbed her eyes. "I don't think I could get through an interview without breaking down."

Exactly what Sebastian wanted to hear. He was counting on tears, but squelched any trace of enthusiasm for her grief.

"I'm not here to make you look bad. If you feel you can't go on, we can stop the interview and let you compose yourself."

Mr. Anderson touched his wife's face and wiped away a tear with his thumb. "It's up to you, honey."

"I'd ask a few questions about what happened, what this place means to you and the gratitude you have for the folks trying to help. You don't have to answer any question you're not comfortable with."

"If we talk to you, won't everyone else want an interview too?" asked Mr. Anderson.

Time for the clincher assurance. "Probably, but you don't have to give them one. You're under no obligation to talk to anyone, including me. You could say, 'We already talked to the CBC and that's our only interview today.'"

Mrs. Anderson sighed and looked at her condemned house. Mr. Anderson ran his fingers back through his grey hair.

"My camera is just right over there. We'd be done in about five minutes."

Mrs. Anderson bit her lip. "Let's do it, John. People have been so good to us."

"Are you sure?"

She nodded and pulled a tissue from her pocket.

"I'll be right back," said Sebastian. He strolled over to Bruce and gave him a discreet thumbs-up.

•

Sebastian's scoop demanded his TV script be overhauled. *Here & Now* viewers deserved uncomplicated, catchy words to complement the gripping video. Time to put pen to paper, though in his case it meant finger to iPhone. He resisted pointing out the irony of Paradise Point in the opening line. Where was the sport in that? He could do better. Give the viewer something clever, something bordering on the poetic. He always read his script out loud. The words had to sound spoken, not written. The ear was the best judge.

They say home is where the heart is.

Both home and heart are broken in Paradise Point.

Still, he couldn't ignore the irony altogether. He'd work in a reference somehow.

Living in a fool's paradise.

"Cruel." He wagged his finger at his iPhone. "Viewers would be offended." He deleted the words as quickly as he had typed them.

Trouble in paradise.

"Pedestrian. Every hack songwriter uses it."

Paradise lost.

"That's the one." Sebastian felt pleased.

"You know, one day that phone is going to talk back to you," said Bruce.

"It already is. It's saying, 'If it's good enough for John Milton, it's good enough for me.'"

"You're writing for the eggheads at the university now?"

"Bruce, I'm trying to raise standards here. It's an epic poem and even though nobody's ever read it, everybody knows the title. The great unwashed will get it. And if any of the pipe puffers are watching tonight, they just might snort approval. It's not the fall of man; it's the fall of a man's house."

And what a day for a fall. The sky was royal blue. The bay belonged in the Caribbean. Turquoise and inviting. A light breeze occasionally caused ripples.

A thunderous rip filled ears. Heads wrenched with whiplash speed. Sebastian gasped. The diagonal house slid, tearing away from the foundation. It plunged towards rocks with the vertical form of a diver wanting a smooth entry into a pool. A skeleton of floor joists whooshed past the edge of the cliff. Crunching and splintering echoed round and round the bluff. The house growled.

Sebastian made a fist, cocked his arm and dropped it.

"YES-S-S-S-S-S."

His fingers madly typed a note to The Desk.

Fire up the bird. House is gone. Have the Money Shot.

Sebastian ran to the satellite truck. "CNN, here I come."

•

Paris in the spring. Was there anything more pleasant? Janice Stone didn't think so. She savoured duck confit and sautéed potatoes, complemented by a glass of Bordeaux from Saint-Emilion. No need to rush. Her flight out of de Gaulle was hours away.

"Regarde ça!" said a male voice behind her.

Janice turned to see a couple at the next table, the beau pointing at the bar, his lunch date heeding his advice. Janice followed suit and saw a bartender mesmerized by a TV sitting on the beer cooler. It showed a house at an odd angle; Sebastian Hunter appeared on the screen.

"Monte le volume!" shouted Janice.

No one moved to turn up the sound. Janice bolted to the bar. The woman on TV sobbed as her husband held her close.

"This house was our dream home. We put our heart and soul into it. I can't believe this is happening."

"I built that house with my own hands. Countless hours of sweat and toil, and for what? I was supposed to die in that house. Now it's the house that's going to die."

The camera gently zoomed back from a stand of maple trees to the sloping house. Sebastian's voice drifted over the Parisian bar.

Paradise Point is now Paradise Lost.

John and Beth Anderson are being cast out of their own Garden of Eden.

The bartender turned up the volume just as gravity hauled the Andersons' house from the foundation. The rumble filled the bar. Sebastian's voice track was silent. When you have the money shot, the best words are no words at all.

"Incroyable!" said the bartender.

"Yes, it is unbelievable," said Janice. She picked up her phone and texted Sebastian.

Saw you on TV in a café along the Seine.

Congratulations, you bastard.

•

Sebastian's phone dinged as he left the washroom. It was a herogram from a producer in Toronto.

Your story had it all.

Jaw-dropping video, real people, ingenious writing.

Easiest vet of my career.

Sebastian enjoyed the flattery, but didn't take such gushing too seriously. The same producer would have savaged him if the bosses at *The National* had uttered a disapproving word.

In the frantic pace of the day he had forgotten to show Bruce the only compliment that mattered. He skimmed his phone along the bar. It stopped precisely in front of the cameraman, like a curling stone drawing to the button.

"All those hours at the shuffleboard table weren't a complete waste," said Sebastian, sitting on the stool. "The virtues of a misspent youth."

Bruce picked up the phone, read the screen and handed it back. "Hell hath no fury like a woman scooped."

Sebastian made a happy sigh. "Janice will never take another vacation."

A bartender approached with two cognac glasses swirling mahogany-coloured liquid. He laid them in front of the barflies.

"Remy?" asked Bruce.

"No, it's Ron Zacapa—rum from Guatemala." Sebastian signed off his tab.

"Rum with no Coke?"

"So little breeding for such a good cameraman. It's better than cognac. It's my celebration drink."

Sebastian and Bruce clinked glasses. Sebastian cupped the snifter in the palm of his hand to circle the rum. He sniffed deeply, letting the glass linger under his nose for a few moments before taking a sip.

"Gorgeous," said Sebastian, as if snuggling with a lover. "You know, they age this stuff on top of a mountain. Twenty-three years above the clouds before it comes back down to earth. That's a pilgrimage I have to make some day."

"After today's story, CBC should fly you there in style."

The puffery got no response. Sebastian gazed past Bruce, smiling at a redhead sitting at the end of the bar. She wore a black dress with a V-neckline and lace sleeves. She smiled back. Her dark eyes said, *Come over.*

"Behind you is a stunning woman," said Sebastian. "She's a Siren singing to me."

Bruce didn't bother to turn around. He had seen that look on Sebastian's face before. "I think I'm about to be thrown overboard." He tossed back a little rum. "Don't forget, we have a chopper booked for eight."

Sebastian sailed over to the woman. He took a seat and sat straight up. She leaned forward. Laughter and smiles peppered their conversation. Her shoe dangled on the end of her foot. Sebastian loosened his tie. She pushed her glass of wine away. They slid off the stools, but Sebastian held back, letting her head to the door first. Her flaming hair swept across her shoulders. A text message left the bar as soon as he did.

Sebastian must be lonely. He picked up a redhead for company.

●

From the air, the Andersons' house looked remarkably intact, despite the fact it was sitting on its roof. Still, it was clear the house had taken a terrible beating. The front wall was torn away, holding like a drawbridge halfway through being let down. Holes had been punched in the floor.

"It must have rolled over twice," said Sebastian into the microphone attached to his headset. The pilot nodded. He made his helicopter hover above the crater left behind when the water receded.

Look at the size of it, thought Sebastian. Big enough to swallow twenty houses.

He tapped Bruce on the shoulder. "Just like Santorini," he said, making a circular motion with his finger. "At least when the volcano blew, the Greeks got a fabulous lagoon out of it."

The playful waters of the Aegean were nowhere in sight, just pools of muddy overnight rain, whipped up by the downdraft of the whirling blades. Jagged boulders dotted the depression. Mountain climbers would have needed ropes to scale the cliff created by the landslide.

"That used to be a grassy slope right to the water," said the pilot. "People would picnic there."

"Look over there," said Sebastian, pointing to a pile of lumber and plywood away from the house. "Probably a shed. I saw one go down in the home video."

"I'll grab a shot just in case we need it," said Bruce. He lurched to the right as the chopper jarred to the left. "Any chance you can hold it steady?"

"Best I can do," said the pilot. "The wind is banging us around a bit."

Bruce braced his shoulder against the door and waved his hand forward. The chopper arced around the basin. Bruce twisted to keep the house in his shot as they flew by.

"Great viz," said Sebastian, "but what am I going to do to put a lump in their throats tonight?"

"Not my department," kidded Bruce. "Try lingerie."

"I wish," said Sebastian, remembering the night before.

•

The sun wasn't cooperating. Sebastian was backlit, making his face dark to the camera. Bruce fussed with a round reflector, warping the silvery fabric to bounce sunlight into Sebastian's face. The shadow disappeared. Sebastian squinted until his eyes adjusted.

"A man with your supernatural power," Bruce said, "should hold some sway over the sun."

"I'm only a god to women."

Bruce laughed and let the reflector fall to his knees. Sebastian's face went black again, but his grin betrayed how pleased he was with his hyperbole.

"Pride is the worst of the seven deadly sins," warned Bruce.

"I'm sure a particularly warm corner of Hell has been reserved for me. On the plus side, you'll be roasting by my side."

"I can't see enough of the house behind you. I'm going to move up the hill."

Bruce held the reflector like a steering wheel and with a couple of contortionist arm twists the flexible ring collapsed in on itself. "Bring this," he said, handing the shrunken reflector to Sebastian. Bruce grabbed the camera handle, put his free hand under the tripod head and lifted the whole contraption. Sebastian sauntered behind, practicing his script by talking to the wind.

"John and Beth Anderson must pick up the pieces of their lives without picking up the pieces of their house. It's not safe to go down there. The earth is still angry and can't be trusted…. Are you ready, Bruce?"

"Almost. I need a white balance."

Sebastian offered a toothy smile, the sort found on Colgate commercials. He was blessed with TV teeth alright—straight and snow-white. Sebastian loved to flash them and his smile melted hearts nightly.

"Very funny," said Bruce.

Sebastian flipped open his reporter's notebook and held it in front of his nose. A ridiculous-looking but vital step to ensure that his teeth or any other part of him wouldn't have a blue tint. Bruce zoomed into a blank page and filled his screen with white. A simple button push locked the colours of Sebastian's rainbow into place.

Bruce unfurled the reflector with an abracadabra flick of the wrist

Sebastian took a breath and gazed into the camera lens.

"John and Beth Ander—" The corner of his eye caught movement. A cat scooted behind Bruce, brazenly marching towards the barricade tape.

"Bruce, the cat."

Bruce dropped the reflector and swung the camera round. The cat pranced like a trotting race horse, with its tail and ears pointing straight up. It paced under flapping yellow tape emblazoned with the word Danger, snaked around rubble and dodged a piece of two-by-four with nails poking out. The cat froze at the brim of nothingness, peering over the edge. It crouched and leapt.

"I hope curiosity doesn't kill the cat," said Sebastian. "Let's see what it's up to. I'll grab the sticks."

How many times had they done this cha-cha together? Bruce flicked the quick-release and bolted with the camera. Sebastian cradled the tripod in his arms and matched Bruce step for step. They skirted around the circumference of the flickering barrier. They had at least a hundred metres to run before reaching a decent vantage point. Trouble closed in from the side. John Anderson was on an intercept course.

"Mr. Hunter, I want to—"

Sebastian didn't break his stride, pretending not to hear. Anderson scowled and cantered after them.

"This goddamned thing never gets any lighter," complained Sebastian as he spread the tripod's legs. Bruce slammed the camera into place. There was a reassuring click. He checked the bubble level and adjusted the tripod head; the world was now horizontal. Sebastian scanned the cliff.

"Over there, just beyond the shed, almost to the bottom."

Bruce caught the cat in his lens, following the jumps from ledge to ledge. It broke into a gallop down the last incline, stopping by the shed, ears twitching. It ducked inside.

"Can you see it?" asked Sebastian.

Bruce strafed the shed with his zoom lens. "You're not going to believe this. It's not, *look what the cat dragged in*, it's *look what the cat dragged out*."

Sebastian lunged for the viewfinder. He blinked to make sure he was actually seeing what he thought he was seeing—a kitten in the cat's mouth. Momma was climbing out with her baby.

"The news gods are smiling on us," said Sebastian. "*The National*, two nights in a row."

Sebastian could not have scripted the ascent any better. Momma dropped her baby twice, but each time picked up her kitten by biting the nape of its neck. She moved tentatively, choosing a longer route than the one down to avoid jumping over crevices. The cautious trek was agonizingly slow, but minutes could pass in seconds with editing tricks. Video dissolves would shrink the journey into a spellbinding vignette. Sebastian had struck gold.

"Come on," said Bruce, "let's move. She's almost to the top."

Their scramble kicked up dust, some of which blew over Mr. Anderson who had politely stood back watching Sebastian and Bruce get increasingly excited about something.

"I just wanted to say—"Anderson began. Sebastian dodged by and gave a little wave of the hand.

"But—" continued Anderson. Sebastian kept his head down.

The news whirlwind settled on its original spot, eyes and camera riveted on the brink of the hole.

"I really don't like cats, but in this case I'm willing to make an exception," said Sebastian.

John Anderson closed in, back arched, fur standing on end.

"Mr. Hunter, a word please."

Sebastian walked away from the camera, motioning for Mr. Anderson to follow.

"We're recording, so I don't want our voices picked up."

John Anderson was yesterday's star. Right now, he's an aggravation.

"Mr. Hunter, I was extremely disappointed in your story. You said you'd let us say thank you to everyone, but you didn't. Our thank you was cut out. Why?"

"Producers!" Sebastian gave a despairing shrug. "They're impossible to deal with."

"I don't understand."

"I'm not the boss of what gets on the air. A producer vets my script. We fought like cats and dogs. We scratched and clawed each other over every word in the script. I lost."

He peeked over Mr. Anderson's shoulder. Still a cat-free zone.

"We did play your thank you later in *Here & Now*."

"An afterthought. No one else in the rest of Canada saw it. And my sister in London certainly didn't see it."

"London?" Sebastian's eyes popped.

"Yes, she was watching the BBC."

"The BBC." Sebastian's voice rose on C.

"All she saw was poor Beth crying and our house falling over and over. You lied to us."

"I argued to have your thank you included." Sebastian hung his head in sham contrition. "I just feel terrible. I'm not the kind of reporter who goes around breaking promises. I'm truly sorry."

Mr. Anderson straightened his back. His fur lay flat.

Bruce waved an arm. The cat came back, kitten in mouth.

"Do you know who owns that cat?" said Sebastian, pointing at the rising news star.

Mr. Anderson spun round. "That's a stray. It was hanging around our shed just before the landslide. She was yowling. I let her in to get her out of the storm."

"Incredible! What compassion. Giving shelter to a homeless, pregnant cat." Sebastian emphasized homeless and pregnant. "People should know this."

"I don't know." Mr. Anderson squat like a baseball catcher. "Here puss, puss, puss."

The feline rescuer and her charge ignored him.

"They seem okay, don't they?" said Mr. Anderson as he stood.

"I won't let a producer tamper with the story this time."

"Maybe I should just quietly fade away."

"You're modest to a fault, Mr. Anderson. Everyone feels awful about what happened here. Help me show that good has come out of disaster."

"Just a quick interview," said a resigned Mr. Anderson.

•

John Anderson couldn't shake the feeling that he had made a terrible mistake by stepping in front of Sebastian Hunter's camera a second time. He needed a little something to take the edge off.

He poured himself two fingers of Scotch—twelve-year-old Macallan. He loved its vanilla flavour and resolutely believed single malt should be served straight in a tumbler. His hotel room had only plastic cups so he borrowed a real glass from the bar. Macallan could make the most wretched of circumstances tolerable and no doubt these were the most wretched of circumstances. He took an affectionate sip.

"If only I could drink my way out of this mess," he said, admiring its amber colour. He laid his glass by a pile of papers: a letter from the Red Cross, insurance documents, an application for disaster financial assistance. Not one promised a new house. The hotel would be his home, at least for a while.

What did the odious Hunter do with my interview? Mr. Anderson opened CBC's website on his laptop.

PURR-FECT RESCUE:
CAT SAVES KITTEN THAT FELL OVER CLIFF

Below the headline was a photo of a contented cat and her kitten lying in a cardboard box filled with blankets. Momma's newborn snuggled into her belly.

The caption read:

> *Hope feeds while Miss Kitty takes a catnap. The exhausted mother made a perilous trek to pluck her baby from certain death.*

"They have names now?" he snorted.

The story burst with sympathy and admiration for the feline: Miss Kitty the traumatized cat, Miss Kitty the brave cat, Miss Kitty the nurturing cat. John Anderson didn't see his name until two-thirds of the way through. It was attached to a larger-font quote pulled from the story and placed in its own box with giant quotation marks in the background. It screamed for attention.

> *"I had no idea she was pregnant. I just thought she was fat."*
> – John Anderson

Mr. Anderson slumped in the chair. He topped up his Scotch before scrolling to the comments section. The thread went on and on: ninety-eight comments in all.

CatsCradle
Where do I send money? Miss Kitty is a heroine and deserves to be looked after.

BadAss
Bet ya the fat cat who saved his own neck first doesn't care.

HellCat
A heartless bastard who left Miss Kitty and her kittens to die.

DarlingDave
Jumpy Johnny didn't know she was pregnant. Don't be such a sourpuss.

MadDog
If he had any doubt he could have checked her nipples. LOL.

BadAss
He should be flogged with a cat.

CatsCradle
You're as bad as he is. Leave all cats alone.

BadAss
A cat-o'-nine-tails, you moron.

MadDog
Catfight. Excellent. LOL.

ScarlettRed
Meeeoooowww!

DarlingDave
Have a heart. Don't forget, Jumpy Johnny is homeless too.

MadDog
Maybe he could live in a cathouse. LOL.

HolyMoly
Tie him up and let Miss Kitty use him as a scratching post.

BadAss
Where do I sign up? I'm not pussyfooting around.

Mr. Anderson shook his head in disbelief. "I'm a hated man."

He emptied the glass of Scotch and poured another, this time not bothering with any finger measurement. His eyes shifted to the column entitled Must Watch. The headline Born Lucky accompanied a picture of Miss Kitty carrying Hope in her mouth.

Mr. Anderson clicked on the Play Video symbol.

Miss Kitty purred as Hope flopped around before nuzzling into her mother. The kitten suckled with closed eyes, her adorable face filling the screen. Mr. Anderson twitched as he heard Sebastian Hunter's oily voice.

Small enough to fit in a teacup. But already Hope is larger than life. And what a life-and-death story she has to tell.

Home Video flashed across the screen. Mr. Anderson's shed sat on the edge of a bank. A massive chunk of earth tore away from the overhang, triggering the collapse of the entire cliff face. It dropped as if it were an elevator moving to a lower floor. The shed straddled the crack; its front sinking, its back staying put. The video froze and zoomed into the shed's open door. A blurry Miss Kitty shot out in slow motion, catapulting off the ground just as the shed fell into the chasm.

Mr. Anderson was mesmerized by the time-lapse video of Miss Kitty scaling the bluff. He even gasped when she dropped Hope. At the top, men in hardhats cheered; Moms cuddling infants cried.

"The most amazing thing I've ever seen."

"Cats are more human than people."

If that's true, then Miss Kitty must be grieving. She could only save one kitten. The rest of her litter is down there, underneath that rubble.

"They just let them die. It's not right."

"Make the man who owns the shed get them. It's all his fault."

Mr. Anderson's head drooped. *It's all his fault.* The words looped in his mind as he buried his face in his hands. He didn't hear the door open.

"John, are you alright?" asked Mrs. Anderson. He flinched as she squeezed his shoulder.

"You'd think I had put the kittens in a sack with a rock and thrown them off the wharf."

"What are you talking about?" She examined the half-empty bottle of Scotch. "How much have you had to drink?"

"What's wrong with people? No one cares that we could have been killed. No one cares that we lost our house. They're only concerned about a couple of damn cats."

"John, you're not making any sense."

Mr. Anderson glared at Sebastian Hunter's web photo. "How does he sleep at night?"

●

The sailboat shuddered as the bow cut through the surf, coating Sebastian in warm spray. The sun touched the horizon. No doubt the lobster boil had started. The thought of dipping the sweet meat into garlic butter made him salivate. Time to change direction and head back to the yacht club. Sebastian pulled the tiller hard towards him, turning the boat to starboard and into the wind. The sound of fluttering canvas gave way to cellphone vibrations.

Sebastian opened his eyes. His phone quivered on the night table. *Couldn't you wait until I ate the lobster*, he thought. His arm shot out to capture the phone. He held it above his nose, pressed Decline and dropped it on the comforter.

"Who was that?" asked Lindsay.

"A friend. Seven o'clock is way too early for conversation."

Lindsay rolled on her side. She rested an arm on Sebastian's chest, tapping his lips with her fingers. "Peter Mansbridge said your name last night. 'Sebastian Hunter reports.' People coast to coast know who you are. How many people?"

"Millions, if you include the States. CNN picked up the story too."

"You're grinning like a Cheshire cat." Lindsay played with the hair on his chest. "What's it like when they say your name?"

"The first time I heard my name on *The National* it was electric. My skin actually tingled. The sensation made my toes curl. It was like sex. I've never felt more alive."

"And now?"

"It can never be as good as the first time, but I still get a buzz. I love overhearing conversations in bars about stories I've done. I love when people stop me on the street to give me their two cents' worth. I love when the premier goes ballistic because I've embarrassed her again. I'm good at my job, Lindsay. I've made it. I belong."

"And where do I belong?"

Let her down easy. "Lindsay, these last two nights have been spectacular," he said, caressing her cheek, "but I have a life back in the city. It's time for me to go."

A muffled vibration wafted from the comforter. Sebastian pushed the phone into his side, scrunching more batting around it.

"Maybe you should answer that. She's probably worried." Lindsay threw back the comforter and headed to the bathroom.

Sebastian waited until the door closed before grabbing the phone. The screen said ROXANNE. Slide to answer. Sebastian did.

"Hi honey. I've only got a minute. I'm packing. I'll be home this evening."

●

The clerk handed Sebastian his receipt. "We hope you enjoyed your stay here, Mr. Hunter." Sebastian folded the paper and slipped it inside his coat.

"Yes, very much, thank you. Paradise Point is a beautiful spot, except for the landslides."

"Just awful, wasn't it? But that story about Miss Kitty. That was fabulous. My wife is crazy about cats. She cried enough to cause another landslide."

"Don't tell her I said so," he whispered, "but if she's raining tears I'm doing something right." The clerk grinned.

Lindsay stood by the front door. Sebastian mimed drinking a cup. She nodded. He scooted across the lobby towards the café. A sandwich chalkboard by the entrance greeted him with a floral Good Morning and a sketch of a piping-hot coffee.

Sebastian froze. John Anderson stepped out of the café with a coffee cup in each hand. He stiffened as he recognized Sebastian.

"Mr. Anderson, I had no idea you were staying here."

"A homeless man has to stay somewhere," he scowled. "And thanks to you, I have to sleep with one eye open."

"What happened?" Sebastian was good at feigning bewilderment. He already knew where the conversation was headed.

"People want to lynch me."

"Excuse us," said a male voice behind Sebastian.

Sebastian and Mr. Anderson stood aside. A man and a woman with a rotund belly headed toward the café, her bulging girth exaggerated by a stretched T-shirt.

"She's not fat, she's pregnant," said the man with twisted lips. His partner's eyes burned into Mr. Anderson as she tottered by.

Mr. Anderson's hands shook, coffee sloshed out of the pinholes in the cup lids. "Everywhere I turn there's venom."

"Producers, again," said Sebastian, throwing up his hands. "I told them, 'The man's been through enough. Don't kick him when he's down.' I pleaded with them. But they wanted the anger; they wanted the nastiness."

"You fed them poison. You filled them with hate."

"They completely ignored your kindness. I don't understand people. It's disgraceful."

"I've lost my home," said Mr. Anderson, his voice quavering. "The insurance company has wiped their hands of it. They call it an Act of God. No one is offering me anything except bile."

"Insurance companies are in the business of screwing people. My father was a lawyer and the stories he told me about insurance companies would make you blanch. Their behaviour is appalling. Somebody should stand up to them."

"Somebody," Mr. Anderson said flatly. "Did you have anyone in particular in mind?"

"I know these last couple of days have been rough on you. I know you've been unhappy with the CBC's coverage, and rightly so. But think of the greater good. You can be a champion for everyone who's ever been shafted by those greedy bastards."

Mr. Anderson ground his teeth.

"Do an interview with me," cajoled Sebastian. "We can make this right. Let me help you."

"I think you've helped me enough already. My coffee is getting cold." Mr. Anderson headed to the elevator.

Sebastian checked the time and weaved through a train of hotel guests and luggage to rejoin Lindsay.

"What was that all about?" she asked.

"Some people don't appreciate what I can do for them."

•

Sebastian dropped his suitcase in the front hall. Roxanne bounced towards him, offering a kiss with her hug.

"It's nice to be home," said Sebastian. He dropped a hand and squeezed a buttock.

"Stop that," Roxanne said softly. She pointed at the wall separating the front hall from the dining room. "Company."

"Who?"

"Dad's in town, so I invited him and Donna over for supper," said Roxanne.

Oh no! Dozy Dan and Dour Donna. Two members of Roxanne's family on the same night, either of whom could suck the air out of a room. Together, suffocation was guaranteed. Still, it could have been worse.

"Where's your mother?"

"She's busy tonight. Choir practice."

Thank God for small mercies. No Prudish Penelope tonight. Sebastian followed Roxanne into the dining room. Dozy Dan and Dour Donna stood by the china cabinet sipping red wine.

"Dan, how nice to see you."

"And you, Sebastian." The two men shared a warm handshake.

"Donna, so glad you could make it." She turned her cheek. Sebastian gave her an air kiss with the flimsiest of hugs. Roxanne handed Sebastian a glass of Bordeaux.

"A toast," said Dan. "To family and the ties that bind."

They clinked glasses. "You certainly love that toast," said Sebastian with a strained smile. "You use it every time we get together."

"That's not often enough. There's nothing more important to me than family."

"Back and forth to Toronto every week is a tough slog," said Sebastian. "And expensive for the Holy Mother Corp. I'm surprised CBC doesn't make you move."

"They bring it up from time to time. I keep saying no. We're not giving up our house and garden."

"Oh yes," said Sebastian, "the famous strawberries. I can't wait."

Sebastian sipped his wine, watching the bird of prey out of the corner of his eye. Donna opened her talons.

"Sebastian, I hear you were into the red in Paradise Point."

"Excuse me?"

Donna crossed her arms and smiled smugly. A kill with just one swoop.

"If you mean red hot, was I ever. Got two stories on *The National* and CNN."

"That's not what I was referring to," cawed Donna. "I heard you were bankrupt, morally bankrupt."

"Donna," admonished Roxanne.

"That's okay, Roxanne. She's right. I was a red rag to a raging bull."

"What do you mean?" inquired Dan.

Sebastian relayed the story of the reviled Andersons and his tense encounter in the hotel lobby. He portrayed Mr. Anderson as a bull trying to gore a matador.

Dan and Roxanne tut-tutted; Donna rolled her eyes.

"By the sound of it, it wasn't just his house that went over the edge," said Donna. "You must have done something wrong."

"I'm sure Sebastian was only doing his job," said Roxanne. "And he doesn't have the last say about what gets on the air. Now, could we please have an evening without an argument over the ethics of journalism?"

"*Ethics*," shrieked Donna. "*The ethics of journalism.* That must be the world's shortest book. The opening sentence goes, 'Find people in misery, and make them more miserable.'"

Roxanne and Sebastian dropped their heads. It would be a long evening.

"Your cat story," interrupted Dan, "was the talk of the newsroom in Toronto."

Sebastian felt himself grow taller.

"Real cute story," added Dan.

Sebastian bristled at the word cute.

"I was too busy to see it myself, but everyone said it was riveting. They were pointing at the monitors."

"I didn't think you ever left the tenth floor of the Broadcast Centre. What were you doing mixing with the peons?" It was a running joke between the two men—reporter vs. vice-president. Sebastian always got the better of the banter.

"I was just passing through. A bit of trouble in the Jerusalem bureau. I can't get into it."

Sebastian tucked the nugget away. Such intelligence would be fodder for gossip or advantage.

A timer beeped in the kitchen. "Dinner's ready," said Roxanne.

"I'll help you, sweetheart," offered her father.

Sebastian's eyes pleaded, *Take me with you.*

Roxanne ignored the signal. "Try to get along while we're gone." The resignation in her voice indicated that she thought prospects for peace were slight.

Donna laid her wine glass on the white tablecloth. She said nothing until a pot cover clanged in the kitchen.

"I keep hearing things about you that I don't like," she said.

"Don't believe everything you hear."

"I don't want my sister hurt."

"Neither do I. I love Roxanne."

"You love yourself."

"It's better than self-loathing."

The kitchen crew reappeared carrying bowls brimming with cubes of beef, diced carrots and pearl onions, all resting in a rich, brown sauce.

"Take a seat everyone," said Roxanne.

"Beef bourguignon," said a beaming Sebastian. "My favourite." He winked at Dour Donna.

[two]

The *Here & Now* newsroom was a paradox: a place mired in disasters, scandals and corruption, yet it looked like it should be selling home insurance. A sea of identical cubicles built with waist-high, grey panels and vanilla desks. Sebastian's cubicle was as bland as the rest, devoid of colour apart from a red chair.

A few deft maneuvers with the mouse and he had a new collection of photos for his screensaver. The folder was entitled Money Shots. He set the slide show speed at medium: the space shuttle Challenger exploded high above Earth, a young man blocked a column of tanks in Tiananmen Square, United Airlines Flight 175 slammed into the World Trade Center, John and Beth Anderson's house slid into a crater.

"That's a little pretentious, don't you think?" said a familiar voice beside him. "Your falling house deserves the same status as a terrorist attack which kills over three thousand people?"

"I'd put *your* world-famous money shot there if you had one," Sebastian replied without looking at the speaker. "Welcome home, Janice."

"I bought you this." Janice handed him a snow globe containing the Eiffel Tower, Notre Dame Cathedral and the Arc de Triomphe.

"Oh, you shouldn't have." Sebastian shook the globe like he was trying to thicken a can of cream. A blizzard swirled around the Paris icons.

"I was torn between that and a pair of boxer shorts with a Metro map printed on them. I figured the boxers wouldn't be appreciated at home, so I went with traditional tacky."

"It's a classic and deserves a place of honour." Sebastian turned to the souvenir corner of his desk and opened a space between a monkey's face carved out of a coconut and a cigarette lighter sporting a picture of a smiling Chairman Mao with the phrase Better Red Than Dead.

"A rose between two thorns."

He peeked at the wall clock. 9:30. "Meeting time." He grabbed a gift-wrapped box as he stood.

"What's that?" said Janice pointing.

"A birthday present for Evan. Something befitting a man of his age."

Sebastian and Janice walked side by side down a hallway lined with award certificates in glistening silver frames. "My heart is still on the French Riviera," she said. "I saw Tom Cruise on the red carpet in Cannes. I tried not to swoon, but dizziness was in the air."

"Angelo should have been there to catch you, but I hear it didn't work out. He seemed like a decent guy."

"What would you know about decency?"

En garde, thought Sebastian.

"Angelo, decent? He dumped me over the phone. Took the dog and walked out the door before I got home."

"I guess he decided which bitch he wanted to live with."

Janice's jaw dropped. "Touché." She bowed her head. Match— Sebastian.

"Did you find Jean Reno on that beach? Inquiring minds want to know."

"I had fun. A girl can only mope for so long. It's amazing how Chablis and sunshine can cure the blahs."

A chatter of multiple conversations greeted Sebastian and Janice as they walked into the boardroom. Such boisterous din in such boring décor. Empty beige walls, except for a white board and a sixty-inch flat-screen TV used almost exclusively for video conferences.

Sebastian and Janice took the last empty seats around the table. A full house meant trouble—a slow news day. No one out the door yet. The crowd was its usual mix of producers and reporters, though producers outnumbered reporters two to one. The habitual imbalance fuelled what's-wrong-with-this-place rants whenever reporters gathered for happy hour. The boss producers sat at the far end of the table behind open laptops.

"The power couple looks unhappy," whispered Sebastian. Executive Producer Evan Forbes and his news wife, Zoe Patel, were engaged in quite a bit of head shaking. Evan surveyed the room.

"Hey, Janice, welcome back. Could your hair get any blonder?"

"It's hard to avoid the sun in southern France. I'm refreshed and ready to go."

"We'll suck the life out of you before the day is done."

"Happy Birthday, Evan," said Sebastian waving the gift. "We all chipped in. You only turn fifty once."

Evan peered suspiciously as the box was passed down the line. Birthday cakes were common, but birthday gifts were unheard of. Evan poked the box with his pen.

"It won't explode," said Sebastian.

Evan tore off the wrapping paper. "Prostate self-examination kit," he announced. The room erupted into laughter.

Evan gingerly lifted the lid, and pulled out a blue latex glove and a tube of KY Jelly. He stretched his arm and squinted at the small print on the box. "Bend over. Insert finger into rectum. Cough. If you feel something bigger than a walnut, kiss your ass goodbye."

Hoots and clapping swept around the table. "Zoe, give Hunter the worst story on the list," ordered Evan.

"The *worst* story on the list. Every story is the worst," moaned Zoe, as she flung copies down the table. "My kingdom for a hostage taking."

Zoe was the Assignment Producer—author and keeper of the outlook; that critical list of known news events and potential ones. Every newsroom in the world starts its day with one.

Her drawn face emphasized that today's list was indeed ghastly. Not an ounce of heartache, not a modicum of triumph, no heroes or villains, no breathtaking rescue, no drug boat seized, not even a bit of TV silliness like a squealing pig race. This would be a torturous day.

"You don't have another house falling over a cliff in your back pocket do you, Sebastian?" asked Zoe.

Sebastian always had a *next* story. "I'm hearing some wild stuff about the premier. Let me make some calls."

"Does it involve the horizontal mambo and a man who is not her husband?"

"I wish," said Sebastian shaking his head. "That would be so much easier to prove."

"Anyone have any ideas they can deliver by six o'clock?" asked Zoe. Her gaze circumnavigated the boardroom. Fidgety reporters everywhere. Janice squirmed in her chair.

"The city is rezoning part of the downtown," said a rookie reporter. "They want more restaurants and bars—"

"Stop. You had me at rezoning," said Evan.

"There's rubber chicken in someone's future," threatened Zoe, followed by a pregnant pause.

"Shirley, can you go to Rotary? The transportation minister is the guest. His flak says the speech will be a shopping list of upcoming projects—roads to be paved, bridges to be built. All old news. The Rotarians will be snoring by dessert. Let's see if we can get a rise out of him. Ask him why his brother's construction company was just awarded two huge contracts."

"Also ask which one mom loved best," said Janice. She was rewarded with chuckles.

"Number two, the chief of police is raising a flag for the Cops for Cancer campaign this morning."

"I'm no expert, but aren't cops supposed to be against cancer?" asked Sebastian.

"Let's just send a camera," said Evan, sounding bored. "We'll pull a clip and some pictures."

"It's education week," said Zoe. "The education minister is reading to a grade-three class this morning."

Gloom swept over the room. This was sugar-sweet news.

"Time for the magic ring," said Janice softly to Sebastian as she slipped an imaginary band on a pinkie. "She can't see me."

The education minister had two children of her own and knew how to entertain kids. Worse, the teachers had just signed a three-year contract with a nine per cent wage increase, guaranteeing that Miss Debbie would be a welcoming host as the education minister entered her classroom. The chances of photogenic disaster were shockingly low.

"Maybe one of the youngsters will have an episode of projectile vomiting," said Sebastian.

"Harris, that's yours," said Zoe. "Turn it into a yarn about why kids don't know the three Rs these days."

"I'd sooner endure waterboarding," whispered Sebastian.

"Could be worse," said an equally hush Janice. "Could be a story about daycare."

"I see you down there, Janice Stone," said Zoe. "The hospital is cutting the ribbon on a ten-million dollar renovation to the main cafeteria. Deep fryers have been banished. They've turned it into chic bistro stations. You can even order banana flambé."

"Out of the frying pan into the flambé," said Evan. There was a sprinkling of laughter.

"I need an easy day, I'll take it," said Janice. "I've had a growth experience in France and no one here seems to appreciate that."

"Cry me a river," said Sebastian. He sniffed and wiped away a phoney tear.

"We can give it edge," said Zoe, "by reminding everyone that these are the same people who thought it was a good idea to open a Tim Hortons in the hospital. Dig out the old tape. Fat was once fashionable."

Wholesome stories. Press-release stories. Agenda stories. Everything but a scoop. Nobody powerful need fret today. There was unanimous derision at the outlook, but nothing could be discarded, not yet anyway. A black hole loomed at six o'clock and it took an hour of pictures, sounds and words to fill that hole.

Sebastian gave Janice a weary smile and pushed his chair back to leave. Others did as well amid the small talk. No one was in any rush to get out the door. Sebastian's phone buzzed. He scrolled through a message. "Jesus," he blurted. "You're not going to believe this. Guess who was picked up for drunk driving in Florida?" Sebastian's announcement magnetized the room.

"Mickey Mouse?" asked a perplexed Zoe.

"Police Chief Paul Bennett."

"Wahoo!" whooped Evan.

"He was stopped by Orlando police and according to the note, he blew twice the limit."

"Who hates him enough to send us that?" asked Zoe. "On second thought, I don't care."

"We just got a lead story," said Evan.

Sebastian could already imagine the headline.

Tonight…Badge of Dishonour. The Chief of Police is charged with drunk driving.

●

DUI. To the Orlando Police Department, the letters meant Driving Under the Influence. Boring. What could they mean for Chief Paul Bennett?

Sebastian cupped his mouth. "Word football," he shouted to the newsroom cabal. He glommed onto the Nerf football sitting in a kickoff stand and shuffled back, as if he had just received the snap from the centre and was avoiding a tackle.

"DUI," he yelled, lobbing the ball towards Janice. The trajectory took the ball over a row of cubicles into her outstretched hands. She tossed the football back and forth between her fingers while concentrating on the challenge.

"Drunk Unhappy Investigator," she said, before zipping the football to a reporter by the fire hose.

"Detective Undeniably Inebriated," he added to the mix. The ball cruised over a bank of printers to a reporter by the emergency door.

"Doofus Undoes Invincibility." The reporter cocked his arm. "Go deep, Sebastian."

Sebastian ran in slow motion, dodged a burly recycling bin and caught the ball on the downward curve.

"Donut Undercover Imbiber. Touchdown." Sebastian spiked the ball and high-fived Janice.

The cheers came from every quarter, except The Desk. Sebastian picked up the ball and pointed an accusatory end with its crosshair seams at the empty chairs. "Do they do anything besides go for coffee?"

The Desk was the producers' castle—a chain of desks in the shape of a horseshoe, sitting on a riser. Sebastian figured the producers designed it that way so they could always watch each others' backs. TV, radio, online—all the empires within earshot of each other. Lords and masters of all they surveyed.

"I need a camera," Sebastian griped, "and the desk jockeys are off getting caffeine hits. Maybe I should just draw stickmen. I'm trying to ruin a career here and I'm not getting any help."

He paced the breadth of the horseshoe for several minutes.

"You could always call them," suggested Janice, waving a cellphone.

"And interrupt the high point of their day? When you've been put out to pasture, deciding what size coffee to buy is about as much stress as you can handle."

Janice laughed. "Zoe would dropkick you if she heard you talking like that."

"I don't know what happens to them when they get on the desk. They lose all sense of urgency. Caffeine is about the only thing that can jump-start their hearts, but do they have to drag me down with them?"

"Here comes the brain trust now. I dare you—tell them what you really think of them."

Four cocky producers carrying coffee cups like Olympic torches entered the far end of the newsroom. Sebastian pulled a phantom zipper across his lips. "Speaking the truth can be a career-limiting move." Janice clucked and flapped her arms.

Sebastian pounced the instant Evan, Zoe, and their coffee mates plopped into their chairs.

"Peter Mansbridge will be saying my name in five time zones tonight." Sebastian had a flashback of Lindsay being enamoured with his fame and his body.

Evan sipped his double-double. "I gather you've got good news, or is there another reason for that grin?"

"Two sweet moments, only one of which matters now. I love talking to American cops. They tell you everything. Sgt. Hernandez with the Orlando Police Department read me the file. The chief got picked up a week ago. A patrol car sees him cut off a car. There are screeching tires and a horn blaring. The cop flicks on the lights and gives the chief a blast with the siren. He pulls over. The cop smells alcohol as soon as the chief drops his window."

"'Have you been drinking tonight, sir?' asks the cop."

"'Two beers,' says the chief."

"Not the first time the cop has heard that line. The chief is glassy-eyed and he's slurring. They bring him back to the station to blow."

"The breathalyzer reading was…," Sebastian paused for dramatic effect; all the producers leaned forward, "point one six."

Evan and Zoe high-fived.

"The chief was charged with DUI," said Sebastian. "Fingerprints, mug shot, court date—the whole enchilada."

"That's Mexican, not Cuban, but I'm sure Sgt. Hernandez would forgive you," said Zoe.

"They held him for eight hours to let him sober up and then released him on his own recognizance."

Sebastian's phone buzzed. His fingers danced across the screen.

"It's Christmas," said Sebastian, kissing his phone. He flipped the phone around to his audience, revealing a glum-faced Paul Bennett with *Orlando City Police* superimposed across his chest.

"Now that's a mug shot," said Evan, taking the phone for a closer look. Zoe pushed aside the monitor swing arm to get a better view. The remainder of the coffee brigade crowded behind.

"Did they know they'd arrested a chief of police?" asked Evan.

"Not at first. They found out when they ran his passport. Sgt. Hernandez said it was funny, actually. The arresting officer and Bennett were falling over themselves apologizing to each other."

"'I'm sorry I had to arrest you,'" said Sebastian facing right.

"'Don't be ridiculous, I'm the one who did wrong,'" said Sebastian facing left.

"'Still, I don't like locking up another police officer.'"

"'Nonsense. You only did your job. And very professionally too.'"

"Did he offer any explanation to the Orlando cops?" asked Evan.

Sebastian shook his head.

"Send the mug shot to the web guys and write up some copy. We won't post it until you've got the chief."

"I'll head him off at the pass. Who's riding shotgun?"

"Take Teddy," said Zoe. "He hasn't been on a shoot yet today."

"Am I hearing this right?" said a bass voice behind Sebastian. The Desk went quiet. Sebastian spun around to see an annoyed Garrison Hill. The senior journalist in the newsroom and co-anchor of *Here & Now* had the floor. "You're going to ambush the chief of police."

"What would you suggest, Garrison, an appointment?"

"Actually, yes." Garrison held up a copy of CBC's Journalistic Standards and Practices. "The policy says an ambush should be a last resort."

"How old is *that*?" mocked Sebastian. "They don't even print those anymore. The policy I read *online* says if a person is involved in a crime and he could run away, we don't have to tell him we're coming. Give the chief a warning and he'll head for the hills."

Garrison puffed his cheeks. "The man obviously has a problem."

Sebastian flicked his hands in a so-what gesture. "So does every druggie dragged into provincial court."

Garrison slammed the journalistic policy guide on his desk. "What about the dignity of his office?"

"The *what*?" snorted Sebastian. "We're not in the dignity business, Garrison. We're in the news business."

The anchor looked at Sebastian with contempt, but the younger man continued. "Maybe he should have thought of that *before* he got drunk and decided to drive."

Garrison thrust a finger at Sebastian. "You're going to crucify the chief of police in public." His voice was booming. "He doesn't deserve it."

Sebastian pointed at a window. "Out there, in the real world, we go after scoops, scoops which entice thousands of people to watch *you*." His finger stabbed the air in front of Garrison's nose. "You've gone soft, Garrison. Do you think for one second that his arrest won't squirt out? If I don't nail him, someone else will. Fortune favours the bold, not the out-of-date."

Garrison scoffed. Sebastian crossed his arms. The Desk was mesmerized by the head butting.

Sebastian turned to Zoe. "Tell Teddy to saddle up the horses. We're shootin' up the cop shop."

●

Sebastian and Teddy plunked their equipment down outside police headquarters, just metres from a lectern and PA speaker. The chief's media-relations officer tapped the microphone. Amplified pops filled the courtyard.

The provincial and police flags fluttered in the blue sky. A third flagpole stood empty. An officer in a dark grey uniform laid a folded Canadian Cancer Society flag on a small table. He adjusted the silver buckle on his snow-white belt, a white that matched his gloves. Police cadets unfolded chairs for the dignitaries and taped nametags on the backrests: Lieutenant Governor, Mayor, Minister of Health, President Canadian Cancer Society, Chief of Police.

Fight or flight? Sebastian was confident the chief would stand and fight, at least for a couple of embarrassing questions, but he plotted possible escape routes, just in case. There were really only two—the chief could run to his own car in the parking lot or scamper back inside police headquarters.

Or he could shoot me. Sebastian laughed to himself.

"What are you doing here, Sebastian?" Constable Patricia Russo had swooped in on his blind side.

"I have a thing for women in uniform, Patricia."

Constable Russo had been the force's media contact for over a year. She could smell trouble.

"If I had a suitcase full of cocaine, I'd understand why you'd be here. If I had the riot squad decked out in shields and batons, I'd understand why you'd be here. But all I have is a Cops for Cancer flag raising. So why are you here?"

"Can't tell you. But I need to talk to the chief right after the ceremony."

"That's not the way it works," said the constable. "No disclosure, no scrum."

"Your rules, not mine."

"You expect me to agree to an ambush." Her body went rigid.

"I'll chase him, if I have to. Think of the dignity of the office. It won't look good on camera."

Sebastian knew he had her trapped. A chief of police running away from a TV reporter. What a public relations disaster that would be. No, she would not turn her boss into a cowardly lion.

"I'll set it up," said the constable through clenched teeth. "I'll remember this the next time you come looking for something."

Sebastian scoped the parking lot. No sign of the competition. His TV camera was still the only one there. *The Telegram* had sent a photographer, but still photos of a happy chief raising a flag posed no danger to his exclusive. The ambush would be his alone.

An officer broke his ramrod stance and pulled the front door open. Chief Paul Bennett led an entourage out of police headquarters. Teddy filmed his every step. The chief wore a full dress uniform—a red band on his hat, a red belt, and a red sash across his chest.

Any redder and he'd be a Mountie.

The guests of honour ambled toward their chairs. The chief stopped to mingle with a group of officers. Teddy circled like a shark swimming around prey, capturing every handshake and smile. The chief patted a few shoulders.

Constable Russo waded in and drew the chief aside. She pointed at Sebastian. His stern face nodded. They whispered as she walked the chief to his chair, then she stepped up to the microphone.

"Ladies and gentlemen, welcome to our annual Cops for Cancer kickoff. This is our tenth anniversary—ten years of your police force going beyond the call of duty to help our community."

Sebastian used his index and middle fingers to form a scissors shape, closing them twice—his gesture for cutaway shots. The camera panned from Constable Russo to shoot faces. The lieutenant governor yawned. The mayor checked her watch. The cancer society president fumbled through pages on his lap. The chief stroked his chin.

"This year the money we raise will be used to send kids with cancer to camp," said Constable Russo. "And to tell us all about that is Aiden Singh with the Canadian Cancer Society."

Polite applause trailed him to the microphone.

"Thank you for inviting me and a special thank you to Chief Bennett. Cops for Cancer sends kids to magical places. Chief, we couldn't do it without your compassion, your decency, and your leadership." Everyone in uniform clapped loudly. "We need more cops like you."

More cops like you. Definitely.

Sebastian subtly drew a finger across his throat. The throat slash meant cut. No point in shooting speeches that would end up on the cutting-room floor. There was only one speech he wanted, only one speech that would make the grade. Teddy didn't turn the camera back on until Constable Russo introduced today's media martyr.

Chief Paul Bennett stood behind the lectern. "Good morning, everyone. Cops for Cancer is one of my favourite campaigns because being a police officer is more than putting the bad guys in jail. Though, I certainly like to do that." Everyone laughed.

"A dozen police officers have signed up for the shave-off. They're going to be as bald as Kojak." Even the drowsy lieutenant governor joined the laughter. "Telly Savalas used to say, 'Who loves ya, baby?' The answer is—we do. Thank you, from all of us." The chief saluted the soon-to-be-barbered cops.

"People think police officers are brave, and that's true. But I'll tell you who else is brave—kids fighting cancer. They stand up to danger every day. They are fearless." The chief's voice cracked.

"It just breaks my heart to see children…innocent children…," he wiped an eye and swallowed, "fight for their lives."

Nice touch, thought Sebastian.

"Anything we can do to make their lives better is a good thing. Bald is beautiful. So let's raise that flag."

Sebastian and Teddy hustled to the flagpole. Teddy had abandoned the tripod to shoot from his shoulder. Being nimble was more important than being steady.

The flag zipped to the top. The crowd cheered. The chief tied off the rope and turned to his media stalkers.

"Sebastian, I heard you were going to chase me." The guests of honour glowered.

"I'm glad it didn't come to that." Sebastian felt disdain from every direction. "Chief, tell me about your encounter with the Orlando City Police."

The chief's Adam's apple bobbed. He turned away, as if composing his thoughts. The friendly faces around him looked baffled. Eyes flickered about for an explanation but saw only shrugs. The chief stood tall, almost at attention. Instead of making eye contact with Sebastian, he stared down the barrel of the gun on Teddy's shoulder.

"A week ago I was charged with Driving Under the Influence by the Orlando City Police," said Chief Bennett.

The mayor dropped her purse. She took a giant step to the side and ducked down before reaching back to pick it up. The lieutenant governor's aide-de-camp pulled him aside as he frantically waved at his honour's limousine. The cancer society president put a hand to his ear though no one was actually calling him. There were exaggerated nods and a brisk exit.

"This has been an extremely stressful time for me and my family."

A shocked face accompanied every police badge.

"Since the matter is before the courts I have no other comment at this time."

The chief quick-marched towards the front door with Constable Russo protecting his left flank. Sebastian and Teddy followed in hot pursuit then manoeuvred themselves in front of the skedaddling pair. Teddy and his camera faced the chief. He walked backwards, matching the escapees' spurt. Sebastian walked forward, guiding Teddy by keeping hold of his jacket between the shoulder blades. The reporter kept his eyes on the path ahead, glancing back just long enough to shout a question. "Chief, why were you drinking that night?" The scurry of footsteps was the only sound Chief Bennett offered.

The Cops for Cancer team and their guests parted like the Red Sea. The journalist-led phalanx barged through the opening. People scrambled to stay out of the way. Chairs were upended. A woman tripped over one. The sound of a bone breaking welded with a scream of pain. Walkie-talkies squealed. "Injured woman outside police HQ. Call an ambulance."

"Are you resigning?" yelled Sebastian, as he applied pressure to Teddy's back. The cameraman stopped, but kept his lens trained on the chief. The chief ignored the question and broke neither his gaze nor his step. He and the constable slipped through the door. Teddy continued filming through the glass until they swerved out of the lobby.

Sebastian spied Constable Russo in an upstairs window on the way back to the van. She made a finger gun and pulled the trigger.

●

The marble statue of the Virgin Mary looked down from her pedestal in the Basilica courtyard at the approaching van. Her serene face showed no sign of disapproval; no condemnation of the news crew coming into her gaze.

"You're Catholic, aren't you?" asked Teddy.

"A lapsed Catholic," said Sebastian.

"What do you think she'd say about the ambush?" asked Teddy, pointing to the Virgin while keeping the other hand on the wheel.

Sebastian reflected for a moment. "Blessed are they who are persecuted, for they shall lead the news."

Teddy let out a belly laugh. A tire dropped in a pothole, throwing the two men into their taut seatbelts.

"Mary obviously didn't see the humour," said Sebastian.

Traffic on Harvey Road was sluggish. Cars from both directions flowed into Tim Hortons, filling the drive-thru lanes.

"Let's stop for a coffee," said Sebastian. "I'll buy."

Teddy pulled up to the door, letting his partner hop out. Inside, Sebastian witnessed a miracle—the customer corral was empty. Perhaps the Virgin Mary appreciated humour after all. He followed the short, sharp turns to the Please Wait Here sign at the front. The lone clerk served a woman at the counter.

"A medium coffee with one cream and a toasted multigrain bagel with herb and garlic cream cheese. I'll have that to go, please."

"We don't sell multigrain bagels."

"Really? But it says up there," said the customer pointing at the menu, "that you have twelve-grain bagels."

"Right, but we don't have multigrain."

Sebastian smacked his forehead.

"I'll have a twelve-grain bagel then."

"Do you want anything on it?"

"Herb and garlic cream cheese."

"Is that for here or to go?"

"To go. No, maybe here. On second thought I don't have time. Make it to go."

"Did you say coffee?"

Sebastian groaned. *Did this guy flunk out of toll-booth school?* He contemplated the chaos if the clerk were on the drive-thru window. There'd be coffee rage. Shots fired. Someone would die.

"Next, please," said the clerk, as the customer stepped aside to wait for her bagel.

Sebastian sallied to the counter.

"Two…medium…black…coffees…to…go…please." He enunciated each word.

"You look familiar," said the clerk, searching Sebastian's face for recognition. "Have we ever met?"

"I don't think so."

"Gerry's wedding last summer. Was that it?"

"I don't know any Gerrys."

"Wait now." He stopped in mid pour. "You're on TeeeVeee." His smile was as wide as the brim on his Tim Hortons visor.

"Yes, you've got me."

"Don't tell me. You're, um, you're…oh, I know it…give me a hint."

"Sebastian Hunter," blurted Sebastian.

"Right, Sebastian Hunter. NTV News." He jacked up the volume on NTV News.

"No, CBC. *Here & Now.* The newscast of choice for purveyors of fine coffee everywhere."

"Never watch it." He finished filling the cups.

"Bagel with cream cheese," shouted a server by the toaster. She handed a bag to the bagel lady.

"Your job must be easy," said the clerk, reaching for the cup covers. "You only work a couple of minutes a day."

Sebastian fantasized stabbing the clerk multiple times with a Tim Hortons plastic knife.

"You're right. It is easy. I should try something hard, like serving coffee." He dropped two toonies on the counter and didn't bother waiting for change.

Sebastian stormed across the parking lot, climbed into the van and slammed the door.

"The mouth-breathers are out today, Teddy."

●

Janice and Bruce trudged through the hospital corridor. Bruce balanced a camera in one hand and a tripod in the other. Janice walked off-kilter, carrying a duffle bag crammed with lights, microphones, cables, and batteries.

"Do you have a body in here?" snarled Janice.

"We're going right by the morgue, I don't see a problem."

"Seriously, Bruce, do we really need three of everything?"

"The van is a mile away. If I don't have it, you can be guaranteed I'll need it."

"I'm going on strike." Janice dropped the kit bag on the floor and stretched her back. An orderly pushed an empty stretcher towards the X-ray department.

"Maybe we can borrow that," kidded Janice. Her phone buzzed. "Damn. Sebastian is at it again."

"What's he done now?"

"Caused a train wreck at the cop shop," sighed Janice. "What a streak he's on."

"At least we get a free lunch." Bruce's eyes twinkled. "And this army marches on his stomach."

The sign at the end of the hall said Grand Opening—Peggy's Place.

"Hi Janice," said the perky greeter. "So glad you could come. It's a great day for community health."

"I can't think of anywhere else I'd rather be."

The greeter tapped multi-coloured fingernails on her clipboard.

"What's that?" asked Janice.

"I went a little crazy on the nail art," said the greeter, splaying her fingers. "Cherry, strawberry, pineapple, kiwi, and watermelon." She pointed first to her pinky and went down the line to her thumb.

"Peggy's Place is all about fresh everything," she said with schoolgirl enthusiasm. "These are the fruits of my labour." She fluttered her fingers.

The rattle of cutlery blended with the banging of plates. "Coming through," said a woman sporting a hairnet and pushing a trolley loaded with tableware. A colleague stacked plastic trays just inside the entrance.

"They're non-slip and made of fibreglass," said the greeter with zeal. She waved at a woman wearing a svelte, pinstripe suit. "That's the foodservice director. She wants to speak with you." The director pressed out a wrinkle in her jacket before wandering over to Janice.

"Hi Janice, I'm Scarlett Unger," said the director. The greeting was wrapped in a plastic smile. "So glad you could come. It's a great day for community health."

"So I've heard."

"How about those fingernails? We have a lot of fun here."

"I can tell."

"Janice, I know you're one of CBC's top reporters," said Ms. Unger, escorting the media inside, "and I would never presume to tell you how to do your job, but I thought I should point out a few things. First of all, don't call it a cafeteria."

"No?" said Janice with skeptical eyebrows.

"No, absolutely no, mademoiselle. It's a café-bistro."

A rose by any other name would smell as sickly sweet, thought Janice. "Really?"

"Would a cafeteria have a pizza oven and a sauté station?" Ms. Unger swept her hand around the room as if to announce Behold. "Nothing here is canned or frozen. Would you like a free-trade, organic coffee?" The director batted her eyelashes.

"No, thank you. We have to set up our gear. By the way, who's Peggy?"

"A long-time employee. You'll have to excuse me. I have a few last minute details to sort out. Remember, it's a café-bistro."

Janice waited until the director was out of hearing range. "Remember, it's a café-bistro," she said in a nasal refrain.

Bruce laughed. "Steel yourself, darlin', your tribulations aren't over yet. Look over there."

Doctors with stethoscopes hanging around their necks congregated near the deli bar. "Please tell me that's not Angelo," begged Janice.

"I believe it is. Imagine, a urology resident in a hospital. What are the odds?"

"He's going to regret being here."

Angelo was holding court, his audience charmed by his quirky hand movements and accompanying story about a patient receiving a terminal prognosis. Janice held back, waiting for the punchline. "'Could be worse,' he says, 'it could be Ebola.'" The cluster roared.

"Dr. Dickhead, what a wonderful surprise," hurled Janice. The laughter died.

"Time for rounds," said a doctor on the edge of the tempest. She and the others drifted away.

"Jesus Christ, what was that all about?" snapped Angelo.

"Revenge. Only a dickhead would break up with me over the phone."

"And that gives you the right to debase me in public?"

"Frankly, yes. You're cute when your veins bulge like that." Janice reached for his forehead.

"Don't." He cuffed her hand away.

"You used to like my touch."

"I used to like everything about you."

"Why didn't you tell me in person?" Janice sounded more bruised than angry.

"I was afraid you'd start throwing things."

"Sebastian was right, you *are* a coward."

"Discretion is the better part of valour."

"I…love you."

"You love your job. You can only be devoted to one thing and that's TV news. There's no room for me." Angelo paused. "I heard you went to France."

"You should have been with me."

"It wouldn't have worked." His pager buzzed. "That's probably the doctors you unhinged. They're trying to rescue me. We should talk. Can we have dinner?"

"Okay. Something on a sizzling platter, though I'm warning you, I might dump the whole thing into your lap."

"I'll alert the burn unit, just in case."

Janice filed past two women in white aprons and hairnets speaking in secretive voices. "Isn't it awful what's happened to Peggy," said one. Janice froze and pivoted on her back foot.

"Excuse me, what's happened to Peggy?"

The woman nonchalantly checked to see if anyone was paying attention to their confab. "You didn't hear it from me, but Peggy won't be here today."

"Disgraceful," said her gossip companion.

"Why?"

"You should ask Scarlett Fever over there," said the first tattler, frowning at the foodservice manager. "She's infected this place with nastiness."

"What do you mean?"

"Peggy's been working here for thirty years. You won't find a sweeter woman. Always smiling and good for a joke. Everybody loves her. The hospital ran a contest to pick a new name for the cafeteria. Peggy's Place won. Peggy was over the moon."

"So far I'm not hearing any nastiness."

The woman fidgeted with her apron.

"Tell her, Mary Ann," said her friend.

"I'd go to jail to protect a source," said Janice with backbone.

"Peggy is always on the food lines. You know, out front. Well, Peggy is, ah, big-boned. Really big-boned, if you know what I mean. She can't stop eating. Scarlett Fever didn't want a fat woman being the face of a new fat-free cafeteria. She went crazy, didn't she, Betsy?"

Betsy chimed in. "Her nibs calls Peggy into the office and practically orders her to lose weight. Told her she has a responsibility to slim down. Told her she has to do her part to promote the new café-bistro." She put air quotes around café-bistro. "Said it was all on Peggy's shoulders. Can you believe it? And that's not the worst of it."

The women handed off to each other like tag-team wrestlers. Scarlett Fever was about to be pile-drived and leg-dropped.

"Poor Peggy was in tears when she told me," said Mary Ann. "God love her, she tried to lose a few pounds. She even ate carrot sticks, and she hates carrots. But nothing worked. She got so stressed she went on sick leave. She's home today, probably crying her eyes out. It's just not right."

"Scarlett Fever treats everyone below her like dirt," said Betsy, "but if you're a manager, she's kissing your ass, pardon my French."

Manna from heaven.

"Would you have a number for Peggy?" asked Janice.

Mary Ann took a pen from her apron pocket and jotted down the number on a paper napkin.

"Thank you, Mary Ann. You've just made my day a lot better and hers a lot worse," sneered Janice in Scarlett's direction.

Janice made a beeline for Bruce. "I need lots of shots of Scarlett, preferably bossing people around."

"What's up?"

"She's a witch who eats fat people alive."

"Locked on target and firing," said Bruce, spinning the camera.

I love my job, thought Janice.

•

Dawdlers blocked the sidewalk and Sebastian was running late. He ferreted his way through the crowd. "Excuse me," he said as he side-swiped a woman's shopping bags, those humongous bags that chic boutiques fill with small, expensive items. They swung in front of her feet; she stumbled.

"Asshole," she bawled.

Sebastian waved, but didn't look back. The Halong Bay Restaurant was in sight, his favourite place for Vietnamese food. Everything was made from scratch. They had shrimp patties he'd die for. High turnover, no credit cards accepted, and usually no reservations taken, but the owner always made an exception for CBC celebrities. Sebastian could see Roxanne standing alongside the cash register with an assortment of waifs and strays waiting for tables.

"Hi, honey. Sorry I'm late." He gave her a peck and joined the lineup.

A waiter skittered from the kitchen carrying bowls of steaming noodle soup. "Excuse, please." The line cracked to let him and his tray through. The aroma of lemongrass lagged behind. Sebastian scooped a handful towards his nose.

"Is it true?" asked Roxanne in a subdued voice.

"Is what true?"

"That you made the chief of police cry today?"

"Cry? No," said Sebastian in his usual volume. "He welled up, but not because of anything I did."

A woman showed her date something on her smartphone and pointed at Sebastian.

"What exactly happened?" asked Roxanne, trying to look nonchalant.

"The chief got sentimental when he talked about kids and cancer. But that was during his speech before I said boo to him."

"Define boo."

"I got Bennett to confess to drunk driving," crowed Sebastian. "He went from hero to pariah in five seconds. People scattered like ants. I took out a police chief today."

"Shush," scolded Roxanne.

A lady closed her purse and raised an eyebrow to her husband.

Roxanne's flustered eyes darted around the restaurant. "You're going to be the most hated man in the city."

"Why?" said Sebastian with genuine surprise. "I'm not the one who drove drunk."

"No, but you're the one who upended the Cops for Cancer kickoff. And you're the one who made the chief choke back tears."

"I did not make the chief choke back tears," said Sebastian, his voice rising.

No one else in the queue said a peep. Ears strained to eavesdrop.

"That's not the way it's going around town," said Roxanne. "They're saying awful things on Twitter. Someone called you an insensitive bastard."

"Are you going to believe 140 characters of wild rumour or are you going to believe the man you're sleeping with?" Roxanne didn't answer. "You are still sleeping with me, aren't you?"

"For now. I'll wait and see if a mob shows up outside the house with pitchforks and torches." Roxanne turned away for a moment. "Why do you think the chief filled up?"

"I have no idea. It really doesn't matter."

"You just don't get it, do you? Something was obviously bothering him. You could have been more empathetic."

"I can be as empathetic as the next reporter."

"You have no idea what the word means."

"I admit that a Cops for Cancer event isn't an ideal location to ambush a police chief about drunk driving, but it was my only chance to get him. Do you think the chief asks, 'Is everything okay? Do you mind if I arrest you?' before he slaps on the cuffs? Come on."

"He gets bad guys off the street."

"I get bad guys off the street too. Are you saying that it's okay for a cop to drink and drive?"

"Of course not. I just wish you hadn't goaded the chief into crying."

Sebastian chafed. "I did not goad the chief into crying." His peeved voice carried into the restaurant. Even people at the back stared. Roxanne put her hand over her eyes.

The owner gave an agitated wave to a busboy and pointed at a table tucked away in a nook. The busboy piled dirty dishes into the centre of the plastic tablecloth before tying the four corners into a knot. He wedged the bundle into an already overflowing tub.

"Sebastian Hunter," said the owner. "Come, please."

Sebastian allowed Roxanne to go first. He glanced back at the lineup.

"I sure told her." Only the men laughed.

●

"Thank you, Peggy," said Janice into her phone. "I'll be over as soon as I'm finished here." She heard sniffles and a frail goodbye. Janice casually moved to the bulletin board and unpinned a poster.

A ragtag crowd in white aprons, jackets, and floppy chefs' hats gathered near the microphone. They were just fifteen minutes from serving their first lunches in the sunshiny café-bistro.

"Ladies and gentlemen, if I could have your attention, please," said hospital CEO Carla Gallo as she settled in behind the microphone. "Thank you for coming to the opening of our new café-bistro. It's a…," Janice matched the words, "great day for community health."

The CEO droned on about a holistic approach to wellness, the banning of deep fryers, and the emphasis on tasty, nutritious food. Not a word about Peggy.

A chef and a cashier stretched a ribbon in front of the CEO.

"Three, two, one," counted down the crowd. Gallo deftly snipped the ribbon with a pair of scissors. There was a flurry of camera flashes. Bruce framed his shot to include the foodservice director rabidly applauding her boss.

"Any questions?" asked Gallo after the ovation petered out.

Time to talk about the elephant not in the room.

"The name over the door says Peggy's Place," said Janice. "Where's Peggy?"

Scarlett gave the CEO a reassuring nod.

"I'm afraid Peggy isn't well today. We had the grand opening booked and couldn't really delay it. We wish she were here. We named it Peggy's Place because no one deserves it more. Peggy is a valued employee who's given us a career of selfless service. We think the world of her."

The answer elicited an approving smile from Scarlett.

Janice unrolled a glossy poster announcing the grand opening of Peggy's Place. Join Us for an Exciting New Dining Experience. Three pencil-thin women held out plates of food. Janice turned the poster towards the chunky CEO.

"None of these women is Peggy. Why isn't she on this poster? It's her place after all."

"I don't really know. Scarlett, can you explain?"

Scarlett's smile vanished. A murmur swayed through the sea of white uniforms. Scarlett stepped forward and stood by her boss.

"It was designed by an ad agency. By the time I saw the poster, it was too late to ask for changes." Mary Ann and Betsy hooted at Scarlett's exaggerated sincerity. Janice rolled up the poster as if she were wringing a neck.

"Would it have anything to do with the fact that Peggy is, and these are her words not mine, carrying extra pounds?"

Scarlett pinched her face. A worker on the hot buffet line lifted a pan, steam billowed in the background.

"I don't know what you mean."

"Peggy told me, that you told *her*, she was fat and she had to lose weight."

There was a collective gasp in the café-bistro. The CEO's face went grave.

"That's…not…true," said Scarlett, punctuating her response with short breaths. "I…never…said…such…a…thing. That's…a…lie." She wobbled, then steadied herself by holding the microphone stand. She let go a belch. "Excuse…me." A nurse rushed to Scarlett's side and led her away.

The CEO was paid 425,000 dollars a year to provide stout leadership. Her hand had a perceptible tremble.

"Ms. Gallo, you have an eating disorder unit in the hospital. Should a woman who struggles to lose weight, who compulsively overeats, be coerced into going on a diet?"

"No, absolutely not. Ordering someone with an illness to go on a diet is callous and completely unacceptable. We help people with eating disorders. We don't bully them."

"But Peggy says she was bullied. And she received no offer of help. She says she's sick at home because your foodservice manager browbeat her."

The CEO listened with pressed lips and an upturned chin. "I can assure you that I knew nothing of this, and if what you're saying is true," she said blackly, "I won't tolerate it. Now if you'll excuse me."

Gallo deserted the microphone. Her getaway left a panorama of dumbfounded faces.

"Peggy's Place—where more than the food gets skewered," said Janice quietly.

●

Sebastian and Evan had a date with The Executioner. For condemned men, they had a sprightly step. They ignored the journalism awards hanging on the corridor walls, many of which they had a hand in winning. The awards wouldn't help them now. The Executioner was out for blood.

"It's better if you keep quiet and I do all the talking," said Evan.

Sebastian cupped his hand to his ear. "I think I hear, 'Off with their heads.'"

"They really don't pay me enough to put up with this shit. A pox on both your houses."

The walk between The Executioner's office and the newsroom was mere metres, but the philosophical distance couldn't be measured.

The sign on the open door read Alicia Gorski, Regional Director. Hers was the biggest office in the building with a view of the university campus and a parkway. Perhaps a buxom jogger would bounce by and tantalize Sebastian's senses. It was the only reward he could anticipate.

Evan knocked. Alicia stopped typing and closed a file on her computer.

"Gentlemen, come in," she said, taking off her reading glasses. "Close the door and have a seat."

Two leather chairs sat empty on the peon side of her oak desk. No invitation today to sit at the cozy conference table by the windows. She used that table for friendly chats. Sebastian peeped through the glass as he approached a chair. Outside, the warm temperatures had sprouted students in shorts and T-shirts. The bookcase behind Alicia offered only saccharine children's pictures.

Alicia picked up the remote and turned off the television. The piercing sound of an approaching siren permeated the office.

"I took a phone call—"

"One second," Sebastian butted in. He looked out the window with a wistful gaze. "They're playing our song." He fanned himself as if overcome with dewy-eyed nostalgia. A police car with lights flaring sped past pulled-over cars. The siren receded.

"Sorry to interrupt. You were about to say something."

Alicia's face was flush. "I took a phone call from a very upset president of the Canadian Cancer Society," she said. "Sebastian, he accused you of embarrassing the lieutenant governor, destroying their flag raising, hounding the police chief, and somehow breaking a woman's wrist. What do you have to say for yourself?"

"It seemed like a good idea at the time."

"Good *idea*," zinged Alicia. "Do you think it's your job to piss people off?"

Sebastian loaded a snarky rebuttal, but Evan shot first. "Alicia, Sebastian has done nothing wrong. I sent him there on an assignment. Did the cancer guy happen to mention that the guest speaker was a police chief charged with drunk driving? Were we supposed to ignore that? This was our best chance to get him."

Alicia leaned forward. "It was Cops for Cancer for heaven's sake. Part of my job is forming partnerships with community groups. We flip pancakes for the homeless and collect turkeys for the hungry. I would have thought that the CBC could get behind cops helping kids with cancer, but apparently we can't."

Sebastian wasn't listening. He daydreamed about Chief Bennett's hasty retreat. Alicia pulled a thick file out of a drawer and dropped it on her desk. The thud sapped Sebastian's reverie.

"This is not the first time I've had calls about you," she said, tapping the file. "The justice minister went crazy when you asked about his son's unpaid parking tickets, the head of the Board of Trade didn't appreciate being called a slum landlord, and the chief judge chewed my ear off when you reported he flunked his first bar exam."

Sebastian imagined the disgruntled parties booing. "I comfort the afflicted and afflict the comfortable. It's an old maxim, but I like it."

"Alicia, pissing people off is part of the business," said Evan. "It's an occupational hazard. Sebastian has a story that everyone is going to be talking about tomorrow. It's a rock-solid exclusive and it's damn fine TV, if I do say so."

"What am I supposed to do with these people?"

"Do?" said Evan. "Do nothing. Let them vent, give them the Journalism 101 lecture and direct them to the ombudsman if they're still mad."

"You've got to give me more than that. Certain members of the newsroom seem to lack esprit de corps when it comes to CBC's philanthropy. They're nowhere to be seen when good deeds are being done."

"I give at the office," said Sebastian.

"That's not enough for today's society," countered Alicia. "People like reporters to have a good heart, not a black heart. We need public support and everybody in this building needs to understand that. We can't always bite the hand that feeds us."

A knock interrupted Alicia's sermon. Alicia's assistant poked her head in. "Sorry to barge in, but the chair of the hospital is on the phone demanding to speak with you. He's so upset his words are garbled. Something about Janice wrecking a ribbon cutting."

Alicia tossed a pen in the air. It spun end over end, landing on Sebastian's complaint file. "First, a flag raising and now a ribbon cutting. Is there anything wholesome that the CBC doesn't demolish?"

"Let no good deed go unpunished," said Sebastian. Evan slyly flicked his foot and tapped Sebastian's shoe.

"We'll pick this up later," said Alicia. "I have another fire to put out."

Evan closed Alicia's door on the way out.

"I don't need to come to work to be kicked surreptitiously," said Sebastian, "I get lots of that at home."

"I'm trying to keep you out of trouble and your smart-aleck comments aren't helping."

Sebastian gave a dismissive wave.

"You could throw her a bone, Sebastian. Do something for a charity. It might even make you feel good."

Sebastian was absorbed in his email. "There's a string of notes slugged Goose is Cooked. What the hell is that about?"

"I have no idea, but I like the sound of it." Evan was fleet-footed; Sebastian was his shadow.

Zoe had a phone propped to her ear using a hunched shoulder and a crooked head. She held up a just-a-minute finger.

"Right," she said hanging up, "The Alert Desk is looked after."

Sebastian felt a cramp in his stomach. Why was she calling Toronto?

"The whole hospital is in an uproar. Janice uncovered a deliciously ugly story about a sweet kitchen worker with an ogre for a boss."

Evan rubbed his hands together. Sebastian bit a knuckle as he listened to the details.

"From famine to feast," said Zoe. "We start off the day with nothing and now we've got two fabulous yarns. The Lord always provides and today we've been particularly blessed."

"Amen, sister," said Evan.

"My story is still the lead," insisted Sebastian. Zoe and Evan exchanged speculative glances but said nothing. Sebastian paced in front of them.

"I'm the only reporter who has the chief—the only reporter. Every media outlet in town was at the cafeteria. Everybody has what Janice has."

"Not quite," interjected Zoe. "Janice has an exclusive too. Only Janice has Peggy and she has quite the tearful story to tell."

Sebastian slapped the counter. "A weepy scullery maid trumps a disgraced police chief. You can't be serious."

"She does today," said Zoe. "Janice has the victim and the villain. You only have the villain. Janice wins! Sebastian, I hate to kick you while you're down, but Toronto thinks so as well. They want Janice's story for *The National* and they're only taking a voiceover and clip from you."

"Evan, feel free to pull rank here."

"Sebastian," said Evan, "it ain't over 'til the fat lady sings, and the fat lady has sung."

"This is the thanks I get for putting up with a regional manager who wants to put me on Ritalin."

Sebastian crumpled two pieces of paper into balls and cuddled them in one hand. "I go into the lion's den, get the scoop," he held out the fanciful scrotum, "and when I come back I get my balls cut off." Sebastian used his free hand to slice the air sideways. "Shing," he sang.

Sebastian tossed the make-believe testicles to Zoe. "I won't need these anymore."

He held his knees together and waddled back to his desk. "Neutered reporter, coming through."

●

Janice typed on her phone as Bruce drove towards the station.

"I don't think Peggy has ever heard the phrase 'Work some fat off,'" said Bruce.

Janice laughed. "You're evil. I like that in a man."

"Scarlett Fever probably said, 'It's a big deal' and Peggy heard 'Eat a big meal.'"

"Stop that."

"Snack pack is definitely not in her vocabulary."

"Enough."

Janice finished her text and hit send.

Angelo, must cancel dinner. Sorry. Have live hit on The National. Tomorrow?

Janice checked her lipstick in the visor mirror. If only a perfectly applied cosmetic could make an answer arrive. She turned up the radio. Bruce always had it set on one of those stations where the DJs stopped playing music made after 1999. The nasally voice offered either pity or jest, Janice couldn't decide which. The waiting is the hardest part, he sang. Her phone chirped.

France changed nothing. It's always tomorrow. I'm busy.

Janice flung the phone into her purse.

•

Sebastian sat on the leather sofa where Roxanne had already installed herself, legs curled under her buttocks. She sipped a glass of red wine. A 2014 Rioja stood on the coffee table—the pricey bottles stayed in the cellar on a Tuesday evening. The TV remote sat orphaned on the coffee table. No need to boost Peter's diction. He would not be uttering Sebastian's name on this night.

Good evening. I'm Peter Mansbridge and this is The National.

The theme music launched and Mansbridge guided viewers through the fear and loathing headlines—an exchange of rocket fire in the Gaza Strip, a police crackdown on gays in Moscow, and an alarming drop in Canada's polar bear population.

And Janice Stone tells us about a hospital cafeteria that doesn't allow fat with the lean.

Video of Scarlett Unger marshalling the food line dissolved into pictures of Peggy dabbing her eyes with a tissue.

"A cry-baby in the headlines," snorted Sebastian. "What are we coming to?"

"Shhhh. I want to hear this."

A thin boss orders an overweight worker to lose weight.

"I've got a big heart and she broke it."

Sebastian sat back. "Just when I think I've got this business figured out, they change the rules."

"What do you mean?" Mansbridge lost her attention; Sebastian held it now.

"Getting the villain should be more important than getting the victim. Janice only has the villain running away. No confession. No explanation. We're not going to hear Scarlett Unger's side of the story at all. Just what a disgruntled employee accuses her of saying. I, on the other hand, have a police chief admitting on camera that he drove drunk. I just can't understand their thinking."

Crises from around the world flowed into the living room. Five minutes passed, ten minutes.

"They buried Janice," said Sebastian.

A picture of Paul Bennett appeared on the screen behind Mansbridge.

"You're up, honey," exclaimed Roxanne. Sebastian raised his glass to toast himself.

Yesterday, he was an admired police chief. Today, Paul Bennett is an admitted drunk driver. Bennett was charged in Orlando, Florida. He blew more than twice the legal limit. He was on vacation at the time. Back home today, he apologized. Bennett has been suspended with pay.

"Why did they bother?" scoffed Sebastian. "Fifteen lousy seconds of copy. No video, no clip. Idiots."

"You can't win them all," said Roxanne, soothing his deflated ego with a shoulder rub. "You're too good to keep off the air for long. Daddy says Toronto is having a serious look at you. You'll get a national job soon. Just be patient. You've got the gift."

You've heard of racism and sexism, well there's a new ism this evening—fatism.

"Oh, Janice's story," said Roxanne, cranking up the volume.

A manager in one of the country's largest hospitals ordered one of her employees to lose weight, or else. Joining us live is Janice Stone.

Janice's face filled all fifty-five inches of Sebastian's smart TV. Her voice resonated through his home theatre system. A brassy, confident Janice Stone had stolen his throne.

Peter, what started out as a simple ribbon cutting ended up being a public relations disaster that has offended the overweight, the underweight, and everyone in between.

"She looks poised, don't you think?" said Roxanne. Sebastian picked a cuticle off a thumb.

Janice's taped report rolled. Peggy sat at the kitchen table with a pile of crumpled tissues by her side, her eyes puffy and red. She wore a blue top and grey bottom.

"She's wearing shrunken sweatpants," jeered Sebastian.

"They're called cargo capris. Be quiet."

Peggy Brown has trouble standing up sometimes. She suffers from bad knees. But today, she stood up for herself like never before. And in doing that, she took down a bully.

"I'm plus-size, I'm big, I'm fat. That still doesn't give her the right to make me feel small."

The video switched to inside the cafeteria.

The 'her' is Scarlett Unger, Peggy's boss. Unger was the food service manager in charge of a multimillion dollar renovation. The cafeteria's menu also got a makeover. Fat was out. Apparently, Unger forgot that she should have stopped with the food.

Back to Peggy in her kitchen. The fridge hummed in the background. Two gigantic bags of chips sat on the counter.

"She called me into the office, and said something had to go—me or the weight. She said, 'You're an embarrassment.' I couldn't believe it. I've tried to lose weight lots of times, but I can't give up the chips."

Roxanne sat still. "That poor woman."

Sebastian sighed and gulped his wine.

Peggy's humiliation didn't stop there. That's because the cafeteria she was about to be thrown out of is named after her.

"That's outrageous," shrieked Roxanne.

"When they said they were going to name it Peggy's Place, I was so happy I cried. It was the proudest day of my life."

"Cue the tears," said Sebastian. The camera gently zoomed in to capture one rolling down Peggy's cheek.

"I'm fed up with people telling me to lose weight. It hurts. It's like a knife in my heart."

Roxanne whimpered. Janice appeared live on the screen again. Street lamps illuminated the hospital behind her.

Peter, just a short while ago, hospital CEO Carla Gallo spoke to reporters. She offered her sincere apologies to Peggy Brown. She said the new cafeteria is most definitely Peggy's Place, not Scarlett's Place. And that Scarlett Unger has resigned to pursue other opportunities. Janice Stone, CBC News.

"Peggy should still sue," said Roxanne.

"Fat chance," said Sebastian, picking up the bottle. "More wine?" Roxanne laid her glass down on a coaster. "I'm going to bed."

•

Sebastian stopped outside the entrance to Bannerman Park. The air was muggy and he felt sweat running down his back. Stately trees inside offered shade from the melting sun, but he hesitated in stepping under the wrought-iron arch.

"Couldn't I just grow a moustache in November?" he asked. "That passes for philanthropy at the CBC."

"You can't back out now," said Roxanne. "People are counting on you. Besides, it'll be fun. And if you're really good, I'll buy you an ice-cream afterwards."

"What am I—six?"

"Sometimes. Come on, there's already a crowd."

"Nothing like an execution to bring out the mob."

Sebastian and Roxanne rambled through tulip beds.

"You know," said Roxanne, "your father would enjoy this."

"I'm sure he would. What father doesn't love to see his son publicly humiliated?" He let Roxanne's hand go.

"I don't think he'd get the sarcasm. I'm simply suggesting that you should take advantage of these chances."

"Life is not a Norman Rockwell painting, Roxanne. Stop trying to paint one."

"Amazing how words can be coated with frost when it's twenty-eight degrees."

Sebastian exhaled audibly. "I'm sorry. I know you're only trying to help. It's just… some things are better left alone."

The mob had gathered near a shaking bouncy castle; the kids' caterwaul made Sebastian grateful for birth control. Parents ignored the pandemonium, seeking solace in cups of coffee and conversation. A man on stilts outfitted in red pants, black tails, and a top hat giant-stepped through a plume of barbeque smoke. Whiffs of grilled kielbasa sausages tormented Sebastian's taste buds.

"I know what I'm having for lunch," he said.

"Mom," yelled Roxanne, waving.

Hesitation blossomed into outright regret. Bad enough he had agreed to a public affront, but Prudish Penelope would witness the burlesque show. Her adulation of all things Sebastian could only balloon and there's only so much hero worship a future son-in-law can handle.

Mother and daughter kissed and embraced. Sebastian dutifully hugged Penelope and gave her a fluffy kiss.

"Sebastian," she said, clasping his hand, "this is so good of you."

"It was Roxanne's idea. Penance for being a contrarian."

"Roxanne, you're too hard on him."

"Just mending fences, Mom. Showing the CBC that he really does have a soft side."

"Mr. Hunter," said a man fast approaching and carrying a purple T-shirt. He shook Sebastian's hand as if he were shaking a martini. "Thank you again for doing this. The Alzheimer Society really appreciates it."

"There's nowhere else I'd rather be on a hot Saturday," said Sebastian. Roxanne gave him the eye of death.

"We've done up special T-shirts. All our celebrities are donning purple. That's our colour."

"What do you think, Penelope? Should I make this a proper wet T-shirt contest?"

Penelope tittered and dropped her eyes.

"No need to be bashful." Sebastian peeled off his own T-shirt, exposing sheen skin. Droplets of perspiration drizzled down firm pectoral muscles.

"Mercy," said Penelope, fanning herself with an open hand.

Sebastian donned the purple T-shirt and modelled for the two women. They nodded to each other. Roxanne touched the letter C on the T-shirt.

"I like the font," she said. "CELEBRITY DUNK."

"Maybe it should say CELEBRITY HUNK," teased Penelope.

"Mom," said Roxanne, turning one syllable into three.

Sebastian rolled his shoulders back, swelling his chest. "Do you have matching shorts," he joked.

"Yours are just fine," said Roxanne. "You don't want to be arrested."

"You're incorrigible," said Penelope, smiling.

The organizer checked his watch. "We should go. It's almost show time." He led his troop to the upwind side of the barbeque. A round dunk tank sat on the grass, awaiting the first dunkee. A city worker topped up the water with a garden hose.

"Nice and chilly," he said.

"At least it's clean," replied Sebastian, peering through the plastic window.

"That cage is made of steel," said the organizer, pointing at the chain-link wire surrounding the seat. "There's no danger from a wild pitch."

The organizer picked up a bullhorn to wrangle the crowd. "Our Celebrity Dunk is starting and the first victim of the day is Sebastian Hunter of CBC. So come on over folks and dunk the TV star. Three balls for five dollars."

Roxanne gave Sebastian a good-luck kiss and held up her phone. "I'll capture every sopping minute for Facebook."

Sebastian circled to the back of the tank, slipping off his sandals before climbing a short ladder and mounting the seat hanging over the water.

"Don't hold the seat," advised the organizer. "You could nip your fingers when it falls. And lean forward a bit."

Sebastian rested his hands on his lap. He noticed a stir in the crowd. A path opened. Premier Susan Robinson and her entourage swaggered through.

Just when I thought it couldn't get any worse.

"We asked the premier to be one of our celebrities," said the organizer. "She said no, but when she heard you'd be here she insisted on throwing the first balls."

"Morning, Sebastian," said Robinson. "Don't you look good in a cage." The premier's minions laughed.

"Bet you throw better insults than pitches, Premier."

"There's nothing wrong with this girl's arm."

Robinson held the ball with an underhand grip, as if it were a softball. She set her feet shoulder-width apart, slightly staggered. She bent at the hips as her throwing arm shot straight up, like a missile ready for launch. The premier took an explosive stride, her arm whipped in a vicious circle, her body twisting sideways as she uncorked the ball. Sebastian never saw it leave her hand; he only heard the clank when it hit the target. His seat collapsed and water filled his nose. Clapping and jeers greeted him and his coughing jag when he stood up.

"Strike one," sang the minion glee club. An obsequious aide handed the premier another ball.

"I used to pitch for the provincial softball team," boasted the premier. She dug a toe into the ground like she was on the mound.

"They put on the big target. The one they use for kids," taunted Sebastian. He squeegeed his hair. Water drained from his drenched shorts. He reset his roost and dangled his feet over the water.

The windup, a cannonball pitch, a slam-bang splash, water slopped out of the tank. Sebastian saw hyenas laughing through the bubbles.

"Strike two." The glee club had picked up new members. Spectators cheered the premier. "Dunk, dunk, dunk," chanted a few.

Sebastian shivered and wiped water out of his eyes. He assumed his precarious repose again.

"People who live in glass houses shouldn't throw balls, Premier."

Sebastian focussed on the premier's pitching hand. Her spread fingers caressed the ball, perhaps muscle memory searching for seams. He once read that Ted Williams could read the spin on a baseball in midflight. All Sebastian saw was a white streak. Water encased him. He sat cross-legged on the bottom and waved to Roxanne and Penelope through the window. Roxanne put a hand over her heart; Penelope blew him a kiss.

"Strike three," howled the glee club. "You're ou-u-u-t-t-t."

The Premier high-fived her lapdogs. She took a hundred-dollar bill from her pocket and dropped it into the donation jar.

"Worth every penny," she told the organizer before disappearing into the hullabaloo.

●

Thank God for turfed cabinet ministers. So full of spite for their former boss. So willing to pass along the dirt they would have taken to their own graves before their ignominious exit. Nothing spurs animosity and late-night phone calls like a cabinet shuffle and a good firing. Sebastian couldn't wait for Zoe to ask if anyone had any story ideas.

"Alright, let's get going," said Zoe.

Sebastian sprung to his feet. His announcement demanded theatre. He had a full house; the boardroom was padded with reporters and producers.

"Point of order, Madame Speaker," he said.

Zoe grinned. She knew the routine. While Sebastian's antics sometimes aggravated her, she enjoyed playing along in this venue. His political satire just might deliver a climax worthy of a lead story.

"Order, please. The chair recognizes the honourable Leader of the Opposition to Everything."

"Thank you, Madame Speaker," said Sebastian with a grandiose air. "As all members of this honourable house know, I don't spread rumours."

"Hear, hear," said some honourable members on Sebastian's side of the table. They slapped the table in approval; free hands grabbed bouncing coffee cups. Sebastian's nodding head kept time with the thumping.

"But when it comes to our holier-than-thou premier, I'm willing to make an exception."

"Shame, shame," cried honourable members on the opposite side of the table.

"This particular rumour is so delicious, so mouthwatering, that I would be remiss in my job as a purveyor of scandal if I did not share it with my colleagues."

"Oh, oh!" said honourable members on both sides of the table.

"Madame Speaker, it's come to my attention that the holier-than-thou premier has a problem of the proboscis variety." Sebastian snorted while holding his nose high.

"No way," said Zoe.

"Yes, Madam Speaker, it is shocking to say the least. I'm sure all honourable members in this honourable house, with the possible exception of the Minister of Dignity…," Sebastian held up a publicity photo of Garrison Hill, "would condemn this outrageous behaviour. The only positive spin I can possibly see, Madame Speaker, is that the premier is so concerned about the welfare of drug addicts in our province that she is personally ensuring they get access to the finest cocaine possible."

Sebastian sat down amid raucous table-banging.

"Typical CBC, Madame Speaker," observed Evan. "Negative. Only interested in the negative. And thank God for it." Evan leaned forward in his chair and rested on elbows. "As entertaining as that was, what can you prove?"

"At the moment—nothing." The entire room slumped. Eyes turned away. Janice twirled a ring on her finger. Sebastian scrambled to recapture his audience. "My sources are solid, but they won't go on the record. The premier has had a relapse into imprudent behaviour. And she's in complete denial, apparently. The knives are out, but only in the shadows. I need time to coax them into the light. I've got to pound the phones."

"Let's talk after the meeting. In the meantime, not a word leaves this room."

Sebastian felt exhilarated. He would smack the doubt right off their faces.

You put water up my nose. Just wait until I prove what you're putting up yours.

●

A plaque by a flower pot read Trinity House. Sebastian stooped to examine the yellow and purple flowers.

"What do you call these?"

"Pansies," answered Roxanne.

"They're quite attractive, aren't they?" Sebastian touched one. "They have blackfaces—a politically incorrect flower. Imagine. Are they annuals or perennials?"

"Annuals."

She was the most unenthusiastic gardener Sebastian had ever questioned. "We should plant some in the backyard," he said.

Roxanne laughed.

"What's so funny?" asked Sebastian.

"Are you the same Sebastian Hunter who stood on the deck and announced to the garden, 'Live or die, it's up to you.'"

Sebastian straightened up. "I've decided gardening can't be any more painful than visiting my father."

"It's *just* once a month. Sit down and have a chat."

"I'll end up doing all the talking, I always do."

"And that's hard for a reporter?"

"Just a few minutes. Okay?"

"We're in no rush," soothed Roxanne. "Whatever you want."

The sliding glass doors swished open. A cooking show blared from the TV in the front lobby.

"Careful with the salt or it will end up tasting like the Dead Sea," joked the chef.

"Must be an in-house channel," said Sebastian.

Three women slouching in wheelchairs appeared stupefied. Only one bothered to eyeball the visitors.

"Hello," she said in a frail voice.

"Hello, nice day," said Roxanne. The grey-haired woman brightened up. Roxanne and Sebastian followed the signs to Oak Wing, passing the cafeteria along the way. The menu promised shepherd's pie and green peas for supper. The meal was still half an hour away, but several residents had already been wheeled in. Caregivers dressed them in bibs. The men wore sensible, solid colours while the women had happy, bright prints.

"It's so depressing in here," moaned Sebastian. "This is what we have to look forward to—zombie television and gruel for supper. And you end up wearing most it."

Roxanne sighed. They turned the corner and dodged a speeding snack cart.

"He's acting up today, Sebastian," said a woman in a blue smock as she sprinted away from a man shuffling behind.

"Come back and I'll give you something really sweet," said Sebastian's father.

"You're not allowed to chase the women," said Sebastian calmly.

"Who are you?" he snapped.

"Sebastian. I'm your son. And this is Roxanne, my fiancée. You've met her before."

"Roxanne? Isn't there a song about you?"

"A different Roxanne."

"Are you sure you're not a hooker?"

"Absolutely."

He turned to Sebastian. His eyes wrestled to recall the face. "And who are you?"

"Sebastian."

"I have a son Sebastian. Never see him."

"Dad, it's a beautiful day. Let's go outside and feed the ducks."

"Ducks! I love duck. Do you think we'll have duck tonight?"

"No, it's shepherd's pie."

"Are you staying for supper?"

"No, another time. We have plans this evening."

"Hang on to my arm, Mr. Hunter," said Roxanne. All three took baby steps down the hall, passing a door with the name Tobias Hunter. A shallow case with a glass front hung on the wall. Inside was a photo of Tobias sitting behind a birthday cake with two lit candles. A six and a zero needed to be blown out.

Tobias squinted. "Is that me?"

"Yes, and this is your room."

"What do I do?"

"You used to be a lawyer," said Sebastian.

"Did I make money?"

"So much, it was criminal." Roxanne elbowed Sebastian in the ribs.

"Where's Olivia?"

"Mom's busy today." The answer was an incomplete truth. His mother was busy alright, busy looking after her new husband. She divorced Tobias five years earlier, after he was convicted of stealing from his clients' trust accounts. Sebastian always figured his father traded one prison for another when he was admitted to Trinity House.

The door to the garden was locked. Sebastian punched the code into the keypad. Five, two, three, nine—the most open secret on the wing. The bold-font numbers were written on a piece of paper pegged to the bulletin board, available to everyone who could comprehend them. The lock clicked open.

A parade of ducks started quacking the instant they saw the trio. Roxanne tossed a handful of rice near the tulips and the ducks veered off, clearing a path to the bench. Sebastian waited until his father sat down before telling him about his recent stories.

"So this cat is climbing out of the crater with a kitten in its mouth…." Sebastian stopped talking when he realized his father wasn't paying attention, wasn't even looking at him. He was leering at Roxanne.

"Just checking out her ass," said his father with a sly grin.

"You're not dead yet."

"What's your name?"

"Sebastian. I'm your son."

"What do you do for a living?" Roxanne and Sebastian exchanged knowing looks.

"I'm a TV reporter."

His father harrumphed. "Yes, I remember. Vultures. Muckrakers. Preying on the innocent."

"The judge didn't see it that way."

"Sebastian," chided Roxanne.

Sebastian rubbed his eyes. He knew better than to argue, but the words couldn't be reeled back.

"There were cameras everywhere. Microphones shoved in my face," shouted his father. "You and your kind crucified me."

"Just relax, Dad. Everything is okay."

"My son—a reporter. What a disgrace. What an embarrassment. I knew you'd never amount to much."

"Time for us to go, Roxanne," said Sebastian as he stood up. Roxanne tied a knot in the rice bag and slipped it into her pocket. Her flock of pecking ducks waddled back to the pond.

"Come on, Dad, we'll take you inside." It was a command. The trip back was much faster than the one out. Sebastian never let go of his father's elbow until Tobias was deposited in his recliner. The TV remote sat on the dresser, next to a box of chocolates and a photo of Sebastian. Sebastian brought the TV to life. The CBC news was on.

"Change the channel," ordered Tobias.

[three]

Sebastian put his feet up on his desk. Time for a quick game of Angry Birds. His finger stretched the virtual slingshot on his iPhone and released it with a boing. The wingless bird arced through the air, smashing into a fortress. Building-blocks tumbled, pigs' heads rolled and Sebastian scored 500 points.

"How goes the battle against the greedy pigs?" asked Janice over the wall dividing their cubicles.

"Great. I'm making more pigs homeless than the Big Bad Wolf ever did." Sebastian kept flinging birds. "Where are you coming from?"

"The hospital. Peggy Brown made a triumphant return today."

"So it's true, pigs *do* fly," said Sebastian. "But they still make very unlikely birds."

"Peggy was floating on air. I've never seen a woman so happy. It's amazing how a grovelling CEO can make you feel better."

"They should try that at the CBC."

"You can see the applause, the hugs and the tears this evening."

"He can do better than that," said Evan after sidling up behind them. "He can even read the intro."

"What's up?" asked Sebastian as he laid down his phone.

"Samantha called in sick. I need you to co-anchor with Garrison."

Sebastian slouched in his chair. "This works so much better if I'm replacing Garrison rather than Samantha. The last time we both wore grey suits. We looked like a gay wedding cake."

"I can do it," said Janice, eyes blinking. "I'll wear something splashy and we'll get a father-daughter vibe going."

Sebastian hopped to his feet. "No. I'll sort out the suits with Garrison."
Evan nodded and moved to leave.

"Evan, if you have a moment?" Sebastian craned his neck to check
Garrison's desk at the far end of the newsroom. The seat was empty. He
turned his back to the sprawling cubicles. "I'm a little concerned about
Garrison. People are starting to talk about his performance."

"Talk?"

"Yes, talk. This is awkward," he shrouded his words despite the
veil of the newsroom commotion, "but I was at a barbeque over
the weekend and Garrison's blunders were the main entertainment.
People were imitating him."

"They say imitation is the sincerest form of flattery."

"Trust me, this was not flattery, it was mockery. Remember
when he forgot his contacts and squinted through the entire newscast.
I spent the whole evening fending off slit-eyed drunks saying, 'I'm…,'"
Sebastian scrunched his face and waited another second, "'Garrison
Hill.'"

"Look, he's fifty-six and doesn't see as well as he used to. The
teleprompter needed a bigger font. The problem's been fixed."

Sebastian leaned forward. "You can't fix his ongoing blunders."

"We all make flubs."

"He's making an art form out of them. There's no room for anyone
else on the Christmas blooper tape. Do I have to remind you what he
said instead of Funk Island?"

Janice giggled. Evan rubbed his hands down his face. "That was a
good one."

"People kept asking me, 'Where's Fuck Island? I want to go.' I don't
like saying this, but he's turning us into the Canadian Boob Corporation.
He's not first with the news; he's first with the screw-ups."

"He still has flashes of brilliance."

"So do Alzheimer's patients. But then again, Garrison is the only
person on *Here & Now* who my father likes. What does that say?"

"Maybe you should leave your father out of it," suggested Evan.

Sebastian didn't break stride. "It's like Father Time sitting next
to Samantha. In twenty-five years there have been five Samanthas, but
only one Garrison. She stays forever young while he gets old. Everyone

calls him Garrison Over-the-Hill. We need a succession plan."

"We have your resume on file," said Evan, pointing to a cabinet smothered in dust.

"He could leave with honour. One of those special assignment jobs they give anchors who overstay their welcome. Something like— Sticking Point with Garrison Hill. A topical debate every week. Or how about—We Stand on Guard? Profiles of soldiers who served in Afghanistan and their struggle to reintegrate into Canadian society. No heavy lifting and a healthy dollop of fame."

"Garrison Hill is the senior anchor of *Here & Now*. He's not going anywhere, at least not today. Now, I've got work to do and so do you." Evan headed back to The Desk.

"Your naked ambition knows no bounds," warbled Janice. She tightened the knot in Sebastian's tie. "I like that in a man."

"Only voodoo can get us out of this mess," said Sebastian. "Maybe I could arrange a little heart attack."

He took a push pin from a corkboard and shoved it through a publicity postcard. A smiling Garrison Hill was impaled through the heart.

•

Sebastian steeled himself for the conversation. Ever since their blow-up in the newsroom, encounters with Garrison had been cool at best and testy at worst. Still, the discussion couldn't be avoided. He strode past beige cubicles to Garrison's green emporium. Garrison tipped a watering jug around a leafy plant.

He must think we're doing a gardening show. Tonight's top story— Holland has a new tulip.

"Hello, Sebastian," said Garrison, as he reached up to the top shelf. Plants hid the entire partition. Water glugged; just a little in each pot. His plants' thirst required daily excursions to the staff kitchen.

"This is lemon balm. It can tolerate full sun or full shade. It's always happy, no matter where it is. I find the scent calms me."

"That's great," said Sebastian, looking at the front page of the *Globe and Mail* lying on the desk. "Garrison, I was wondering what colour suit you're wearing tonight?"

Garrison wore smart casual pants and shirts most days, usually changing into a suit late in the afternoon. He concentrated on a plant with white leaves. "This is a peace lily. It really improves the air quality around my desk. The newsroom can be so stifling. Would you hand me the spray bottle, please?"

Sebastian passed a bottle with a blue handle. Garrison squeezed it vigorously below the air-conditioning vent. Mist wafted towards Sebastian. He grabbed the newspaper off Garrison's desk and fanned.

"If you're finished preparing the set for British Gardens, could we discuss suits?" Sebastian tossed the newspaper aside.

"You inquired about the colour of my suit." Garrison held up the spray bottle. "This must be a sign."

"So, you're wearing blue then?"

"Sure," said Garrison without conviction.

"I'll wear grey."

"Fine. We wouldn't want to be the Bobbsey Twins."

"My worry exactly," said Sebastian. "I'll leave you to save the rain forest."

"By the way, Sebastian, when you're writing your copy today, watch your verb-subject agreement."

The caution nailed Sebastian's feet to the carpet. "Excuse me?"

Garrison sat down. "I notice you sometimes have a little trouble sorting it out." He clicked on a file. Sebastian circled back and leaned over Garrison's shoulder. Garrison pointed to a line on the screen.

"See, you say here 'The legacy of Chief Bennett's indiscretion are embarrassment and hypocrisy.' It should have been 'The legacy of Chief Bennett's indiscretion is embarrassment and hypocrisy.' The subject is legacy. Legacy is a singular noun."

"That's it? That's all you took from my report about a drunk police chief—one little mistake. Incredible."

Garrison leaned back in his chair, resting his intertwined fingers on his stomach.

"If you're going to crucify a man, you might as well use proper grammar."

•

The landline phone on Sebastian's desk rang for the first time in days.

Call display told him it was Joan, the receptionist. The only other calls to that phone were wrong numbers for an electronics shop. Even if Sebastian answered with a forceful "Newsroom," he might still hear, "I need a fifty-volt capacitor." Sebastian had long given up saying, "You've dialled the wrong number." That was usually greeted with skepticism and demands for proof. No, it was simply easier to take the order. Keep the shoppers happy. Occasionally, Sebastian would offer two-for-one specials. "Yes sir, slow-blow fuses are on sale today."

"Hi, Joanie."

"Sebastian, there's a woman in the lobby waiting to see you."

He was wary of unexpected visitors. This woman in the lobby might spin a conspiracy theory and dump a box of documents on the front desk. Or she might moan about the power company cutting off her electricity, even though she hadn't paid a bill in months. Scoops never walked in off the street unannounced. Only nuisances did.

"Is she a crazy?"

"No, I'll offer her a coffee." Joan's all-clear code. It was safe to go downstairs. He had five minutes before Roxanne picked him up.

Sebastian grabbed his trench coat. The morning sun had given way to drizzle. He bypassed the elevator and took the stairs, his footsteps amplified by the cavernous lobby. He rounded the corner at the bottom and turned to stone—caught in mid-run like a statue memorializing an Olympic athlete. The woman sat in a red chair, a flaming red that matched her hair. What was that hair doing here? What was *she* doing here? She sorted through her purse. She hadn't seen him. Sebastian retraced his last step in a backwards, slow motion.

"Here he is," said Joan with her usual cheery voice.

The woman tossed her hair. "Sebastian." She vaulted out of the chair and rushed to hug him.

"Lindsay," said Sebastian feigning enthusiasm. "What a wonderful surprise. What are you doing here?"

"I apologize for not calling, but this was a last-minute trip. I'm doing research at the university."

Sebastian shuddered imperceptibly. Roxanne worked at the university library.

"I'm so close I thought I'd stop by. Do you have time for a coffee?"

"Well, actually I was just on my way home. I have to pick up a suit," said Sebastian touching his chest. "I'm hosting the show tonight."

"That's fantastic," she beamed. "I loved your drunken cop story, by the way. You are *bad*."

"How long are you in town?"

"A few days. It depends on how much progress I make." She moved closer. "I'd really like to see you."

"Sebastian, I think that's your ride," said Joan.

Sebastian and Lindsay both peered through the all-glass porch. He recognized his Acura, Roxanne at the wheel.

"I'm sorry, I have to go."

"How about lunch tomorrow?"

Sebastian swept towards the door and put on his coat.

"Not sure. I'll text you. Bye."

"I have…" The click of the closing door lock drowned out, "a new number."

A hug and a hightailing in under a minute—a personal best. Sebastian's unbuttoned coat flapped as he sprinted to the car.

"Hi, honey," said Sebastian, kissing her on the cheek.

Roxanne pulled away from the curb. The CBC shrank in the rear-view mirror.

"Who was that?"

"The woman in the lobby?"

"Yes, the woman who hugged you."

"I met her up in Paradise Point when the house fell over the cliff. She was friendly."

"Very friendly, apparently."

Sebastian lowered the window, just a crack, to let out the air of disapproval.

"Appreciative, I think. I showed her around the satellite truck."

"Watched your report go up to the bird, did she?"

"It was a big thrill for her. I said, 'If you're ever in town, look me up.'"

"What's her name?

"Lindsay Moore."

"What's she doing here?"

"She said research at the university."

"I'll keep my eyes open for her."

The windshield wipers squeaked. Roxanne adjusted the timing after she stopped at a red light. A bus drove through the intersection. A jumbo CBC logo rolled past, followed by a colossal Garrison Hill and Samantha Cormier. Arms folded, faces stern. *BREAKING NEWS and ALL THE RULES.* "What a moronic slogan," said Sebastian. "When did Garrison ever break the rules?"

●

Sebastian was late. He liked to be in the studio half an hour before newscast time to sort through the inevitable technical glitches and rehearse the headlines. But today mediocrity kept him at his desk.

"Who writes this shit?" huffed Sebastian as he rewrote the intro to the lead story. The answer was someone on The Desk. Some producer who forgot that the intro is hype, like the huckster outside a Barnum & Bailey Circus tent shouting, "Come inside and see the bearded lady."

He pounded the keyboard with two fingers. The clatter filled his corner of the newsroom.

"Sebastian," shouted Evan from the horseshoe, "the clock is running, get downstairs."

Twenty minutes to air, Sebastian hit Print All Scripts, bringing the printer in the studio to life. He dashed to the stairwell and skipped down the steps, avoiding a somersault by sliding his hands along the parallel railings.

"Look out below," he called to the video librarian at the bottom. She pressed her back against the wall and Sebastian hustled by.

Sebastian pushed open the heavy studio door. He stopped by a mirror and checked his tie—a royal blue tie that jumped off his cream-coloured shirt. They blended nicely with his grey suit. It was a prized possession from a vacation in Hong Kong. The camera would love the combination.

The printer behind the *Here & Now* set furiously spit out pages. Sebastian grabbed an inch-high pile of scripts. They were a precaution in case the teleprompter failed, but they also allowed him to easily skip ahead to upcoming intros for one last read, something Garrison Hill never seemed to do given the frequency of his bungles.

The *Here & Now* set divided the studio the way the wall once divided Berlin. On one side: dreariness, a colourless world kept grim by dim lighting, black curtains, and unpainted plywood. On the other side: glamour, lights capable of guiding a plane through fog, and bold red letters shouting *Here & Now*. Splashes of blue, dissected by crimson lines, surrounded jumbo televisions. Robotic cameras spun in front of a glistening black-top desk with regal chairs. Just one step transported Sebastian into the magic kingdom.

You've got to be kidding me.

Sebastian dropped his scripts on the anchor desk. A startled Garrison Hill peered over the reading glasses hanging on the tip of his nose. His look demanded an explanation for the jarring entrance.

"Garrison, you said you'd wear a blue suit."

"I thought you were wearing the blue."

"No, remember up in the newsroom, you looked at the blue handle on your spray bottle and said, 'This must be a sign.' You were supposed to wear blue, not grey."

"Sorry, it slipped my mind." Garrison examined his tie. "At least I got the right colour in the tie," he chuckled. "We both have excellent taste in ties."

"Yes, I'm sure the Society for Unimaginatively Dressed Couples will give us an award."

"Don't worry about it," admonished Garrison. "People don't care if men wear the same suits. It happens all the time. Women wearing the same clothes get all the catty comments. We get off easy."

Spoken like a man who has never heard of Twitter trolls.

Sebastian visualized biting photo manipulations. Gay wedding cake toppers starring Garrison Hill and Sebastian Hunter: Dancing Garrison and Sebastian, Kissing Garrison and Sebastian, Crossing the threshold Garrison and Sebastian.

Thankfully we're not wearing top hats.

Sebastian clipped tiny dual microphones on his lapel and plopped into the empty chair behind the desk. He adjusted the volume on his earpiece, his link to the director in the control room.

"Don't the two of you look sweet," said the voice in Sebastian's ear.

"You make a handsome couple. I think I'm going to cry."

"Roddy," said Sebastian, as he raised his middle finger to the camera, "don't make me come in there."

Sebastian logged onto his laptop. *Here & Now* scripts are living creatures. Last minute changes happen daily. And occasionally, someone has the audacity to undo what he has done. Sebastian always gave himself enough time to change the words back. He glanced at Garrison's screen. His co-host was playing Solitaire.

"Red eight on black nine," said Sebastian.

Another newscast where I'll have to carry him on my back.

Sebastian and Garrison rehearsed the show-opening twice, the last run-through finishing just a minute to air. Sebastian and Garrison alternated the headlines with Sebastian going first. The lead story was his. Sebastian had uncovered yet another embarrassing example of government favouritism.

"This is for real," said Roddy in both men's earpieces. He counted backwards from ten. The *Here & Now* theme poured into Sebastian's ear. He kept time with his foot to the pounding drums, while swirling animation revealed video of a paving machine laying asphalt.

"Tonight...It pays to have the blues. The Tory government will pave its own districts first."

Garrison's voice jumped in behind.

"Giving drive-thru a whole new meaning. A drunk driver takes out a Tim Hortons."

Sebastian watched security footage of a car crashing through a window and plowing into the counter, spraying donuts high and low. The video inspired Sebastian to create an unspoken, alternative headline.

The cop and the cruller. Chief Bennett gets the late-night munchies.

"Barely keeping their heads above water. Homes in Airport Heights are flooded."

A hose wriggling out of a basement window created a backyard brook next to a pile of waterlogged boxes and furniture.

"Got to get his mousse. He tried to steal a hunting rifle. He ended up with hair gel."

The perp walk of shame: a sheriff escorted a handcuffed man in an orange jumpsuit past the media horde. The video ended with *Here & Now* swooshing across the screen. A camera gently narrowed the live shot of Sebastian and Garrison in the studio.

"Good evening everyone and welcome to Here & Now. I'm Garrison Hill."

"And I'm Sebastian Hunter. Our top story tonight, the government is going on a paving spree, but only in its own districts. For every mile paved in Liberal districts, at least two will be paved in Conservative districts. And some Liberal districts won't get any asphalt at all. The premier denies that it's favouritism. But a Here & Now investigation has discovered that being on the right team means a smooth ride."

Sebastian watched his own report on the monitors. He smiled as the premier fumbled through an implausible explanation. Geology made roads in Liberal districts more expensive to pave than roads in Conservative districts, she explained, so the Liberals were getting their fair share after all. But Sebastian had uncovered an engineer's report which showed the cost per kilometre was the same everywhere. The flummoxed premier promised to investigate.

"Gotcha," said Sebastian.

Garrison ignored Sebastian's self-congratulation and continued typing on his computer. The senior anchor didn't look up until Roddy told both men, "Ten seconds." Sebastian scowled off camera as Garrison read his first intro.

"A drunk driver parked his car inside a Tim Hortons this morning. Police say when they arrived, the driver rolled down the window and asked for a double-double. Instead of coffee, he got a breathalyzer test. He blew double the legal limit…."

Sebastian scrolled through Garrison's upcoming scripts. There hadn't been a Garrison gaffe in a couple of weeks. Perhaps he needed a nudge in the right direction. Sebastian read the kicker, the last news script in the block before the weather. The kicker signals a change in direction. Death and mayhem are temporarily suspended. Viewers are treated to an uplifting story. Better still, a funny story.

This is not funny enough, thought Sebastian, it needs a screw-up.

He typed one into the kicker.

The newscast plodded along. Two dozen homes had their basements flooded when a contractor punctured a water main. A thief tried breaking into a gun shop, but accidentally dropped through the ceiling of a hair salon next door and landed on a case of mousse.

Sebastian bounced with excitement as the kicker rolled up the teleprompter. Garrison's face brightened to match the bright story.

"City workers are busy uprooting flower beds. They're planting more perennials this year. And the flower of choice is the concubine."

Garrison's face flagged; perhaps he realized he had blundered yet again. Sebastian turned away and bit a knuckle to stop himself from laughing out loud. The audience saw video of a work crew pushing wheelbarrows full of blue and red flowers. Garrison paused the teleprompter using the control pad on the desk. His eyes oscillated between the paper script in his hands and the digital script in front of the camera. Sebastian relished the cock-up concentration.

"A concubine flower bed. That really would be something wouldn't it? That should have been columbine. Columbine is the city's flower of choice this year."

Garrison's adlib dovetailed into the written script.

"Columbine flowers come in many colours. The plant tolerates drought well and it's ideal for rock gardens. The city grew the plants from seed in greenhouses over the winter."

Camera two spun around, providing a wide shot of both Garrison and Sebastian. Garrison wore a self-deprecating smile.

"Garrison, where exactly is the city getting those seeds? I think a lot of guys would like to buy some."

Both Sebastian and Garrison let out hearty laughs.

"Let's ask meteorologist Rhonda White if the columbine," said Garrison emphasizing the last word, *"will be getting any rain over the next few days."*

"You boys," said Rhonda squelching her laughter. *"There's no hope for either of you. Unfortunately, for the columbine,"* Rhonda imitated Garrison's emphasis, *"we're in a heat wave."*

"It certainly feels like a heat wave inside the studio," said Garrison.

"That's all the sultry talk," said Sebastian, attempting to wring one more laugh out of the latest Garrisonism.

Garrison grimaced. His forehead glistened. A bead of perspiration ran down his temple. He rubbed his chest.

"I'm sorry, I don't feel well."

Sebastian dropped his smile. Rhonda stopped giggling. Garrison slumped in his chair.

"Garrison, are you alright?" Sebastian touched his shoulder. Garrison didn't move, didn't speak. His chin rested on his tie knot.

That was the last image viewers had of Garrison Hill. After that, they saw a *Here & Now* slide. Roddy had cut the cameras.

"Call 9-1-1," he shouted into Sebastian's ear. "I'll get the defibrillator."

Sebastian's shaking finger dialled 8-1-1. He dialled 9-1-1 on the next try.

"Emergency services," said the voice.

"Send an ambulance to the CBC. I think Garrison Hill is having a heart attack."

"It's already on its way. We've had calls already."

Sebastian and Rhonda stared at the motionless Garrison. He looked like he was dozing.

"Is he breathing?" asked Rhonda in a stressed octave.

"I don't think so."

"Do you know CPR?"

Sebastian shook his head. He heard running behind the set. Roddy and a contingent from the newsroom scrambled past the cameras. Roddy bounded up on the riser, tossing the defibrillator on the desk, splaying Garrison's neat pile of unread scripts. He put two fingers on Garrison's neck, just beside his Adam's apple.

"I'm not getting a pulse," said Roddy. "Help me lie him down."

Sebastian threw his chair off the riser to make space. The wheels clanged on the concrete floor.

Roddy pulled Garrison's chair away from the desk. Garrison tilted like a falling tree. A slew of arms grabbed him amid shouts of "Watch his head." They gently laid Garrison on the riser.

"Sebastian, your jacket," demanded Roddy. Sebastian hesitated. Roddy's eyes implored speed. Sebastian slipped off his Hong Kong suit jacket. The one made by Sam's Tailor on the Kowloon Peninsula. The same store where George W. Bush and Bill Clinton had bought suits. Sebastian carefully draped the jacket over an arm and passed it over. Roddy balled it up and stuffed it under Garrison's head.

Sebastian drifted behind Roddy. Apparently, it wasn't enough that Roddy could do the work once done by fourteen people, thanks to computers and automation. He also knew how to save a life.

"Begin by removing all clothing from the patient's chest," intoned the defibrillator's electronic voice. Buttons flew as Roddy tore open Garrison's shirt. His tie, turned noose, landed on Sebastian's shoe.

Roddy followed successive commands—attaching pads to Garrison's bare skin, one on a collar bone and a second on a breast bone.

"Shock advised," said the machine. "Charging, stand clear." Sebastian stepped back.

Roddy pressed a button with a lightning-bolt symbol. Garrison's body convulsed. No response, no breathing. Roddy tried chest compressions. He was blowing into Garrison's mouth when the paramedics wheeled a stretcher into the studio. They whisked Garrison away with the newsroom crowd in tow, everyone except Sebastian.

He waited until he heard the studio door close before bending over Garrison's laptop. Sebastian maximized the tab for *Here & Now*'s lineup and chose the story slugged *City Flowers*. The script which Garrison tripped over appeared on screen. Sebastian erased concubine and typed columbine. He hit refresh. The Modified By box displayed hillg. Garrison's fingerprints were the only ones on the script.

Sebastian picked up his rumpled jacket off the riser. He hooked a finger under the collar and shook out the wrinkles before slinging the jacket over his shoulder. Worry and anxiety were spectators outside. He should join them.

Red lights slashed across the parking lot. For the first time in his career, Sebastian wasn't shooting a stretcher being loaded into an ambulance. It would have been overkill. Garrison's graceless exit was already being recorded from every conceivable angle on a legion of iPhones.

Janice sidled over to Sebastian. "You're the Grim Reaper," she whispered.

•

Sebastian poured Ron Zacapa into a cognac glass. He coiled the rum as he read the headline.

Here & Now Host Garrison Hill Dead at 56

A publicity photo of a smiling Garrison standing by the *Here & Now* desk stretched across CBC's webpage. The same desk where he had his last laugh, where he took his last breath. Sebastian raised his glass in salute and sipped.

"Garrison, you give new meaning to the phrase dying on the air."

The story quoted Garrison's moist-eyed wife outside the emergency department of the General Hospital.

"*The doctors declared Garrison dead on arrival. They said he didn't suffer.*"

He died from an apparent heart attack, but there would be an autopsy just to be certain. His wife explained that Garrison had been battling high cholesterol for years.

Television and Garrison had been married longer than Garrison and his grieving widow. After graduating from Ryerson University, Garrison landed a job with a television station in Barrie, Ontario. He never looked back; he only looked into the camera. In thirty-four years, he never once dirtied his hands with newspaper ink, never once suffered the faceless anonymity of radio.

"*I love the smell of the greasepaint and the roar of the crowd,*" Garrison jokingly said in a 2014 interview.

The crowd certainly roared its approval on this night. Tributes saturated the Comments section, but Sebastian didn't bother reading them. He typed "anchor dies laughing" into Google. YouTube video of Garrison's exit topped the results. The viewer tally sat at 84,324. And he was only dead two hours. Thumbs Up—2,445. Thumbs Down—135. Sebastian gave thumbs up to the computer screen.

"If you live by the sword, you die by the sword. Even better if you die in high definition."

The front door opened.

"I'm in the office, Roxanne," yelled Sebastian. He returned to the CBC webpage and clicked on the link Your Condolences on the Passing of Garrison Hill. He heard footsteps on the hardwood behind him.

Roxanne laid a hand on his shoulder and squeezed with the gentleness of a concerned fiancée. Sebastian reached across his chest to hold her hand. Heavy sigh.

"They loved him, Roxanne. We loved him."

"I know." She kissed the top of his head. "How are you feeling?"

"Numb. I did everything I could to save him. I rolled up my jacket and laid it under his head. Then I ripped open his shirt to let Roddy slap on the defibrillator pads. We couldn't get a spark out of him. Roddy even tried CPR. I was just about to take over when the paramedics showed up."

A tear rolled down Roxanne's cheek. Sebastian wiped it away with the same thumb used to endorse the YouTube video.

"How awful, dying in such a public way."

"I know. There was no dignity, Roxanne. He was a good man and he deserved better—a longer career and an even longer life. It was all cut too short. No one can ever replace him."

"I'll get a glass and we'll toast Garrison together."

"I don't know if he'd approve of rum," said Sebastian. "Garrison didn't drink. It was his only failing."

"You say the sweetest things."

Sebastian's phone vibrated as Roxanne headed to the china cabinet—a text from Janice.

Been thinking, Grim Reaper is boring.

Stealer of Souls? Angel of Death? Ferryman of the Dead?

Sebastian glanced at the photo on the desk. He and Roxanne laughing, their hair blown back, both listing to starboard behind the helm of her father's sailboat.

Ferryman of the Dead has a nice ring to it. ☺

•

A bouquet of angelic white roses sat in the centre of Garrison's desk. Sebastian smelled the flowers. Fragrance free.

All show, no substance. Typical Garrison.

Sebastian sensed he was being watched. Janice and Rhonda walked toward him, heads down.

"Don't look at the eyes," said Janice. "Don't look at the eyes." Her second caution was louder. The two women giggled and shielded their eyes with upright hands.

"Don't make me kill again," threatened Sebastian as they passed by.

"Sebastian, do you have a minute?" Evan stood in his office doorway.

"Well at least you're brave enough to look me in the eye."

"Ah yes, the evil eye. I've heard all about it."

"So far today a husband asked me to dispatch his wife, and a wife asked me to dispatch her husband. Get this—they're married to each other. I warned them—no two-for-one deals."

Evan laughed.

Sebastian picked a push pin off Evan's desk and pointed the tip at a staff photo. "Is there anyone you need to have a heart attack?"

"No, that's very kind of you, but I don't want to bury anyone. And neither should you. Instead, I need you to praise Caesar."

"I'm not following."

"I was talking to Sharon Hill. Garrison's funeral is on Saturday. Sharon asked if someone from the newsroom would give a eulogy. I was just drawing in the breath to say, 'I'd be honoured' when she suggested *you*."

"Me." Sebastian wore a startled face.

"Exactly what I thought. Apparently, Garrison was talking about retiring. Told her the torch had been passed to the next generation. He mentioned you as a likely successor, despite the fact he considered you an arrogant SOB. Sharon wants you to represent the newsroom. What was I going to say? 'I think that's a bad idea because Sebastian may have willed your husband's death.'"

"I only wished for a mild heart attack, not a fatal one."

"Garrison wasn't close to anyone in the newsroom. I couldn't offer Sharon an alternative. If you don't want to do it, you're going to have to tell her yourself."

Sebastian leaned back in the chair.

An audience for the taking.

"I'll do it for Sharon. I truly admired Garrison."

"Right. You keep that up."

"Don't worry; they'll laugh, they'll cry, it'll be better than *CATS*."

•

Sebastian drove around the parking lot at Carnell's Funeral Home three times. Every spot was taken. He parked his Acura on the grass underneath a No Parking sign and headed for the door. Janice walked out wearing a yellow skirt.

"It's great for TV, but I don't think of yellow as a funeral colour," said Sebastian.

"I'm wearing black unmentionables."

Sebastian feigned shock and fanned himself.

"Have you finished writing the eulogy?" asked Janice.

"Not completely. I want to run a few things by Sharon, but I'll have Garrison Hill canonized before I'm done. A lover of mankind and God's gift to journalism."

"There's a crush of people inside. You'd better go or you won't see her before midnight."

Garrison Hill—Salon A. Sebastian obeyed the arrow and turned right towards the din. But he didn't recognize anyone standing in the hallway. He passed through a gauntlet of boisterous conversations before pausing to sign the guest book. Sebastian scanned the salon from the doorway, but couldn't see Sharon through the cracks in the throng. He weaved his way towards the casket, occasionally getting a flicker of recognition from the mourners.

Let's see if the mortician is any better at applying makeup than Garrison.

Sebastian ignored the kaleidoscope of photos on the picture boards. He laid a hand on the open casket.

He's a dead ringer for somebody, but not Garrison Hill.

Sebastian read the brass plate on the casket—Alistair O'Keefe.

Garrison's cock-ups are contagious.

"Mr. Hunter, thank you so much for coming," said a voice.

Sebastian turned to see a twenty-something brunette. She wore a fetching black dress and a necklace with a teardrop pearl. Her puffy eyes were enchanting.

"It was the least I could do. I'm so sorry for your loss."

"I recognized you when you came in. I'm Alistair's daughter, Judy."

Sebastian extended his right hand and peeked at her left. No ring. Her handshake was gentle, none of the stiffness he encountered from the power skirts he interviewed. He didn't let go. The handshake became handholding.

"Your father was a good man. It's tragic he died so young." Sebastian finally let her hand slide away.

"How did you know my father?"

"We met once while I was shooting a story."

"Dad never mentioned it. He always grumbled that he never met anyone famous. Building engineers rarely do."

Sebastian smiled. "He was very helpful. Our lights kept blowing the circuit breakers. He came up with a fix. I remembered him when I saw his name on the notice board in the lobby." He glanced at the photo display. "You have your dad's eyes."

"That's very kind of you." Judy welled up. "I didn't think I had any more tears left."

"I'm sorry. I didn't mean to upset you."

"That's alright. I'm a crier at the best of times. I even cry during Hallmark commercials." She elegantly pulled a tissue from a dress sleeve and sponged a tear.

"A tear as beautiful as that necklace."

She stroked the pearl. "Dad gave me this on my twenty-first birthday."

"He obviously thought the world of you."

"Come over and meet the rest of the family."

"I'd love to, but I'm expected at Garrison Hill's wake and I'm already late. Call me when you're feeling up to it. Let's have a coffee."

Sebastian hesitated outside the salon long enough to type Judy O'Keefe into his reminder app. In memoriam research was required. Google would be his wingman.

•

The sidewalk leading to the Anglican Cathedral teemed with men and women in dark clothing. Sebastian and Roxanne passed a cop directing cars away from the already-full parking lot.

"I hope they saved a spot for the premier close to the doors," said Sebastian. "She really gets annoyed if she has to walk more than the length of herself."

"That's not a very benevolent observation from someone who wrote a eulogy full of benevolence. It is full of benevolence, isn't it?"

"Of course it is. I'm all heart when it comes to Garrison. Less so with the premier. She likes to make a spotlight entrance."

"She didn't look lazy when she dunked you," said a droll Roxanne.

"I guess my baptism didn't purge all my wicked ways."

"She didn't wash away your confidence. I heard you practicing last night. You sounded good."

"I've re-written the eulogy half a dozen times. I went from being too funny to not being funny enough. I think I've got the right balance now."

"And the right suit. You look handsome."

Sebastian pulled down his jacket sleeves. "Dark blue—good for TV, weddings, and funerals."

A minibus from Trinity House pulled up in front of the church. A gaggle of elderly women hobbled off the bus. Sebastian had never seen such a collection of canes, walkers and oxygen tanks.

"There's Garrison's fan club. He certainly had a way with the ladies."

Roxanne jabbed her elbow into Sebastian's side. "Be nice."

"He lived for his fans."

"Very funny. You don't have to mask your grief with black humour, Sebastian."

A group of teenagers in hockey sweaters scuffed their way through the doors.

"Was he a coach?" asked Roxanne.

Sebastian shrugged. He looked across the street. Three TV cameras sat on tripods; every station in town was there. CBC agreed to provide the pool feed inside the church.

I'll be on every TV in the province.

"Sebastian," yelled Janice as she bustled between the parked cars.

"Pretend you don't hear," said Roxanne. "Keep walking." She clamped onto Sebastian's arm and towed him forward.

"Who's not being nice now?"

"I've tried to like that woman, but can't," hissed Roxanne. "She has a nasty streak."

Janice jostled through the churchgoers and caught up to the fleeing couple. "What a crowd. Every *Here & Now* fan must be here. And even some non-fans. I just saw the premier on the far side of the parking lot. She was bitching at her husband."

"Told you," said Sebastian to Roxanne.

"Roxanne, you're certainly a brave woman," said Janice.

"What do you mean?"

"Sitting next to Sebastian in God's holy sanctuary. When the lightning bolt strikes, you're bound to be singed."

Roxanne looked puzzled. Sebastian acted puzzled.

"Remember the Tenth Commandment—Thou Shalt Not Covet Thy Neighbour's House. Sebastian is after Garrison's house, so to speak."

Roxanne appeared as baffled as before.

"The anchor chair," explained Janice.

Roxanne pursed her lips. "Excuse me for a minute. I see Evan and I should say hello."

Sebastian waited until Roxanne pitter-pattered away before speaking. "Avarice is a mortal sin. I'm trying to keep it in check until after the funeral."

"You should be thankful I didn't say Thou Shalt Not Kill. I'm assuming Roxanne doesn't know that you're the Ferryman of the Dead."

"I didn't think she'd see the humour."

"Are you going to The Ship after the funeral?"

"Absolutely. Evan says he's buying the first round. Let's all raise a glass to the teetotaler."

"I should let you rescue Roxanne before Grandpa Evan puts her to sleep with his war stories."

Janice climbed the church steps, her dress hugging her hips and thighs. Sebastian ogled every accentuated curve.

Thou Shalt Not Covet Thy Neighbour's Ass. Surely God didn't mean that one.

"Sightseeing?"

His head gyrated. Roxanne stood by his side.

"Fashion critique," said Sebastian. "Who wears a tight dress to a funeral?"

Roxanne raised a hand. Sebastian fortified himself for a finger wag. She straightened his tie instead.

"Okay, let's go in."

•

Garrison Hill's nephew stood at the pulpit. He was not much younger than Sebastian. "The twenty-third Psalm was one of Uncle Garrison's favourite passages."

Sebastian reached inside his jacket and touched folded papers, reassuring himself that the eulogy hadn't disappeared from his pocket.

"Don't fidget," whispered Roxanne.

"Yea, though I walk through the valley of the shadow of death," said the nephew with throaty inflection, "I will fear no evil." His gaze landed on Sebastian.

"Thou preparest a table before me in the presence of mine enemies." The tone was even more ominous. He added unsynchronized hand movements to the rest of his reading, never wavering from his bedrock cadence.

Somebody at Toastmasters turned this guy into Pastor Darth Vader.

"And I will dwell in the house of the Lord forever."

Garrison's sister limped to the pulpit. "Too much wine after the wake," said Sebastian. "Tripped over the sidewalk. She's taking it hard."

"Oh dear," said Roxanne in a low voice.

"The reading is an excerpt from Psalm 139."

The sister excelled at monotony.

"Surely thou wilt slay the wicked, O God."

Yet another set of condemning eyes. Sebastian checked his feet to make sure they hadn't turned into cloven hoofs.

"Search me, O God, and know my heart: try me, and know my thoughts: And see if there be any wicked way in me, and lead me in the way everlasting."

Garrison's sister hobbled to her pew, making way for the priest in his white robe and purple stole.

"Garrison Hill," the priest rhapsodized, "was a devoted father and husband, and a winning hockey coach. But most people knew him as the host of *Here & Now*. A visitor to our living rooms every night—a journalist you could always trust."

Roxanne squeezed Sebastian's hand before he headed to the pulpit.

The Bible was open. Sebastian pressed out the fold in the eulogy right over Psalm 139. Garrison's wife and two shapely daughters sat in the front pew with beseeching eyes: please make Garrison come alive, please ease our pain, please make us proud.

The podium creaked as Sebastian gripped it with both hands. He inhaled, but stalled when he caught an unexpected face in the crowd— Paul Bennett, sitting behind Garrison's widow. Not in his police chief uniform, rather a black suit.

At least his suit is sober.

The priest cleared his throat. Roxanne mouthed the word *go.*

A sunbeam landed on the casket spray. Sebastian gestured towards the circle of light surrounding the purple and pink flowers resting on top of Garrison.

"God's spotlight. Could there be any better sign that *everyone* watched Garrison Hill?"

Laughter rolled through the congregation and encircled Garrison's family. Mirth pushed sorrow aside.

"When I was growing up, there was a rule in our house. We had to finish supper by six o'clock so Dad could sit on the chesterfield with a cup of tea and watch Garrison Hill. Mom and I were there too. *Here & Now* was a family event. And every family up and down the street was doing the same thing."

Heads nodded.

Sebastian had picked a spot on the back wall, just above the crowd. He focused there, occasionally arcing left or right. He looked no one in the eye, but from their point of view he looked everyone in the eye.

"Garrison never lost his hold on the audience. When I became a reporter, a Mountie once told me that he gave up going to houses between six and seven o'clock. Trying to interview a witness during that hour was an exercise in frustration. Garrison Hill was on the TV and nobody would pay any attention to a cop."

Titters abounded.

It was time for the pièce de résistance—the story that had turned

Garrison Hill into a CBC legend.

"It was just minutes to air and a sputtering Garrison ran into the studio. Arms swinging and papers flying." Sebastian flailed his arms. "The script assistant was in full pursuit. Garrison stopped by a camera and turned around to finish his conversation. What he didn't realize was that his pants' pocket had hooked a knob on the camera. He set off for the anchor desk like a lightning bolt and ripped the front of his pants wide open."

Sharon Hill placed a hand over her mouth to hide her laughter. Her daughters' faces shared both tears and wide smiles.

"There was no time to change, so Garrison simply dropped his pants and told the director to keep the shots tight. He read the entire newscast in his underwear."

The priest guffawed. The church roared. A few people clapped. Sebastian subdued his own laughter, practicing false modesty for the bewitched congregation. He waited until the last chortle faded.

Cue the tears.

"Garrison Hill was the kind of journalist we all should be."

Sebastian oozed admiration. He sprinkled Garrison quotes and complimentary adjectives into eager ears.

Self-deprecating—"It's only TV news. Nobody died."

Decent—"Let he who is without sin cast the first sound bite."

Professional—"Let the facts stand in the way of a good story."

All uttered without the slightest blush.

"Husband, father, colleague…friend." Sebastian's voice cracked. "Garrison Hill had two great loves in his life—his family and TV news. We will miss him terribly. He may be gone, but he is not fading to black in our hearts."

Sebastian let his words hang before folding the eulogy. He heard sniffles and slurps. There were enough tears to fill the baptismal font. A woman in the back with an oxygen tank wheezed. Sebastian stopped at Garrison's casket, laid his hand on it and bowed his head. Sharon Hill said thank you between sobs. He slid into his pew and curled his fingers around Roxanne's outstretched hand. Someone behind patted his shoulder and said, "Well done."

Sebastian followed the sunbeam from the casket to a stained-glass window: Christ adorned with a halo preached to kneeling disciples. A gold banner swirled below—Admonish the Sinner.

•

The cathedral's bell tolled over the city. Fifty-six clangs—one for every year of Garrison Hill's life.

The pallbearers wheeled Garrison's casket out the stately doors towards an honour guard of teenage boys wearing hockey sweaters. Six Wildcats down a side, all standing at attention, their sombre faces littered with zits. The line went from tall to short as it jutted out from the cathedral. Every player held a stick, blades on the pavement as if reaching for a pass.

Roxanne slipped her arm through Sebastian's. "This is so sweet."

"Present sticks!" said the boy with a C on his sweater. The two lines lifted their sticks in unison, like military officers raising swords for an approaching bride and groom.

"Just like an Arch of Sabres," said Roxanne.

"Good Canadian boys," said Sebastian in his best Don Cherry impersonation.

Garrison and his pallbearers passed under the arch. The runts closest to the hearse strained to keep their sticks aloft, their hands shaking. Garrison had preordained his cremation. His family would spread the ashes at their cottage, his favourite summer destination.

Sebastian rubbed an eye.

"Are you feeling alright?" asked Roxanne. She touched his shoulder and drew him in.

"I'm fine, really."

"It's okay to be sad."

"It's just a speck of dirt."

"Don't bottle it up."

"Roxanne, I'm past the tears."

"Excuse me," said a woman clutching a purse with a tissue poking through the clasp. She smelled of liniment. Her hair was tinged blue.

"I'm sorry to bother you. I'm with the group from Trinity House. I just wanted to say that was a marvellous eulogy."

Sebastian turned jovial. "That's very kind of you. Thank you."

"I'm Bertha."

"Bertha, I was honoured to do it. Garrison was a great man."

"We watched him every night on the big-screen TV in the lobby. Everyone except Hilda, that is. She likes channel five."

"One of God's great mysteries. But on a day like this, even an adversary is welcome," said Sebastian pointing to the NTV camera.

"I have no idea what Hilda sees in those people. We vote her down all the time and keep *Here & Now* on."

"I've always said Garrison had good fans at Trinity House."

The pallbearers slid the casket into the hearse. The hockey players tapped their sticks on the parking lot, the way they tap the ice when somebody's number has been retired.

"We tried to convince your father to come along. We thought the outing would do him good and of course he could see *you*." Bertha dropped her eyes. "He said no."

"Dad's not much of a hockey fan."

The woman chuckled. "Such wit. You must get it from your father. He says the funniest things sometimes."

"Yes, always a laugh with Dad."

"Well, your father missed a wonderful tribute. Garrison would have appreciated it. He was such a gentleman."

"He was indeed, a real gentleman."

Sebastian spotted Chief Bennett by the hearse.

"Would you excuse me. I see an officer next to that gentleman, and I should talk to him."

Death lifts us up where we belong.

Bertha held Roxanne's hand. "He's so handsome. Don't let that one get away, dear."

"Don't you worry, I won't."

●

The pallbearers laid their white gloves on top of Garrison's casket. Janice and Evan stood unobtrusively beside the TV cameras, perfectly situated to see Sharon Hill embrace her daughters, tears trickling. Sharon kissed her fingers and touched her husband's nameplate.

"If only I could be the kind of person who inspires such tenderness," said Janice.

"Tenderness needs cultivation," said Evan. "It doesn't grow in hostile conditions."

"If I wanted that kind of empathy, I'd be with Sebastian."

"He's already taken. How did Roxanne get tangled up with him, anyway?" asked Evan. "She seems so…nice."

"Too nice. She's a Stepford Wife. Perfect hair. Perfect dress. Perfect in every nauseating way."

"A saucer of milk for one, please," said Evan holding up a finger to the oblivious funeral director. "She's certainly beautiful."

"I'd be too if I troweled on the makeup like that," sneered Janice. "She must have cemented her eyes shut. She can't see the real Sebastian."

The hearse lumbered away. Sharon Hill made a tiny wave goodbye, the sort that parting lovers do when one is not looking.

"Yet another woman who thinks Sebastian is a saint," said Janice. "She has no idea that the man who praised the love of her life wished him gone."

"If you tell her, she'll never forgive you. She has the illusion her husband was loved by all. Why spoil it?"

"I won't. Condolences only. I'll see you later at The Ship."

Janice examined her dress. Straight lines, no clinging. She waited for a break in the stream of mourners hugging Sharon. Her own hug left an air pocket between them.

"Sharon, I'm so sorry for what's happened."

"That's very kind, Janice. It was a wonderful service, wasn't it?"

"Sebastian canvassed everyone in the newsroom. He certainly had great stories about Garrison. He tied them up with a big bow. That's what we do after all."

"I hate to say it, because I cringe at TV news sometimes, but it was a well-produced funeral."

The two women shared a laugh. Janice spied Sebastian stepping over hockey sticks, swooping in on the police chief.

"Sebastian's stalking Paul Bennett. That'll be uncomfortable. They haven't seen each other since Sebastian upended the Cops for Cancer event."

"It's so sad about the chief. He's a good man."

"How did Garrison and the chief know each other?"

"They knew each other…socially. Let's just say they were brothers-in-arms."

"The kind of brothers-in-arms who help each other quit something?"

Sharon studied the blue sky. "I can't say. Confidences were undertaken. Promises made. You understand, don't you?"

"Perfectly," said Janice.

●

"Chief," hollered Sebastian. "Chief Bennett."

Paul Bennett spun around to face his pursuer. Sebastian extended his hand. The chief's stayed hidden in his raglan pocket. Sebastian enjoyed the awkwardness of his hand taunting Bennett.

"Well?" tormented Sebastian. The chief grabbed his hand like a train coupling.

"No Cops for Cancer to ruin today, Sebastian?" Bennett compressed his grip.

Sebastian torqued his grasp. "You're surly today, Chief. Perhaps you need a hair of the dog. That'll sooth your nerves."

Their locked hands quivered.

"I'm holding a dog right now—one of the hounds of hell," said Bennett.

"I'll take that as a compliment. Always remember, my bite is worse than my bark."

The handshake broke. Sebastian stretched his fingers.

"Let's call a truce, Chief. I can help you. But it starts with an interview."

"How do I know that you're not recording me right now?" His wary eyes descended on the CBC camera in the distance.

"You know me well enough to know that I do in-your-face ambushes. You're not being recorded."

"Go on," the chief said cautiously.

"Come clean about what happened in Florida, apologize, and you might still have a future around here."

"You spoke to the police in Florida. They gave you all the information you're entitled to. If I have any more to say about it, I should say it to a judge."

"What about the court of public opinion, Chief? MADD is screaming for your head on a silver platter. You have to live here afterwards. Who's going to hire a disgraced police chief? Somebody might if they hear you say you're sorry. People can be very forgiving."

"Your concern about my welfare is touching." The chief ran his fingers through his hair. "What would be involved?"

"A sit-down interview in your living room. Home sweet home. You wouldn't look like a menace to society. You'd look contrite. You'd be the repentant chief, surrounded by his loving family."

"My daughter is off limits," snapped Bennett.

"Alright. Just you and your wife. Do one interview with me and no one else. Any question is fair game. In return, you get sympathy and understanding, and maybe you'll save the little bit of reputation you have left."

"I'll think about it."

The cortege meandered out of the parking lot onto Church Hill, the hearse leading them uptown. Garrison had an appointment with a crematorium.

"I'm intrigued, Chief, why are you at Garrison's funeral?"

"I admired his journalism, which is more than I can say for some others." The chief turned on his heels and marched away.

"Don't bite the hand that feeds you."

[four]

"Now that's a money shot," Sebastian boasted. The glow from the night table lamp flooded the bedroom.

"I hope that money shot won't be a screensaver," said Janice as she rolled her tawny body out of bed.

"I am nothing if not discreet," said Sebastian.

Janice finished wiping herself and tossed the hand towel into the laundry hamper. "We made need another bath." She reached inside the night table. Sebastian heard clinking. Janice lay back down holding two wine glasses and a bottle with a cork barely pushed into the lip.

"Do you always keep wine by your bed?"

"Doesn't everyone?" She poured. "Here's to rivals." The glasses dinged.

"Delicious. What is it?" asked Sebastian.

"Chianti."

He stopped sipping. "You're not going to eat my liver with some fava beans, are you?"

"Oh no, I intend on eating something quite different."

Sebastian flashed a conceited smile. He held the wine up to the light and swirled. Streaks formed on the inside of the glass.

"Good legs," he said as the droplets rolled down.

"The French call them tears."

"Either way, Roxanne would enjoy them."

"What do you see in her anyway, besides her impeccable taste in wine?"

"She's everything that you're not. Caring, decent, sensitive."

"And those things matter to you?" scoffed Janice. She dipped a pinky finger in her wineglass and cleaned it with a long draw from her mouth. "Is she trusting?"

Sebastian blessed himself. "To a fault."

"If she's all of these wonderful things, why are you here?"

"I'm attracted to your ruthlessness. Roxanne lacks a certain passion. It burns here."

Janice picked up the bed lamp by the column and laid the world between them. The lampshade was a vintage map. She loosened the knob and spun the shade like a globe.

"It's ours for the conquering," said Janice. She placed her index finger on England; her fingertip turned red as the light passed through the skin.

"I'll take London. All of Europe is mine."

Sebastian rotated the lampshade half a turn.

"Beijing. China is swaggering. Japan is nationalistic. North Korea is crazy. Someone's going to start a war."

Janice walked her fingers across the Pacific Ocean and over North America. "Washington would be fun. World power and sex scandals. A girl can't ask for more than that."

Sebastian made a bomb-dropping whistle as he sent a twirling finger into the Middle East. "Jerusalem is a hot spot. The missiles are already flying there."

"Here's to great careers still to come," said Janice. They toasted world domination.

Janice returned the lamp to the night table. "How does Roxanne fit into your plans?"

"She'll go wherever I go. Roxanne adores me."

"The abused woman never leaves," said Janice shaking her head. "She might adore you, but she doesn't know the *real* you."

"We all have different faces for different people."

Both Sebastian and Janice drank.

"Tell me," probed Janice with pillow-talk indulgence, "what's the thing you love most about your job?"

The question prompted a cunning smile. Sebastian had been asked that same question many times—relatives, fans, moderators, friends, even Roxanne wanted to know. He always lied. Until now.

"I don't have to be nice all the time."

"I like that in a man."

Janice laid her glass on Sebastian's chest. She slid a finger up the stem to the bulb and pushed it over. Red wine splashed over Sebastian's stomach and dribbled down his side to the sheet.

"How clumsy of me. I'll have to clean that up."

•

Sebastian stepped out on the sidewalk and looked up at Janice's apartment. The bedroom light was still on. A dog barked in the distance. Eleven o'clock. Time to wrap up his night of "lamenting" Garrison Hill's demise and head for home.

He pressed the unlock button on his key fob. Only one headlight flashed. Sebastian saw glass on the pavement.

"Jesus. How did that happen?" He checked both ends of the street. No one running away. No one at all, in fact. The street was deserted. He circled the car. No other damage. Sebastian kicked the glass to the curb.

He flopped into the driver's seat. The Acura revved over. Sebastian shoved the gear shift into reverse and backed away from the glass. The tires screeched as the car pulled out.

Sebastian never saw the figure standing by the telephone pole. Never saw the shadow dialling 9-1-1. Never heard the voice tell the dispatcher, "I want to report a drunk driver. He's headed for Elizabeth Avenue. He's driving an Acura with just one headlight. He's a menace."

Gloved hands closed the flip phone and picked up a piece of Sebastian's shattered headlight.

•

The familiar piano riff of "Werewolves of London" reverberated through the car speakers. Warren Zevon was a member of Sebastian's pack. They howled together.

Aaaooo! Werewolves of London.

Aaaooo!

Sebastian broke off his howl when red and blue lights danced around the interior of his car. The rear-view mirror revealed that a police cruiser had turned him into prey. The snare closed with a siren burst.

"Oh, shit."

Sebastian pulled over and lowered his window. He exhaled deeply: once, twice, three times. He checked his eyes in the rear-view mirror. The pupils were bigger than usual. Dilated pupils—betrayer of many a drunk driver.

The cruiser's lights streaked across the neighbourhood. A set of living-room curtains opened for a peek and then fell shut. Two car lengths separated Sebastian from the hunter. He knew the cop was running his licence plate. Standard police procedure—know who is behind the wheel.

The police-car door opened. Sebastian followed the officer in the mirror. She put on her hat, covering her tied-back hair. The colour was lost in the darkness.

"Turn off your car, please." Sebastian did what he was told.

The officer ambled past the hood, twisting just enough to scrutinize the headlights and keep her eye on Sebastian at the same time. She never once turned her back to him.

Sebastian squinted through the dark. A bulletproof vest frustrated his lascivious eyes. They dropped to her belt. She carried an arsenal: pepper spray, nightstick, handcuffs, handgun. His eyes dropped lower. *Body crushing thighs.*

The officer sauntered back to the open window, leaned down and sniffed. She shone a pen flashlight into Sebastian's eyes.

"Were you drinking this evening?"

"I had a glass of wine."

"Only one?"

"Well, maybe two, but over a couple of hours."

"You're driving with one headlight. Did you hit anything this evening, sir?"

"No, I came out of a friend's house and the light was smashed." Under more sober circumstances Sebastian might have added a glib observation about rampant vandalism in the city, but prudence dictated he keep his breath and opinion to himself.

"Where exactly was that?"

"Cherry Hill Road."

"And where are you headed now?"

"Home. Trudeau Street."

"Your licence, registration, and insurance, please."

Sebastian reached inside his jacket pocket and pulled out a patent leather case.

"You have good taste in leather," she said.

Sebastian pointed at her gun holster. "So do you." He handed over the documents.

"Stay here," she demanded.

There would be more computer checks. Sebastian rummaged through the glove compartment for his emergency stash of breath mints. They had burrowed their way past fast-food napkins and assorted iPhone cables to the very bottom. He popped a couple of Tic Tacs.

His phone vibrated. It was a text from Janice.

Can't sleep. Wide awake. Come back. Have wine, don't whine.

Sebastian typed.

Can't. Cop has me pulled over.

Accurate, but listless. He added:

Send lawyers, guns and money.

Sebastian was pleased with his cleverness. He managed to work in a Warren Zevon line before possibly being dragged off to the hoosegow.

"Mr. Hunter, come back to the police car, please."

His smile vanished. His nemesis stood by the open window. He tossed the iPhone face down on the passenger seat. No need to ask what she wanted.

Sebastian had taken a few long walks in his life. The walk to the principal's office after he put his pet ferret in Miss Marlene's desk. The walk down the aisle at a friend's wedding with a fat bridesmaid in a pink taffeta dress. The walk to the podium at the Canadian Journalism Awards to pick up an honourable mention certificate. But none felt as long as the walk to the Ford Crown Victoria with the strobe lights.

The officer passed him a mobile Breathalyzer. Three lights—green, amber, and red. If he blew red, he'd be charged with drunk driving.

"Take a deep breath and then keep blowing until I say stop."

Sebastian put the mouthpiece between his lips and blew hard. His cheeks puffed.

"Keep going, keep going."

His lungs ached.

"Stop."

"What does it say?"

"It says you're a lucky man." She turned the Breathalyzer to show him a green light. "Point zero four."

The officer flipped down her visor. Sebastian's driver's licence, registration, and insurance were tucked behind a band, next to a photograph of bald and laughing police officers huddled around a Cops for Cancer banner. She handed Sebastian his papers.

"Am I free to go, officer?"

"Not quite." She opened a metal binder and passed him a ticket. "Driving without a headlight."

"You've got to be kidding me," exclaimed Sebastian. "You're giving me a diploma."

"Consider this the cost of education, Mr. Hunter."

Sebastian opened the door and stepped out.

"By the way, Mr. Hunter, that's a distinct fragrance you're wearing. Coconut isn't it? I'm sure your fiancée will love it."

●

Sebastian needed stealth. He scrunched his dangling keys and eased one into the lock. The turning tumbler made a loud click. He grimaced. Sebastian pushed the door open and crept through, stretching over a creaky floorboard. To the left was the bedroom. No light. To the right was the bathroom. He turned right.

Sebastian stuffed a towel along the bottom of the bathroom door before flicking on the light. He stripped. A nervous, naked man frowned in the mirror. He smelled a shoulder. His nose hopscotched all the way down to his wrist. Other arm—same olfactory detective work. He rubbed his hair and sniffed his palm.

I smell like Paris Hilton.

He contemplated taking a shower, but decided it would be too noisy. He might wake up Sleeping Beauty. Sebastian opened the medicine cabinet and found salvation—a box of sanitizing wipes. Individually wrapped and promising to kill 99.9 percent of common germs. Roxanne liked to keep a few in her purse, believing you never know when you might get your hands dirty. So true, thought Sebastian. His hair squeaked as he pulled a towelette through his locks. He scrubbed his forehead and worked his way down to his toes, using a fresh swab on each body part and ensuring every centimetre of skin was washed with alcohol. He dropped the used wipes into the toilet and stuffed a fistful of packets inside his jacket. They could be safely disposed of in the morning.

Front done, back next. Sebastian dragged a wipe across a shoulder blade. He winced and sucked through his teeth. He turned his back to the mirror. Red furrows in the skin, tracks left by Janice's nails.

"Sebastian, is that you?" Roxanne's voice floated down the hall.

"Yes, it's me. Sorry to wake you up. I'll be right there."

Sebastian clenched his teeth and dabbed the scratches. He scoured the rest of his back and flushed the toilet as the last towelette fell.

"Turn on the light if you want," said Roxanne as Sebastian entered the bedroom.

"No, that's alright. I can see in the dark. I'm like a wolf."

Sebastian put on his pyjamas, playfully growled, and leapt on the bed. Roxanne laughed as he slid under the duvet. She snuggled in. Her nose recoiled.

"You reek of booze."

"Some drunk at the bar dumped a full drink over me."

"Some drunk at the bar. Knowing your crowd that could have been any one of a dozen reporters."

"I am nothing if not discreet," kidded Sebastian. "You should have come along."

"Nah. I didn't need another night of witty one-upmanship and withering critiques."

"But those are our best features."

Roxanne jabbed Sebastian with her elbow before using it to prop herself up. She cradled her head in her hand so she could gaze at Sebastian. "You did a great job today. I'm really proud of you." She kissed his lips, first with affection, then with appetite. Her hand tugged at the drawstring to his pyjama bottoms. Sebastian covered her hand and held it still.

"*You're* saying no to sex," pouted Roxanne.

Sebastian had never seen such disbelief. "It's been a long day. I'm exhausted."

"Are you the same Sebastian Hunter who says men will always trade sleep for sex?"

"That was a younger Sebastian."

"Is it me?" Roxanne brimmed with hurt.

"No, no, not at all. It's just that I'm feeling a little…downcast."

"It's Garrison, isn't it?"

Sebastian sighed. "Yes. I feel a piece of me was buried today."

"I understand." Roxanne caressed his cheek and kissed it. "It's heartbreaking. Not to mention traumatic. Garrison died right in front of you. Promise me, you'll tell me if you're having any problems."

Sebastian nodded. "You're always looking out for me. I'm a lucky guy."

"Goodnight, honey."

"Good night, Roxanne." Sebastian turned on his side.

Thanks, Garrison. You're more helpful from the grave than you ever were in the newsroom.

•

Hell is a reception room with no distractions.

Sebastian's head swung between doors on opposite sides of the front desk. Clearly, pendulum action was not enough to tempt a lackey into the room.

There was nothing to read except pamphlets entitled Your Action Government. A pile sat on the magazine table, all highlighting the premier wearing a hardhat and turning over a sod with a silver shovel. The caption bragged Jobs for Our People.

Sebastian's iPhone refused to rescue him from tedium. It said No Service. He searched for Wi-Fi networks. None existed. Breaking news would be old news by the time he saw it.

"Why is there no cellphone service?" he asked the receptionist.

"Security," she replied in a deadpan manner, not bothering to make eye contact. She turned a page of her newspaper.

You belong in an episode of *Mad Men*, thought Sebastian. Grey hair, horn-rimmed glasses, and a prim dress. Happy Birthday cards stood on her desk.

You don't look a day over seventy, honey.

Sebastian checked his watch. He had been waiting half an hour. The watch was a gift from his father, presented when he graduated with his Bachelor of Journalism. He didn't like it.

The watch face contained the Indian-Head test pattern—a black and white icon from the earliest days of TV. At first, he considered the retro look dapper. Then Generation Y constantly annoyed him with the question, "What's a test pattern?" It made no sense to them. Imagine, television stations signing on and calibrating your TV with circles and lines. And what was up with the guy wearing the Native headdress? The final indignity came from Dour Donna. She chastised him for insulting First Nations peoples and declared the watch racist. What possessed him to wear that watch on this day?

The receptionist answered her phone.

"You can go in now, Mr. Hunter. The premier is ready for you."

Sebastian leapt out of the chair. He had been summoned to the premier's office with the promise he'd have the scoop of the decade, but he had to come alone.

"Just one thing, Mr. Hunter," said the receptionist, "you must leave your phone with me."

Surrendering a cellphone was standard protocol during the budget lockup every spring. But for a meeting with the premier? Sebastian had never heard of such a thing. Still, the receptionist's sternness implied the request was not debatable. He handed it over.

The receptionist opened a drawer and took out a hammer. She whacked Sebastian's iPhone. The screen cracked like a windshield hit by a flying stone.

"What the hell are you doing?"

"Security."

She bashed it again, so hard the hammer bounced off the phone. She whaled away until the screen was completely shattered.

"Don't worry," she assured Sebastian, "your conversation with the premier will be more than enough compensation."

The receptionist opened a clear, torpedo-shaped canister. She laid Sebastian's crippled phone inside and closed the buckles before standing the canister upright in a tube. Sebastian heard a sucking sound and the canister whooshed out of sight.

"Let me guess—security."

Sebastian faced the closed-circuit camera. He wondered who was watching, who was laughing at him. He gave the prying eyes a profile, kissed a couple of fingers and planted them on a buttock. The premier's door buzzed and Sebastian stomped through.

"Sebastian," said the premier, sitting behind her mahogany desk. "I'm so glad to see you've finally dried out. That dunk tank was so much fun, wasn't it."

"You should try it sometime. I'm sure you'd make a big splash."

The premier's face soured. "Sit down."

Sebastian rolled over a high-back, leather chair and sat opposite the premier.

"Sebastian, you've been making scurrilous inquiries about an unfortunate time in my life." She wagged her finger. "I don't really appreciate it."

"Since you brought it up, Premier, did you snort cocaine in your twenties?"

"I did indeed, Sebastian. And what's more, I've never kicked the habit entirely." She lifted the lid on a writing box and plucked out a packet of white powder.

"Is that cocaine?" asked an astonished Sebastian.

"Oh, yes," she said, shaking the packet.

Reflex took over. Sebastian drove his hand into his jacket pocket and groped for his iPhone. His whole body sagged when he remembered that his camera was dead and buried in a pneumatic tube.

"I consider myself a social user," said the premier. "Special occasions, that sort of thing. And I only use cocaine. Never crack. I'm no Rob Ford. I have my standards."

The premier opened her purse—a sensible handbag, the kind favoured by Margaret Thatcher. She clutched a cosmetics mirror and nail file. A gentle tug broke the packet's seal and she poured a thin line on the mirror.

"It's always more fun to watch myself." She winked. "And a little bump never hurts."

Sebastian's mouth dropped. The premier's intercom buzzed. "Yes, Norma?"

"Premier, would you like some music piped in? Clapton's 'Cocaine' perhaps, or the original version by J.J. Cale."

"Not today, thank you." The premier flicked a button. "She thinks of everything."

The premier used a nail file to break up clumps and smooth out the edges. She took a twenty-dollar bill from her wallet.

"These new polymer bills make a perfect tube," she said, rolling the bill. "No wrinkles."

She leaned over the mirror, inserted the tube in one nostril and closed the other with a finger. "Your tax dollars hard at work."

The blaring snort startled Sebastian. Cocaine flew past Her Majesty's nose and into the premier's. She inhaled the line, vacuuming every grain.

The premier pointed the tube at Sebastian's wrist. "Too bad your Indian head can't take pictures of a cokehead."

Sebastian flung the chair back as he stood up. "Premier, even without video, thank you for the story of my career. It will end yours." He strutted to the door.

"One more thing, Sebastian." He hesitated reaching for the door-knob. "I did the same trick for Janice Stone just before you came in. Except she had her phone. The video was very good quality. I suspect it will be all over the web by the time you get back to the office."

"Bitch!" screamed Sebastian.

•

Sebastian flinched and whimpered under the duvet.

"Wake up," said Roxanne, shaking his shoulder. Sebastian opened his eyes. "Are you alright?" she asked.

He let out a long phew. "What a dream I was having. It was insane."

"Who's the bitch?"

"What?"

"You said the word bitch."

Sebastian chuckled. "Believe it or not—the premier, I think. She snorted cocaine in front of me, right in her office. But I couldn't take any video because they smashed my phone with a hammer. She also snorted coke in front of Janice, only Janice did have a camera."

Roxanne folded her arms. "You were dreaming about Janice Stone?"

"No, Janice wasn't actually in the dream. I mean, the premier told me what she had done. She gave Janice the scoop and sabotaged mine."

"Aha."

"I guess I was so angry I shouted bitch. Maybe Janice was the bitch."

Roxanne fastened the top button on her nightshirt. "So, you weren't dreaming about Janice, you were only thinking about her?"

Sebastian cleared his throat. "Is it me or has it suddenly gotten chilly in this room?" He squeezed Roxanne's shoulders. "Honey, it was a dream, a crazy dream. I can't be held responsible for a dream."

Roxanne headed for the bathroom. "I don't like the idea of Janice being in your dreams. Dreams can be rooted in reality."

"The reality is I don't like being scooped. Nothing more."

He waited until Roxanne left the bedroom before picking up his phone. He deleted the text exchange with Janice.

The bathroom door opened.

"Sebastian," yelled Roxanne, "the toilet's not flushing properly."

●

The plumber panted with each pump of the plunger. Roxanne stood in the bathroom doorway, cringing with every glug.

"We already tried that," she said.

The plumber swung the rubber end of the plunger towards Roxanne. "You certainly clogged it up." Water dripped on the laminate flooring.

"Do you have any rags?" she inquired.

"No. Cleanup is not my job." He stood the wet plunger beside the toilet and reached for a metal contraption. It had a turn-handle on top of a solid tube, with a wire cable and a bulbous auger attached.

He shook it at Roxanne. The auger clanged. "Do you know what this is?"

"No, I don't have a clue."

"This is the heavy artillery. It's called a toilet auger. I use it when a plunger won't unblock a toilet."

He spun a finger on his free hand. "I'm going to corkscrew the toilet. Works like a corkscrew in a bottle of wine."

"I hope you don't use it for both."

"I tease my wife whenever she asks me to open the wine." The plumber had a devilish grin. "I pretend I can't find the corkscrew and suggest using the auger. Drives her nuts every time."

"You've got quite the sense of humour."

"Ya, she loves it. Now, this works best on soft blockages. You didn't drop a hairbrush down there, did you?"

"No, I didn't"

"You're sure?"

"I didn't drop anything down there," snapped Roxanne.

The plumber hauled up the handle and the cable zipped inside the tube.

"You'd be surprised at what I've pulled out of toilets," he said as he maneuvered the auger into the toilet bowl.

Roxanne pinched her nose.

"Toothbrushes, false teeth, eyeglasses, even dolls," he said, cranking the handle. "I'm like a kid with a box of Cracker Jacks. I never know what the prize is going to be."

The plumber spun the handle like a mixing beater, pushing the auger deeper into the toilet trap with each revolution. The clatter ended with a swoosh.

"There's the wad," exclaimed the plumber, making Roxanne recoil. "I thought you said you didn't drop anything into the toilet."

"I didn't," barked Roxanne. She inched forward and peered into the bowl. Pieces of white bobbed about. "Toilet paper?"

"No, not toilet paper." The plumber scooped up a handful of floatables. Water streamed off his fingers. "Wet wipes. You should know better than to throw them into the toilet."

"I did not throw them in the toilet."

"Well, somebody threw them in there. And it wasn't me." He held up a finger. "One, they're not biodegradable." A second finger. "Two, they won't shred." A third finger. "Three, they could survive a thermonuclear blast."

Roxanne opened the medicine cabinet and examined the box of sanitizing wipes. "I don't understand. I never use them here."

"I'm not a detective. I only fix toilets. I don't find out who's using them." He threw the auger in his tool box. It clashed against his plumbing wrenches. Roxanne plugged her ears.

"That's 200 bucks. I prefer cash."

"Will cash get you out of here faster?"

He nodded.

"I'll get my purse."

●

Evan stepped out of his office. "Sebastian, can we see you for a minute?"

"Be right there," said Sebastian.

"Take a seat," said Evan, pointing at the empty chair. He turned to Zoe. "Let's send Carter to court next week and see how he makes out." Zoe scribbled a note on her outlook.

"What's Janice up to?" blurted Sebastian.

"Nothing yet," said Zoe.

"No appointment with the premier?"

"No," replied Zoe. "Should she have one?"

"I want to make sure that she doesn't hijack my story on the premier's nose problem. I'm getting close. Keep her away from it."

"It's prophetic that you should mention Janice's name," said Evan. Sebastian's sphincter tightened. "We've decided what to do in the short-term about filling Garrison's job. We're letting Samantha fly solo all this week as a sign of respect. Starting next week, you and Janice will alternate. One week you'll co-host with Samantha and Janice will do the next. Janice starts Monday."

"So you're trading the gay wedding cake for the *lesbian* wedding cake," said Sebastian.

Evan eased out of his chair and walked back and forth, both hands grasping an imaginary lawyer's robe.

"Now would you tell Her Honour, Ms. Patel, what exactly did Mr. Hunter say that day when he heard two women would be co-hosting *Here & Now*?" Lawyer Evan shook his finger at Zoe. "And remember, Ms. Patel, you are under oath."

Zoe repeated Sebastian's statement verbatim in a jittery voice. "Such an…unfortunate comment. As a proud member of the LGBT community, how did that make you feel, Ms. Patel?"

"I felt objectified," said an indignant Zoe.

"And if Her Honour finds Mr. Hunter guilty of homophobia because of his spurious slur, would you have any recommendation as to the proper punishment?"

Zoe leapt to her feet, her eyes ablaze. "Hang him from the highest tree by his—"

"Got it," interrupted Sebastian, throwing up his hands in surrender.

"Now that we've got that sorted out," said Evan, "maybe you should get back to work."

Laughter followed Sebastian out of the office. He called Roxanne.

"Hello," said an exasperated-sounding Roxanne. Sebastian heard a bang in the background.

"Great news, honey. I'm going to host *Here & Now.*" No response. Sebastian strained his ear. He heard heavy footsteps and a door close.

"Sorry about that," said Roxanne.

"What was the racket?"

"The plumber," said Roxanne. "I'm beginning to think outhouses are highly underrated."

●

Sebastian closed the front door and flipped a bottle of wine like a juggling club. "I picked up something special for supper," he shouted to the kitchen.

"You forgot, didn't you?" yelled Roxanne.

"Forgot what?"

"Donna's play at the Arts and Culture Centre."

Sebastian mouthed *fuck.*

Roxanne rolled out of the kitchen with a plate of sandwiches in one hand and two glasses of wine in the other.

"We agreed to have a quick bite and go. Is box wine okay?"

"Sure. Who wouldn't want box wine over Chianti Classico?" Sebastian rested the bottle on the sideboard. "Another night, perhaps."

They sat down and chose sandwiches. White chicken for Roxanne, dark for Sebastian.

"The plumber unclogged the toilet."

"Great," he said between chews.

Roxanne laid her glass down. "Sebastian, did you throw sanitizer wipes down the toilet?"

Sebastian swallowed. His brain whirled.

"I'm such an idiot, Roxanne."

"Go on."

"It was a stupid thing to do."

"What was a stupid thing to do?"

"I'll never do it again."

"What are you talking about?" Roxanne strangled the life out of her napkin.

"I used the sanitizing wipes…to get makeup off my shirt. It sticks like glue. I was afraid of ruining the shirt if I didn't clean it right away. The alcohol in the wipes works great."

"When did you do that?"

"The night I was hosting with Garrison. The night he died. The situation was so chaotic it was impossible to be careful. The collar was smeared in makeup, inside and out. I had to use a lot of wipes."

"Why didn't you throw them in the garbage instead of the toilet?"

"They stink. I was trying to protect your nose. That cute, delicate nose. The nose that the Mona Lisa should have. Why should your nose suffer for my soiled shirt collar?"

Roxanne sipped her wine.

"It seemed like a good idea at the time," said Sebastian.

"Next time, you can deal with the plumber. And you have to be extra nice to my sister tonight."

Sebastian crossed his heart, while thinking he'd rather stick a plunger handle in his eye.

●

The lobby of the Arts and Culture Centre brimmed with people dressed for show. Sebastian wore his Hong Kong suit. The glint from Roxanne's sparkly dress outshone the waxed and buffed marble floor. She spied Donna in the throng and waved. Donna headed towards them, fluttering past a sign—*The Vagina Monologues.*

She gives vaginas a bad name.

Sebastian braced himself for the inevitable bombardment. "Well, Sebastian," chided Donna, "I never expected to see *you* at *The Vagina Monologues.*"

"*Vagina?*," said a wide-eyed Sebastian. "I thought we had tickets to The *Regina* Monologues. I was expecting to see a play about a nice canola farmer in Saskatchewan fighting the evils of genetically modified grain."

Roxanne poked him in the back. Donna pursed her lips.

"Sebastian, there's a segment in the play written especially for you," said Donna.

"Which one?"

"You'll know it when you see it."

"I look forward to *The Globe and Mail* review," said Sebastian. A bell rang, calling the audience to their seats.

Hunter wins by a knockout in the first round.

The crowd shuffled towards the theatre doors. "I've got to get backstage," said Donna.

"Good luck," said Roxanne.

"Break a leg," said Sebastian.

Roxanne huffed. "That's extra nice?"

"I'll buy her a glass of box wine after the show."

Sebastian and Roxanne's seats were just five rows back from the stage, a perk of being related to a cast member.

"This is going to be fun," said Roxanne.

"Can't wait," replied Sebastian. He squirmed. Dozy Dan and Prudish Penelope spryly stepped through the jumble of legs in the row ahead. They waved hello. Their destination—seats directly in front of Roxanne and Sebastian.

"You made it, Dad," said Roxanne.

"Miss my little girl on stage? Not a chance. Toronto can't beat this."

"The program says there's coarse language," fretted Penelope. "I don't like vulgarity."

"Mom, we're all grownups," said Roxanne.

"I'm sure Donna knows her audience," said Sebastian.

"She certainly thinks she knows you," said Penelope. "People can be so judgmental sometimes."

Sebastian sat back, letting Roxanne carry the full weight of engaging her parents. Dan and Penelope filled the rest of the conversation with platitudes—"momentous evening," "ground-breaking play," "worthy cause." Sebastian drifted away, looking over his shoulder in a panoramic sweep of the audience. Familiar faces dotted the view. People he had interviewed; people he had annoyed. He raised a hand to the finance minister—the most eligible bachelor in government. The minister turned to his date.

Scuffling feet blended with the soft thumps of cushioned seats closing as long-legged men stood to open a path for a woman. "Excuse me," she said. Sebastian's cocksureness shrank. Lindsay Moore perched in the empty seat behind him. She smiled and motioned sideways with her finger: you, her? Sebastian nodded once, then turned to face the stage.

The house lights dimmed. The curtain rose to reveal a dozen women sitting in a semicircle.

A Greek chorus of Dour Donnas.

The Dour Donna stood at centre stage. "Good evening," she said. "And welcome to a night of womanhood." Roxanne beamed.

Sebastian laughed on cue. Tut-tutted on cue. Scorned on cue. He matched all of Roxanne's emotions. And from what he could hear, so did Lindsay.

The word vagina rotated round and round the theatre, picking up speed and intensity. But the tornado wouldn't carry Sebastian off. He stayed trapped in a whirlwind of female empowerment and the blessings of womanhood.

His future sister-in-law pranced about with a wireless microphone. "Cunt," she shouted. Sebastian felt Roxanne stiffen. Penelope's head jerked, as if she had been slapped in the face.

Donna gave Sebastian a haughty expression. "Love that word. Can't say it enough," she said. Her mother looked back at Roxanne, horrified.

"Try it. Go ahead," said Donna.

Penelope buried her face in her hands. Donna darted about the stage like Mick Jagger, playing verbal ping-pong with the theatregoers.

"Cunt," bawled Donna.
"Cunt," bawled Lindsay.
Sebastian sank in his seat. Pockets of women joined the chant.
"Cunt," screamed Donna.
"Cunt," screamed Lindsay.
Donna reinforced each chorus with an air punch. Sebastian had never seen her so happy.
"Cunt," shrieked Donna.
"Cunt," shrieked Lindsay.
The word bounced from stage to audience, from audience to stage. An echo of vitriol passed through Sebastian's ears.
Penelope grabbed Dan's arm and stormed for the aisle. Roxanne's eyes begged for help. Sebastian tilted his head in her mother's direction. Roxanne formed OK with her hand.
Escape. Blessed escape. He snuck one last glimpse of Dour Donna.
Takes one to know one.

•

Sebastian didn't sing in the shower; he played with words instead. He kidded Roxanne that massaging his scalp stimulated his brain. Whatever the reason, saucy headlines bubbled up like shampoo foam. A bit of cruel fun. Worth creating even if they could never be used on air. This morning's sacrificial lamb was a down-on-his-luck man who won 6/49 and then blew the jackpot on booze. He used his million dollars to keep himself and his friends swimming in beer.
Tonight—Lotto Lush. He hit the jackpot; then he hit the bottle.
The circumstances offered wonderful emotions for TV: despair, surprise, euphoria, pleasure, remorse, shame. Sebastian's story would plumb them all. He stepped out of the shower as the tawdry headline trickled down the drain.
Mr. Boozehound's only friend was his beagle. He didn't bother with housekeeping anymore. Sebastian expected tumbleweeds of dog hair, so he dressed in jeans and a plaid-collared shirt; clothes he could wash or throw away later. He'd change into his Hugo Boss suit at the station after his interview. His phone said 6:30 AM. Time to go. Mr. Boozehound's breakfast of champions included a six-pack. Getting the psst

and fizz of a beer can opening was visual number one. Sebastian didn't want to miss it.

He leaned over Roxanne and kissed her goodbye.

She opened an eye. "Be nice to that man."

Sebastian raised a three-finger salute. "Scout's honour." He was duty bound to follow his solemn promise. Except Sebastian had never been a Scout.

The Acura was parked on the road to avoid the ever-annoying driveway shuffle. He laid out the suit bag in the trunk before hopping into the driver's seat. The engine vroomed. He looked up.

"What the fuck?"

ЯƎЯƎT⅃UꓭA

Someone had scrawled scarlet letters across the windshield. Sebastian took tentative steps around the hood.

ADULTERER.

Sebastian's aghast eyes ricocheted around the neighbourhood. The only person seemingly about was Mr. Wade across the street. He pulled out of his driveway in his beloved '69 Camaro convertible. The top and the windows were down. Sebastian stood by the defaced windshield, hoping the angle would hide the communiqué. Mr. Wade stopped alongside.

"Beautiful day for a spin," said Sebastian.

"It certainly is." Mr. Wade stretched in vain to look around Sebastian. "What's on your windshield? I saw something when I was getting in the car."

"It's nothing. Just some graffiti."

"What does it say?"

Sebastian allowed himself a half smile. "Asshole," he said, attaching a titch of laughter to appear bemused. "Probably an NTV viewer."

"There goes the neighbourhood," chuckled Mr. Wade. "See you later." He and Sebastian exchanged waves as he drove off.

Wherever Sebastian turned there was jeopardy. The neighbourhood was coming to life. Mr. Dyer uncoiled a garden hose and sprinkler on his new sods. A construction crew unloaded scaffolding by Mrs. Hayward's house. Sebastian scrambled to park the Acura in the driveway, windshield facing in.

He rubbed a finger down the R. The red felt waxy and stuck to his fingertip. He sniffed a faint aroma of flowers.

"Lipstick."

His thumbs typed *get lipstock off windwhield* on his iPhone. Google knew what he wanted despite his poor spelling and showed 281,000 results.

"For Christ's sake. Is there a pandemic?" He picked the first one.

Step 1 – Mix dish-washing liquid into hot water.

Step 2 – Dip clean cloth in water. Wipe window with small circular motions to loosen the lipstick's oil base.

Step 3 – Rinse thoroughly and dry with paper towels.

Step 4 – If the lipstick stain remains, add ammonia to water and clean window again.

Step 5 – Rub salt over any stubborn smudges. Scrub with toothbrush.

Step 6 – Remove any remaining discolouration with isopropyl alcohol.

"Not the sanitizing wipes again."

Sebastian tore into the house. Check bedroom. Door closed. Dash to closet. Grab bucket. Race to kitchen. Run hot water. Squirt dish-washing liquid. Fill bucket. Throw in dishcloth. Seize paper towel roll. Scour under sink. No ammonia. Shove salt grinder in pocket. Drop supplies at front door. Gallop to bathroom. Confiscate sanitizing wipes. Snatch tooth brush. Catch breath.

"Sebastian, is that you?" He heard Roxanne's feet hit the floor.

"Yes, it's me." Sebastian scurried down the hall.

"I thought you were gone to work. What are you doing?"

He turned the knob on the front door. "Some kids smeared crap on the windshield. I've got to clean it off before I can drive." Sebastian hugged all the cleaning supplies in one arm and grabbed the bucket with the other.

"Would you like some help?"

"No, thanks. I can handle this." He heard a dresser drawer open.

"I really don't mind."

"No. It's a job for one." Clothes hangers shuffled along a rod.

"You're already late. I'll be right there."

Sebastian needed a few precious minutes. Something had to die. He spied a victim on the hallway table—the bird vase. China had never mass-produced a finer ceramic swan. Roxanne loved to put freshly cut flowers in its tail. The colours jumped out of the white porcelain.

"Okay, I'll see you outside." Sebastian swung the bucket and knocked the bird off its perch. It smashed on the hardwood floor. Water sloshed over the shards.

"What was that?" yelled Roxanne.

"What a morning I'm having. I just broke the vase by the door."

"Not the one Donna gave us?"

"I'm afraid so."

The ugly duckling certainly gave a good swan song.

Roxanne wandered out of the bedroom shaking her head. "Go on. I'll clean it up."

"You're an angel." He kissed her cheek.

She examined Sebastian's armful of cleaning supplies. "Don't throw those down the toilet," she ordered, pointing at the sanitizing wipes.

"I swear." Roxanne pushed the front door open.

Sebastian left a trail of soapy water out to the driveway. He plunged his hand into the steaming bucket.

"Jesus Christ," he screeched, whipping out his hand. He shook off the scalding water.

"Stop swearing," yelled Roxanne through an open window. "There are kids around."

Sebastian poked about the bucket with a stick he found lying on the grass. He flung the cloth at the scarlet letters. Splat.

To hell with small circular motions.

He used both arms to push the cloth back and forth like an Irish washerwoman cleaning a floor. ADULTERER became ADULTER. The lipstick stuck to the cloth, but left smudges. He stretched across the windshield. He was now an ADULT. Sebastian ran to the passenger side. More frenzied chafing. The proclamation was gone.

Sebastian balled up the cloth like a basketball. "One second left on the clock. Hunter for three." The cloth arced over the hood. Plop. "Ha-ho. Hunter knocks down a three-pointer. Man, did he nail that."

Hoop dreams gave way to cleaning smears. Sebastian twisted the salt grinder. Grains sprinkled over the windshield.

"That better not be my Japanese sea salt," reprimanded Roxanne.

Sebastian spun around. "It's for a good cause, Roxanne. This is stubborn stuff." He tore off several paper towels and dipped them in the hot water.

"What did they write?"

"Just a nonsensical scribble." Sebastian rubbed clockwise and then counter clockwise. The salt turned into slurry.

"Tell me."

"You said I shouldn't swear."

"Nobody else seems to have been a target," said Roxanne, surveying cars up and down the street.

"Maybe they hate CBC reporters." Sebastian kept destroying evidence.

"Lots of people hate CBC reporters, but they don't go around vandalizing cars. You should call the police."

"I'm sure they'd investigate right after they finish with the drug dealers and the wife beaters."

Roxanne folded her arms. "They should have scribbled *Jerk*."

"Look, this is petty crime and I'm not going to embarrass myself by calling the cops."

"I give up." Roxanne's hand skimmed soap bubbles out of the bucket. The cloth had measles. "What's the red?"

"I'm not sure. Maybe crayon."

Roxanne curved around the car, inspecting Sebastian's cleaning job. She touched the windshield. "Missed a spot." She squinted. "That looks like an A."

"They tried writing Alpha Male, but couldn't spell alpha."

●

Sebastian took the front steps two at a time. Ordinarily, he loathed dinners with Dozy Dan and Prudish Penelope, but after Dour Donna's potty-mouthed performance, this was one dinner he didn't want to miss. A few well-placed jabs might goad Penelope and Dan into an entertaining row. Anything would be better than Dan's tedious musings on the importance of family.

He stalled at the top of the steps and theorized about whether a lipstick-wielding Peeping Tom was following him. An unfamiliar car was parked on the street several doors down. His eyes made futile attempts to infiltrate the sedan. He couldn't suss out if anyone was behind the wheel.

Damn tinted windows. Better to go inside.

Singing seeped into the front hall. The voices belonged to Penelope and Dan; the music belonged to another time.

Sebastian peeked into the living room. Penelope and Dan held unlit candles as pretend microphones. They swayed in time with the music. Dan was misty-eyed; Penelope blinked her eyelashes flirtatiously. The lovey-dovey pair dazzled their audience of one. Roxanne sat enraptured on the loveseat, lightly bouncing in time with the melody.

Sebastian pulled back and shoved a finger down his throat. Imagine, schlock drifting out of his speakers. Worse, he was powerless to stop it. Like a moth drawn to a flame, Sebastian peered around the corner again.

Skyrockets in flight.

Penelope threw her hands in the air and wiggled her fingers. The make-believe fireworks sparkled all around her head. She and Dan strutted around the living room, never breaking eye contract.

Afternoon delight.

"Big finish," squealed Penelope. Sebastian shivered. They stretched out the A in Afternoon. Sebastian covered his ears as they climbed octaves. Their voices cracked.

Afternoon delight.

Sebastian waited until the last notes of the air pollution had dissipated. He clapped as he walked into the makeshift theatre.

"Bravo," he bellowed. "Bravo."

Penelope covered her eyes. Dan gave him an aw-shucks wave. Roxanne sprung off the loveseat and rewarded the blarney with a kiss.

"What a performance," said Sebastian. "Where did that come from?"

"I was going through my box of keepsakes under the bed," said Roxanne, "when I came across the CD. I hadn't thought of it in years. We used to sing 'Afternoon Delight' in the car when I was a kid. I put it on for fun and these two turned into teenagers."

"I used to squeeze your mom's thigh during the chorus." Dan mimed driving a car and pinching a leg in the passenger seat. "That song always makes me frisky."

Penelope's face went rosy. "Dan!"

"Too much information, Dad," said Roxanne.

"Should we leave you two alone?" ribbed Sebastian.

Penelope's colour turned blood-red.

"It's a fun tune," said Sebastian. "I think it's so much classier to leave something to the imagination. Kitschy charm is the best way to go. Forget crudeness."

The jaws on the leg-hold trap were now pulled open. Dour Donna was written on the trigger. Someone would step on it soon and spring the teeth.

"That was a big hit when we were in high school," said Dan.

Sebastian picked up the CD jacket. *Afternoon Delight: The Best of the Starland Vocal Band.* He flipped the jacket over: K-Tel. As Seen on TV.

"The 70s had some great music," said Dan.

Sebastian glanced at his copy of Warren Zevon's *Excitable Boy.* "Yes, it certainly was a watershed decade."

"Mom," said Roxanne, "would you please give me a hand in the kitchen?"

Sebastian's conniving about Donna's thespian antics would have to wait for the dinner table.

"I had a little chat with your boss today, Sebastian," said Vice-president-of-the-CBC Dan.

"Really," said Sebastian, straining not to sound eager.

"I encouraged Evan to use Garrison's death as a chance to reinvigorate the show with youth."

"My feelings exactly," said Sebastian, trying to sound profound.

"Good things are going to happen in your little newsroom."

Little newsroom. You...

"Especially to you."

...wonderful man.

"You've got a bright future." Vice-president-of-the-CBC Dan slapped him on the back.

"Define bright future," said Sebastian.

"I can't disclose personnel matters, not even to my future son-in-law. It's going to take a little while to sort out. In the meantime, just keep doing what you're doing—landing scoops and impressing the bosses." Vice-president-of-the-CBC Dan winked at him.

Roxanne and Penelope sashayed out of the kitchen carrying a bowl of pasta primavera, fresh parmesan, and a basket of focaccia.

"So where's Donna this evening?" asked Sebastian as he grated the cheese.

●

Sebastian came to a standstill. His father's bed was empty. His reclining chair too. Roxanne checked the washroom. Unoccupied. Tobias Hunter was missing in action.

"He's probably in the recreation room," said Sebastian.

They headed down Oak Wing. A man in a wheelchair scuttled their brisk pace. He dragged himself forward using a single foot. He filled the centre lane of the corridor. Passing without contortions was impossible.

"Would you like some help?" asked Roxanne.

"No thank you," said the man, stalling Sebastian's hands in mid-flight as they approached the push handles. "I can manage. It's good exercise."

Sebastian groaned softly. He and Roxanne scuffed behind. A TV blared through an open doorway.

You are the first four contestants on The Price is Right.

The man in the wheelchair stopped to look.

"Excuse us," said Sebastian turning sideways, sliding down the wall. Roxanne followed suit.

"It was either that or heave him out of the way," whispered Sebastian. They heard a piano and singing.

This land is your land, this land is my land.

"Oh goodie," said Sebastian, "campfire songs."

Several seniors huddled around the piano, photocopied song sheets in hand. Tobias Hunter sat off by himself, song sheets on his lap, his eyes empty.

"Hi Dad," said Sebastian taking the seat next to his father. Tobias didn't turn. "Not singing today?" No answer. "Let me have a look. Maybe there's something there you'd like."

He flipped through the songs. "You Are My Sunshine," "Oh, What a Beautiful Morning," "Moon River." Geriatric hit after geriatric hit. He dismissively tossed the song sheets on an empty chair.

"It's the playlist for somebody's life, just not my father's," he said to Roxanne.

"Great job," said the twentysomething piano man to his audience.

"Do you know any Warren Zevon?" Sebastian called out.

"I'm afraid not."

"My father does. He can play too."

The piano man stood up and gestured for Tobias to take the piano seat.

"Come on, Dad. I'll help." Sebastian held his father's arm as they picked their way through wheelchairs and walkers.

Sebastian placed his father's hands on the keys, moving his fingers to the right chords. He covered his father's hands and pressed.

"First G, then D. You remember." Sebastian played more chords then eased his hands away. Tobias continued the tune. He knew it now. His confidence grew with each stanza. His fingers flogged the keys. The back of his hand ran down the black and whites.

His mouth opened. His faced contorted. "I can't remember the words."

"Here we go," said Sebastian.

Poor, poor pitiful me.

Memory gaps filled. Tobias sang along. A father and son duet.

These young girls won't let me be.

Sebastian flashed a smile at Roxanne. He clapped his hands over his head.

Lord have mercy on me.

Woe woe is me.

Tobias and Sebastian romped through the song. Alzheimer's and animosity watched from the wings. Tobias finished with arms flaying. Sebastian grabbed the song sheets off the piano and threw them in the air. "Wahoo." Pages fluttered to the floor.

There was a smattering of applause. Mostly, there were stunned faces. The man with the foot-powered wheelchair arrived. "What's all the fuss about?"

Tobias looked bewildered. "Who are you?"

"Sebastian, your son."

"Oh."

Roxanne held Sebastian's hand. "You brought him back for a couple minutes. It was wonderful. I had no idea you and your father shared a love of Warren Zevon."

"It's the only love my father ever gave me."

[five]

Sebastian felt chuffed. Twitter was effusive with praise. Tweet after tweet loved him. Just one week in the anchor chair and he owned it.

@newswench You're a natural. So relaxed and smart. Easy on the eyes too.

@stompin'dave Garrison who? Here & Now has found its new anchor.

@cbcfan The king is dead. Long live King Sebastian.

"Ten seconds," said the director in Sebastian's ear.

So much exultation, so little time to scroll. The business of reading the news kept getting in the way. Sebastian sat upright and hid his phone. Camera two's red light came on. He delivered clarity and calm.

They are women who have done bad, but now are trying to do good.

Inmates at the Women's Correctional Centre are knitting teddy bears for children traumatized by natural disasters.

The program is called Teddies for Tragedies.

Here & Now's Janice Stone went behind bars to report on these special gifts.

The clicking of needles filled Sebastian's earpiece. The monitor showed hands knitting a teddy bear's ear. Janice's voice sailed over the video.

She once stabbed a man with a knitting needle. That got her jail time.

Stabbing a ball of wool makes the time pass.

She does so much knitting that she has a nickname—Purl, as in purl stitch.

"I bet they have great stitch-and-bitch sessions," said Sebastian to his co-host. Samantha Cormier laughed.

Purl was on camera. *"These kids have nothing. I can knit them a toy. Making kids happy makes me feel better about myself."*

Photos of shoeless children hugging teddy bears drifted through the monitor. Both bears and kids had smiley faces.

They live in Peru, Bangladesh, Sudan—wherever misery lives.

"The justice minister is such a hypocrite," said Sebastian. "If we want to do a story about drugs in prison, overcrowding, prisoners shanking prisoners, we can't get anywhere near an inmate. Privacy concerns, my ass. Somebody knits Winnie the Pooh, and they're pushing the cons toward the camera. We should tell the justice minister to go shove it sometimes."

Samantha checked her watch. "Just ten minutes since your last rant. Could we have a rule, please, that you're limited to just one rant per newscast?"

"You're gagging my creativity. It's your loss."

Sebastian texted Janice.

Nice story. I'm free tonight. You?

He was in the mood for a tryst. His phone vibrated.

Yes. You bring the Chianti. I'll bring the garter…stitch. ☺

"Here we go," said the director. "Outcue is Lakehead Prison."

Janice Stone, CBC News, Lakehead Prison.

Sebastian moseyed into the bumper, the teaser before commercials which promotes what's ahead on *Here & Now*.

After the break, we'll see who's celebrating a special day. Your birthdays and anniversaries are next.

Long-retired reporters had christened birthdays and anniversaries as The Happy Happies. The impish derision passed from generation to generation. The ride to the end of the show would be a coast. The Happy Happies were already on tape.

"The Happy Happies are Pablum," said Sebastian. "When will we kill them?"

"When you're eating Pablum," said Samantha.

The commercials babbled on. It was a convenient time to razz.

Sebastian pressed the intercom button to the control room. "Hey Roddy, need any help getting The Happy Happies to air."

"I'm good," said the voice in Sebastian's ear. "But if I ever need a megalomaniac with a potty mouth, you're first on the list."

"Roddy, a trained monkey could do your job." Sebastian slapped the desk. "Space bar."

Tapping the space bar on Roddy's properly-coded computer would indeed roll The Happy Happies. But that code and the hundreds of others which synchronized cameras, microphones, lights, graphics and anchors with the live and taped reports took four hours of Roddy's time.

"It only takes one hand to eat a banana," said Roddy. "Try not to slip on the peel. You've fallen on your ass enough today."

The Happy Happies rolled the moment the commercials finished.

"Space bar," said Sebastian to his pre-recorded self.

Bring on the cake. Bertha MacDonald turned ninety-four yesterday. Bill and Edna Conley celebrate their sixty-first anniversary on Saturday.

"Which one is Bill and which one is Edna?" asked Sebastian. "Why do old couples look like each other?"

Ralph and Blanche Hayward celebrated their fifty-seventh wedding anniversary on Tuesday.

The photo showed an effervescent Blanche and a forlorn Ralph.

"Couldn't even muster a smile," said Sebastian. "He's a broken man. That's what 57 years with the same woman does to you."

"You think she's happy being married to a sourpuss," said Samantha. "Women are just better actors."

Sebastian's taped voice trudged through an interminable list. The Happy Happies always devoured the last block of the show. Sebastian fired up the Angry Birds app on his iPhone.

Coleen... Colene... Jesus H. Christ...Collena Snow is ninety-eight today.

Sebastian dropped his phone; his eyes crashed-landed on the monitor. They saw a photo of a bubbly Collena Snow, but Sebastian's taped voice no longer glorified her longevity.

God damn it.

"Roddy, it's the wrong tape," Sebastian screamed into the intercom.

I've got to do the whole fucking thing over.

"RODDY."

The screen went black.

"What was that?" Samantha's face blended shock and disgust.

"Somebody fucked up," bellowed Sebastian.

Sebastian imagined bedlam in the control room. Likely harried intercom snippets between Roddy and the media centre, trying to figure out what the hell happened and what to do about it.

Five seconds of black.

Ten seconds of black.

Fifteen seconds of black.

"We've got to do them live," said Roddy. "Apologize, then go."

Sebastian sat ramrod. The list of birthdays and anniversaries rolled up the teleprompter. The monitor dissolved out of black to the studio.

Obviously, we're having some technical difficulties and we apologize, especially to Mrs. Snow. Sebastian sounded uncharacteristically contrite. *We'll start over.*

Take two. Bertha MacDonald and her birthday cake materialized on the screen. Sebastian couldn't shake the tension out of his voice until after Collena Snow's birthday. Three minutes and thirty seconds of special days, punctuated with off camera dabs to his forehead. Sebastian reappeared on camera with just twenty seconds left in the show.

Once again, I'd like to apologize for the unacceptable language you heard earlier in our newscast. We're truly sorry. Goodnight and have a safe weekend.

Samantha's eyes stayed glued to her laptop during the closing wide shot. No benign chitchat or orthodontic smiles between the co-hosts as the *Here & Now* theme played. Sebastian shuffled his scripts. Ten agonizing seconds to seven o'clock. The instant the screen faded to black Sebastian tore off his microphone, flung it over the desk and stormed upstairs.

"Not my fault," snarled Sebastian as he blew into Evan's office. Evan's elbows rested on his desk, his hands in the praying position, fingertips touching his lips.

"There's an idiot down there," spewed Sebastian. "That tape was supposed to be wiped. I've been set up. Someone is out to get me."

Evan curled his hands under his chin. "The only idiot is you. And the only person out to get you is you."

Evan pointed to an empty chair. Sebastian sat down.

"The first rule of TV news is never swear into a microphone. The second rule of TV news is NEVER SWEAR INTO A MICROPHONE. Now get out."

Sebastian slinked to the door.

"By the way," said Evan, "the Twitterites are wondering if Jesus H. Christ is celebrating a birthday too."

●

Sebastian sat alone in the newsroom. His only company was a muted News Network anchor. Her lips flapped silently; her words trapped in the monitor hanging over The Desk. His phone rang. Roxanne was on the other end of a video call. He had his spin ready.

"Hi, honey."

"Please tell me," said Roxanne, "that I dreamt hearing you swear on the air."

"Wish I could."

"What happened?"

"The tech was supposed to wipe the first tape and record the clean version, but he didn't. Brain dead, I suppose. Evan fired him on the spot."

"Oh no," said Roxanne.

Sebastian's explanation was a half-truth. Incompetence never got anyone fired at the CBC.

"Why did so much get to air?"

"Roddy was nowhere near the switcher. I think he wandered off to get a banana. The guy is addicted to them. I can't believe he abandoned his post."

Another blending of fact and falsehood. Roddy stepped away from the switcher not to pursue fruit, but to replace a burned-out bulb in the control room. The perils of being a conscientious one-man band.

"Why were you swearing in the first place?"

Sebastian played turtle with a retractable flash drive, the head ducking in and out of the shell with increasing speed. He disliked the role reversal—the reporter under fire with his own weapons. He had shared too many trade secrets with Roxanne over bottomless glasses of Bordeaux. She employed open-ended questions, questions which couldn't be answered with a simple yes or no. What and Why always extract more. Even outright lies.

"It was a dare. Samantha threw down the gauntlet. Bet me a beer I couldn't get through The Happy Happies in three minutes. I hate losing. I just forgot where I was."

"Are you in trouble?"

"Evan wants to wash out my mouth with soap and water, but I'm okay otherwise."

"Sebastian, I'm worried. You haven't been yourself since Garrison died and now this—machine-gun swearing on the very spot where he went down. Something is wrong."

"I'm fine, really."

"Maybe sitting in his chair triggered something."

"It was a lapse in judgment. Nothing more."

"CBC has employee-assistance programs. Perhaps you should talk to a professional."

Sebastian laid the flash drive down. "Are you suggesting I should join the ne'er-do-wells around here who spend all their time talking to psychologists instead of actually working? I don't need anyone to hold my hand. That would be a career killer."

Roxanne rebounded from the screen. "There's no need to be snippy. I'm just trying to help."

"I'm sorry. I appreciate the concern, but you don't understand. This place exiles damaged goods. Even a whiff of mental illness and it's anchor aweigh."

"It's all confidential, Sebastian. No one would ever know."

"Roxanne, we report on privacy breaches every other day."

"Reaching for a helping hand doesn't carry the stigma it once did."

"Everybody says that. Nobody believes it."

"I give up." Roxanne checked her watch. "I should go. There's a session in ten minutes."

"Enjoy the conference," said Sebastian, trying to sound conciliatory. "I'll pick you up at the airport."

"Thanks. You've had a tough day. What are you doing tonight?"

"I think I'll go to bed early."

●

Sebastian propped himself against the headboard, reading a brochure entitled *Teddies for Tragedies.* "You know, you should have asked those women to knit a teddy for me."

"I don't think an anchor gone ballistic is the kind of tragedy they had in mind," said Janice from inside the walk-in closet.

Sebastian sipped a glass of Chianti. "Sure it is. It says so right here in the brochure. 'Whenever catastrophe strikes somewhere in the broadcast world, the first journalist to suffer is the innocent host. But you can alleviate his pain with a simple gift—a hand-knitted teddy bear.'"

Janice laughed. "They're for children in natural disasters, not anchors in *career* disasters."

"'A teddy comforts these broken men,'" read Sebastian from the bogus blurb. "'They are brought down by the ineptitude of others. They deserve admiration, not scorn.'"

"Sebastian, you are bad to the bone."

He turned off the night-table light and skulked through the darkness to the window. He waited until his eyes adjusted to the shadows before opening the curtain, just a crack. The covert reconnaissance found no spy in the bushes. He picked his way back to bed.

Janice opened the closet door and breezed into the blackness. "Since when did you get shy?"

"Since I acquired a stalker."

"Forget him. You're safe here. But what's done in the dark needs a little light."

Janice pawed through her dresser. A match flared. She lit a candle. "Now, what were you saying about a teddy?"

The candle's luster revealed a red, lace teddy with a plunging neckline and thong bottom. Little bows decorated the straps. Janice posed like a Victoria's Secret model—one hand on her hip, the other on her thigh. She spun around to reveal a lace-up back.

"Now that's a Teddy for Tragedies," said Sebastian. "I need consoling. I need a teddy." He lifted the duvet and Janice slid underneath.

●

Sebastian swiped his security card over the sensor. The lock clicked open.

"I'm still working for the CBC, Joanie," said Sebastian as he entered the lobby. Making the receptionist smile was a routine part of his grand entrance, though today's smile was smaller than usual.

"The feedback around your Jesus Christ tirade is ninety to ten in your favour," said Joan. "Only the bible thumpers want you fired."

Sebastian looked around. There was no one else in the lobby. No one coming down the stairs. "Fuck 'em if they can't take a joke," whispered Sebastian. Joan laughed.

"There's a buzz upstairs, Sebastian. This could be the day."

"Destiny calls, Joanie."

Sebastian grabbed both handrails and propelled himself up the stairs. "Morning, Zoe," he said, passing The Desk.

"It wasn't me," she said.

Sebastian stopped. "What wasn't you?" Zoe pointed to his cubicle. He wandered over.

A banner exclaimed Happy Birthday Jesus. Tacked above—a refashioned copy of *The Last Supper*. Christ's outstretched arms framed a birthday cake with lit candles in the shape of a cross. One hand clutched a cake knife, the other a server. The disciples wore pointy party hats. Several blew noise makers. The bubble above Judas's head said, "That cake cost me thirty pieces of silver."

"I'll get you back," yelled Sebastian to no one in particular, but to everyone within earshot. No doubt his tormentors smirked.

The Last Supper reeked of Janice Stone. How dare she repay virility with lampoon. How dare she reward an orgasm with ridicule. *Next time, Janice, thy kingdom will not come. Where is the Judas hiding?*

Sebastian's eyes lay siege to the newsroom, like a centurion scouting an enemy of Rome to crucify. He found her. The traitor was in Evan's office. The door was closed, but a slight head-tilt let Sebastian see through a window running the entire length of the doorframe. When Janice was agitated, she talked with her hands and right now her hands shouted.

No more musical chairs for Here & Now, perhaps?

Janice's tantrum gave way to a sulk. Her hands fell silent.

Hunter comes out on top in jobs, as well as sex.

Janice stomped out of Evan's office and stopped by Zoe's desk, her hands in full rail again. Zoe laid a frog stress toy on the counter. Janice smashed it with a fist. The frog's eyes bulged.

"Sebastian, can I see you for a few minutes?" Evan stood in his doorway.

News anchor walking.

Sebastian felt taller, more handsome. He could feel Janice's gaze. It followed him into Evan's office. He would go in a peon; he would come out a star.

"First of all, I want to say you've been doing a great job filling in for Garrison," said Evan. "This hasn't been the easiest of circumstances. The man was an icon and never more so than after his death. My mother still tears up and asks how his wife and kids are doing. Never how *my* wife and kids are doing."

"Your mother needs a new anchor to love," said Sebastian.

"I agree. It's time to move on. It's time to bury Garrison. As long as we keep switching the faces on the desk, Garrison will be a ghost in the background."

Sebastian nodded gravely.

"You're a natural performer in the studio. You're smart, funny, quick on your feet; a solid reporter and despite your cock-up on Friday, the audience still likes you. And most importantly, the network still likes you."

Sebastian beamed. He prepared to extend his right hand.

"I'm ready for the chair, Evan."

"I know you are. I also know how disappointed you're going to be."

"What!" Sebastian's chest fell.

"Sebastian, you're not getting the job."

"If it's not me and it's not Janice, who?"

"You can't breathe a word of this until the official announcement later today. It's Ethan Tremblay."

"The CBC's Ethan Tremblay?"

"Yes."

"The Ethan Tremblay in Jerusalem?"

"Yes."

"The Ethan Tremblay who got his balls shot off."

"Yes, the same one."

"What the fuck is he doing coming here?"

"He doesn't want to be a road warrior anymore. He'll be here in a month. In the meantime, you and Janice will continue alternating in the chair."

Sebastian bristled. He frowned at the Gemini sitting on Evan's desk. He imagined snatching the statuette and cracking Evan's skull with it.

"I have a runner-up prize for you. Toronto wants to borrow you for a couple of months once we get settled. You should go. They've got national reporter jobs to fill and they like your edge."

"Always the bridesmaid," said Sebastian before opening the door.

He made himself stand tall. He wouldn't give Janice the satisfaction of seeing his dejection. He passed her desk.

"Dead man walking," said Janice, not lifting her eyes.

•

Sebastian and Janice leaned against The Desk watching a monitor hanging from the ceiling. Channel 124—the closed circuit feed from the studio. The screen was split: Samantha Cormier sat poised in one video box, Ethan Tremblay in the other. The studio director typed *Jerusalem* under Ethan's video cell.

"He is my enemy," said Sebastian in a hushed voice.

"Mine too," said Janice softly.

Sebastian turned to Janice. "The enemy…," to the screen, "of my enemy…," to Janice, "is my friend."

The interview would unveil Ethan Tremblay to *Here & Now*'s viewers as Garrison Hill's successor. Because of the time difference, the chat needed to be pre-recorded. Ethan would be dreaming when the tape aired, while Sebastian would be plotting.

Sebastian turned up the sound to eavesdrop on the satellite confabulation.

"Hi Ethan, can you hear me alright?"

"No problem, Samantha."

"Ethan, you look fabulous."

Sebastian rolled his eyes. "That's a new record. Just five seconds for her to serve up the first vacuous compliment."

"It's not me; it's the golden hour," said Ethan.

He had a yellow cast on his face, compliments of the setting sun. Warm colours filled the Jerusalem sky behind him.

"Ethan, the backdrop is perfect," said Samantha. *"The Temple Mount, no less."*

"Nothing is too good for the yokels back in Canada," heckled Sebastian.

"We're recording here, Ethan. We're going in five." Samantha and Ethan looked straight into their respective cameras, staying quiet while waiting for the cue.

"Joining us now from Jerusalem is the new co-host of Here & Now— Ethan Tremblay. Ethan, congratulations. We're all very excited that you're coming."

"Can't wait to bask in your glory," said Sebastian. He crumpled an abandoned outlook and pitched it at the screen. The paper ball bounced off Ethan's face.

"Thank you, Samantha," said Ethan. *"I'm excited too. I've been away from Canada for twelve years. I've loved every minute as a foreign correspondent, but it's time to go home."*

"I've loved every minute as a foreign correspondent, except for the time I got my balls shot off," mocked Sebastian.

"But your crotch looks normal," said Janice.

"Walnuts," said Sebastian. "I always slip two in my underwear. They're the perfect prosthesis. And I never run out. You can buy them on any street corner in Jerusalem."

"Ethan, reporters would kill to have your career," said Samantha. *"You work in one of the most exhilarating cities of the world, but you're giving it all up to host a local newscast. Why?"*

"Twelve years ago I didn't have kids," said Ethan. *"Now I have two. I think they deserve to see their dad for more than a few days a month. Plus, this city—this country—can be dangerous. I'd like them to live in a place where there's no chance of a bus blowing up."*

"Two children—that's astonishing," said Janice. "Quite the feat for a man who, shall we say, doesn't have any family jewels."

"What is a walnut if not a seed," said Sebastian. "I can't explain the miracle, but walnut gonads behave like the real love spuds."

"Ethan, when will you get here?" asked Samantha.

"We're packing right now and hope to be there by the end of the month," replied Ethan.

"We're coming after Christmas," said Sebastian. "I want to avoid *The Nutcracker Suite*."

"Good precaution," said Janice. "And I also suggest not watching *America's Funniest Home Videos Christmas Special*. They're very fond of testicular trauma."

"Thanks for doing this, Ethan," said Samantha. *"We'll see you soon."*

"You're welcome, Samantha. I'm really looking forward to hosting Here & Now."

The screen went black. Sebastian laid the remote on the counter.

"Nuts to you, Ethan."

●

"There you go," said the waitress, as she laid a coffee in front of Sebastian. He didn't bother to look up; he was too busy reading the smartphone version of his Lotto Lush story, though the web folks opted for the timid headline: Lotto Millionaire Blows It All.

"Our barista is trying some new latte art," said the waitress, fishing for feedback. Sebastian laid his phone down and examined the coffee foam.

"Do I look like a Snoopy kind of guy?" said Sebastian, wearing his best stone face.

"Now that you mention it, no." The waitress bit her lower lip. "I don't suppose you'd like a cat either?"

Sebastian shook his head. "I'm allergic. Has she used up all the ferns?"

"I don't think so."

"I'll have a fern, please."

She reached for the cup. Sebastian held up his hand. "It's okay, he'll have it." Sebastian pointed at Dozy Dan skirting between tables. Sebastian pushed Snoopy away. The two men shook hands.

"Thanks for coming, Dan."

"I'm a little pressed for time," he said, taking his chair. "I have a flight to catch."

Dan glanced at the cup. "Oh, Snoopy," he said with childlike delight. "And he has happy feet."

Sebastian forced a smile. "Yes, they're quite talented here. I knew you'd be rushed so I ordered already. Mine's coming. There was a mix-up in the order."

"I just heard your radio story on that alcoholic millionaire. Absolutely compelling."

"He had a brilliant business plan—buy a million dollars' worth of beer and live off the empties."

"Terribly sad," said Dan, missing the joke as usual.

"Wait until you see him. He's right out of central casting: bloodshot eyes, red nose, hasn't shaved in days and he's wearing a wife beater undershirt."

"Evan says you found his ex-wife."

"She's a piece of work too. It took a while to track her down and convince her to talk, but I can be very persuasive. We're saving her for the *Here & Now* story"

Dan sipped his forgotten coffee. "What's on your mind, Sebastian?"

"Ethan Tremblay."

"What a coup, eh," said Dan. "He'll improve the quality of journalism at *Here & Now* simply by walking into the room."

Sebastian imagined ramming Ethan's head into the bull's-eye of a CBC logo, kicking him in the ass and snarling, "Improve this."

"He certainly comes with a reputation," said Sebastian.

"One fern, just like you ordered." The waitress barged into their conversation. "Anything else? Something sweet?"

"No, thank you," said Sebastian.

"I thought so," said the waitress. "You don't look like a sweet kind of guy."

Dan craned his neck. "A fern. I think you got short changed in the artistic department." He slurped Snoopy's nose.

"Dan, I was under the impression that I would be getting the job. You said I have a bright future."

"You do. The door is open to Toronto, isn't it?" Dan winked. "Look, no son-in-law of mine will founder on my watch, but I never said you'd get the job."

"You implied it."

"If I misled you, I'm sorry." Dan laid his cup on the saucer. "CBC has more than one talented journalist. We had to find a spot for Ethan."

Dan's seriousness triggered a memory, a cryptic conversation in Sebastian's dining room about a bit of trouble in the Jerusalem bureau.

"Why did you have to find a spot for Ethan?"

"I can't get into it." Dan used his teaspoon to scoop foam off the sides of his cup.

"If I say something that's true, take a sip of coffee," said Sebastian. Tacit answers were better than no answers.

Dan raised his cup, letting it hover near his lips.

"Ethan did something he shouldn't have."

Dan sipped.

"He embarrassed the CBC."

Dan sipped again.

"You had to get him the hell out of Dodge."

Dan took a third sip and laid the cup down. "I have to get to the airport."

The two men walked to the cash register. "I'll get this," said Sebastian, pulling out his debit card. He lifted the lid off a jar of chocolate-covered coffee beans.

"Care for some?"

"No thanks," said Dan. "I've spilled enough beans already."

●

Sebastian used the drive home to reflect on how to turn the oblique into the candid. First thing tomorrow, he would canvass the best gossip mongers in the CBC. Thanks to the Training Department he had bonded with dozens of them—reporters from across the country. They had shared band-of-brothers training at the Toronto Broadcast Centre and, more importantly, band-of-brothers drinking along John Street. Some Deep Throat knew what Ethan Tremblay was hiding. Sebastian would turn over the rock and uncover the slime underneath.

Sebastian parked in his driveway and shadowboxed as he ducked left and right up the walk.

"Float like a butterfly, sting like a bee."

He'd win the fight with Ethan Tremblay by a knockout. Sebastian gave the coat tree a left jab and then a straight right.

"Hello, Sebastian."

The greeting landed like an uppercut to the jaw, momentarily dazing him.

"Hello, Donna."

"Picking on a defenceless coat tree. Why not fight someone your own size?"

Sebastian countered with a short, crisp punch. "How nice to see you, especially when you're not shouting the C word."

"Sebastian, please," said Roxanne, charging between the two fighters like a referee about to send them back to their respective corners.

"Hi, honey." He kissed the referee harder than usual, just to annoy Dour Donna. "Mmm, you taste good."

Sebastian steadied himself for another round. "I haven't seen you in ages, Donna. Did you take your little show on the road?"

"Couldn't. We all have respectable day jobs. But it certainly was a fun evening, wasn't it?" said Donna.

"Are you including the part where your mother walked out in disgust?"

Donna moved closer, planted her feet and turned Sebastian into a punching bag. "Disgust! You took advantage of an alcoholic lotto winner. Now that's disgusting. You have no shame."

"This is not the night, Donna," scolded Roxanne.

"I'm sorry, I forgot," said Donna. "I heard you didn't get the big job you were after. I'll leave you alone to lick your wounds in peace."

Donna headed for the door, but paused at the mirror. She took a lipstick tube out of her purse. Scarlet lipstick. Sebastian watched in slow motion—the removing of the cap, the twisting of the base, the head poking up, the deft covering of the lips.

"When did you start wearing lipstick, Donna? I thought you vetoed cosmetics."

"It's an experiment. I'm writing a paper on the psychology of colour. Red is the colour of arousal. It's also the colour of anger. What does red mean to you, Sebastian?"

"I was taught red means stop."

•

No son-in-law of mine will founder on my watch. Sebastian dissected the words. Dozy Dan didn't say, "No *future* son-in-law of mine will founder on my watch." The pledge was predicated on marrying his daughter. An engagement wasn't enough. His arid pontification on family was a coded message: Get on with it—make my daughter an honest woman. Sebastian calculated that his future success would come with a price. And he would pay it.

Roxanne touched his shoulder. "How are you feeling?"

"Like I've been thrown under a bus. I hurt all over. I was cheated. I deserved that job."

"I know you did. You worked hard for it. I'm sorry you didn't get it." She hugged him. "Besides," she said, wearing a wry smile, "I was looking forward to telling people that my fiancé hosted *Here & Now*."

"About that word *fiancé*, I was thinking that my career isn't everything. Family is important too. Maybe we should set a wedding date."

"I'm in no rush to get married," said Roxanne.

Not quite the swoon he had hoped for. "Let's recap the history. I get down on one knee. You say yes. Your mom and dad host this huge party. All our friends are there. You show off your ring. They all coo. And that's the last time either of us mentions the word wedding."

"You don't get a job, so you want to get married. What's all this about?"

"It's just…," Sebastian turned to the window. He focused on a kid walking his dog. Sebastian mentally counted one thousand one, one thousand two, one thousand three. He rotated back to Roxanne.

"It's just…I need you. Journalism is a black pit. I fall into it every morning. You pull me out at the end of the day. You're the decency in my life. I want to show the world what you mean to me."

Roxanne stepped back. Not quite the teary embrace he had hoped for. She was more cautious than adoring.

Sebastian had seen that pensive look before. "Did I say something wrong?"

"Women are always flirting with you."

Sebastian spun an imaginary game-show wheel. The pie wedges clacking past the flapper contained flippant phrases: I'm man enough for all, They're only flesh and blood, Handsome has its benefits. Roxanne tolerated his conceit, knowing he cast the bait in the hope of hooking a live one. Dour Donna offered no sport whatsoever. Roxanne was a much harder fish to land. The wheel ticked past Bankrupt and stopped on Jackpot.

"Who wants a man that no one else finds attractive?" Roxanne's solemn face signalled that his attempt at levity had fallen flat.

"You don't discourage them."

"Roxanne, you have a lock on my heart. I love you. I won't stray. I'll never hurt you."

She moved closer. "If you do, let's just say that Lorena Bobbitt has set the standard for divorce." She exuded grit.

Sebastian graced her cheek. He kissed her the way Rhett Butler kissed Scarlet O'Hara.

"A fall wedding would be nice," said Roxanne.

"Let's celebrate," he said. He loaded a disc into the CD player. Of all the burdens he carried today, this was the heaviest. He pushed play.

Roxanne melted into a glow of recognition.

"May I?" Sebastian held out his arms for a ballroom dance.

"You sure know how to make a girl feel special."

They fox-trotted through the dining room.

Gonna find my baby, gonna hold her tight.

Sebastian synced with the vocals. "Gonna grab some afternoon delight."

He removed his hand from her back and scooped up the bottle of Chianti Classico. He twirled Roxanne; she lifted two glasses off the sideboard.

Slow, slow, quick, quick. Sebastian and Roxanne zigzagged down the hall to the bedroom.

•

Paul Bennett sat on a park bench watching ducks poke about the grass. He heard the occasional quack, but mostly they kept their heads down and stayed quiet.

Maybe I should be doing that, thought Bennett.

A couple holding hands passed in front of him. They paid no attention to the in-limbo police chief. He tapped his fingers on the bench.

"Hello, Chief."

"Hello, Janice." He stood to shake hands.

"Thanks for agreeing to see me."

"I don't know why I did." The chief's eyes spurted around the parking lot.

"If you're checking for a camera, I swear I didn't bring one. We're alone. Well, as alone as you can be on a walking trail."

"I'm not keen on the idea of people seeing us together."

Janice took the sunglasses off the top of her head and perched them on her nose. "I'm a master of disguise."

The chief smiled, just a little. "My encounters with your profession lately haven't been pleasant. I have my reasons to be suspicious."

"I'm not wearing a wire either. You can frisk me if you want. People like to."

He waved her off.

"Care to go for a stroll around the lake?" asked Janice. "We'll have more privacy in the trees."

The chief sauntered past the ducks. Janice matched his pace.

"We could have had this conversation over the phone," said Janice, "but it's better in person."

"I'm listening."

"You need some good PR, chief."

"Your colleague said an identical thing to me at Garrison Hill's funeral."

They heard running feet on the boardwalk and stayed quiet as a jogger slipped by.

"I know Sebastian asked you for an interview. Enough time has passed to have done a dozen interviews. I don't think you're going to give him one, are you?"

"I thought about it, but I couldn't get past one inescapable fact—I don't like the son of a bitch."

Janice laughed. "Chief, remember the old saying—don't get angry, get even. If you really want to stick it to Sebastian, do an interview with me. He'll be apoplectic."

The chief stopped dead. His face filled with astonishment. What a revelation. There was no thin blue line at the CBC.

"I take it that you don't like Sebastian Hunter very much."

"Quite the opposite, really. I like him a great deal. But this is business. He had his chance to get your story, now it's *my* turn."

The chief leaned behind Janice.

"Anything wrong, Chief?"

"Just checking for a dorsal fin." He started walking again.

"People go on TV all the time to apologize for lapses in judgment. Tiger Woods and Bill Clinton both said I'm sorry in front of the cameras."

"I didn't cheat on my wife, I drove…," Bennett stared into the woods, "drunk."

"The point is—an apology is good for the soul and it's good for the image."

"Now you're really sounding like Sebastian Hunter."

Janice cut in front of Bennett. There was no missing her emphatic expression. "I'll tell you the difference, Chief. Sebastian would never have sat on the information that I've been sitting on."

"What do you mean?"

"I know your connection to Garrison Hill."

The chief rubbed his lips. "Go on."

"Stop me when I'm wrong. You and Garrison met at an Alcoholics Anonymous meeting. You went through the twelve steps together. You got off the bottle together. And as far as I can tell, you stayed sober until that night in Florida."

"Garrison took my secret to his grave. I will take his."

"I'm not asking you to betray his secret. Garrison's name never has to come up. I'm only interested in *your* story."

"Why should I? Why should I get on TV and tell people that I'm a recovered alcoholic who faltered?"

"Because if you don't, it's going to squirt out anyway."

"Are you blackmailing me?"

"Not me, Chief," said Janice, touching her chest, "but your background is not safe. Someone else is going to discover it, eventually. Someone not as understanding as I am."

Janice filled the chief's silence. "This story is not over. You've still got your court case. You won't survive as chief. Set the agenda and get ahead of the bad news. Release the details on *your* terms. Apologize. Then climb out of the hole."

The chief's face twitched. He made fitful glances, but avoided eye contact. "I need to talk to my family. Sebastian wanted them involved. You'd want the same?"

Janice nodded. "Sebastian might be a son of a bitch, but he's a smart son of a bitch. He's knows what works on TV. And so do I."

Janice and the chief continued their circuit. Bennett caught a glint in the bushes. He bent down and pulled out a Sleeman beer bottle— clear glass embossed with a beaver and maple leaf.

"Not mine, I swear. Though I'm sure no Canadian jury would believe me."

"Now that's a money shot. And me with no camera," moaned Janice.

Bennett pushed the bottle back between the stalks and wandered away.

[six]

Sebastian rolled two shell-on walnuts in the palm of his hand, over and over. Occasionally, he tossed one up, just a couple of inches. It banged the other when he caught it. He had practiced hours for this very moment. The technique demanded more finesse than strength, but he had an abundance of both. He was giddy with anticipation.

Ethan Tremblay flicked about the newsroom, handing out smiles and handshakes like a politician on the campaign trail. Janice extended her hand. Ethan bowed and kissed it. Janice laughed and tossed her hair.

You wouldn't kiss that hand if you knew where it's been.

A hubbub followed Ethan. Nubile interns giggled while snapping cellphone pictures to be shared later over wild-coloured drinks made with peach schnapps, rimmed with fruit and topped with paper umbrellas. Young reporters joked about not washing the hand that touched King Ethan. Even the wizened and the jaded stood in His Majesty's presence.

Sebastian reread the email reminding everyone of Ethan's arrival. The accolades caused nausea: Former CBC correspondent in London; CBC correspondent in Jerusalem for five years; Fluent in English, French, and Arabic; Reported on the Afghanistan and Iraq wars; Winner of two Canadian Screen Awards; Author of a much-lauded memoir; Awarded an honourary degree from the University of Toronto; New co-host of *Here & Now*.

I suppose the ingratiating bastard can even walk on water.

"Sebastian," said Ethan, "a pleasure to meet you."

"Likewise," said Sebastian, dropping the walnuts into a bowl full of them. He reached for Ethan's hand. "No kissing, please." They shared a laugh.

"Sebastian, your story about the house going over the cliff was on every newscast in Israel. The Israelis were amazed that a house could be destroyed by something other than a Hamas missile. It was riveting TV."

"Thanks." Sebastian offered no reciprocal praise. "I busted my balls on that story."

Ethan mustered a syllable of laughter. "I also know you busted your balls trying to get my job."

MY job. The gall.

"When I passed through Toronto I had a game of squash with your future father-in-law," continued Ethan. "He gave me the background."

"Yes, Dan loves to reveal more than he should sometimes." Sebastian engineered an awkward silence. "So tell me, Ethan—why are you *really* here?"

Like a good lawyer, Sebastian knew the answer before he even asked the question. He had uncovered Ethan's dirty little secret within forty-eight hours of being cheated out of the anchor job. The interrogation was simply to make Ethan squirm, to prove him a liar, to prove that he wasn't man enough, neither in character nor in anatomy, to sit in the anchor's chair.

"It's for family reasons."

"Aha."

"I have the distinct impression you don't believe me."

"Please. No reporter leaves the Bang Bang Club for his family."

Ethan laid both hands on the cubicle wall and bent over straight into Sebastian's face. Their noses were within duelling distance. "My personal business is *my* personal business."

"You leave a place where World War III might break out so you can report on potholes and bake sales. It doesn't add up."

"Maybe that's the kind of journalism you want to practice, but I'll be setting a different standard. And what doesn't add up is why you think you're entitled to a job over someone with ten times the experience."

"You mean ten times the trouble," taunted Sebastian.

Ethan leaned back, perhaps to pull the pin out of a grenade. "Some people work to get where they are. And some people just sleep with the right person."

Sebastian picked up two walnuts and jiggled them. "I've heard that you're a tough nut to crack. But I'm very good at cracking nuts."

He laid the walnuts flat in the palm of his hand—one nestled into the fleshy muscle at the base of his thumb, the other cupped into his fingers.

"First of all, one nut needs to be slightly bigger than the other. Much like a man's testicles. Assuming he still has them, of course."

He fiddled with the seams between the walnut halves.

"The key is to make sure the ridge of one nut touches the ridge of the other."

His free hand cradled the hand holding the nuts.

"Apply sudden, firm pressure."

The push/squeeze combination resembled a spasm.

CRACK.

Ethan flinched.

Sebastian opened his hand. One nut remained whole. He picked away pieces of disintegrated shell from the other.

"Walnut?"

"No, thank you."

Sebastian plucked another nut from the bowl. "I could do this all day."

CRACK.

"Are you sure you don't want one, I have plenty."

CRACK.

Ethan shook his head. "You're not eating them."

"I find it far more satisfying just to break them."

●

Sebastian was entangled in a string of cars trickling by a paving crew. His Acura lumbered towards the portal. A flagger in a pink hardhat glanced at her counterpart at the far end of the construction zone.

"One more," prayed Sebastian.

The flagger spun the sign on her staff; slow turned to stop. Sebastian's escape route was blocked.

"Damn." He smouldered despite the air conditioning. Cars rumbled from the opposite direction. His fingers drummed the steering wheel.

"There's no point in being upset," said Roxanne. "The roadwork needs to be done and they have a job to do."

"I should send Ethan a text: Breaking News—Potholes filled on Elizabeth Avenue."

"Very funny."

"No really, he wants to know. That's why he left the Middle East. The freeze and thaw cycle of road repair is heady stuff. If I don't tell him, I'll regret it later. You know what they say: The road to hell is paved with good intentions."

Roxanne laughed in spite of her inclination to admonish Sebastian for his aversion to playing nice.

"Try to get along with Ethan," she said. "The sting won't go away until you do."

"That won't be easy. He's got a mean streak and an ego that's bigger than mine."

A worker wearing safety earmuffs pulled the cord on a compacter. It rattled to life and vibrated around freshly shovelled asphalt.

"We're going to die here," moaned Sebastian. The only entertainment was watching the compactor crisscross through the windshield. Sebastian's attention drifted to a digital billboard which promised to correct vision with laser surgery for only $490 per eye. The ad dissolved into another. Scarlet letters flared off a white background.

DOES ROXANNE KNOW ABOUT YOUR SECRET LOVE?

Sebastian's eyes bugged. Roxanne concentrated on her smart phone. The compacter spun around and headed back towards the billboard side of the road, Roxanne's side of the road. Wisps of steam drifted by, but not enough to obscure the message. He needed a decoy. Sebastian clutched his stomach and keeled forward.

"Ow," he said.

"What's wrong?"

"A sharp pain went up my chest."

"What kind of pain?"

"Pain, pain. It's hard to describe. A burning sensation."

"That could be a heart attack." Roxanne held up her phone. "I'm calling 9-1-1."

"No-o-o," said Sebastian, vigorously waving his hands. "It's only heartburn." He rubbed his breastbone.

"You can't be sure. Garrison Hill just died from a heart attack. I don't want to bury my fiancé too. I should call an ambulance."

"It's not a heart attack," said Sebastian, his voice rising. "I wolfed down breakfast. This is payback. I'm not dying. I'm just uncomfortable." He gave Roxanne an Oscar-winning grimace and grunt.

Roxanne chucked the phone into her purse. "Don't come crying to me if you find out later that it's a heart attack," she huffed.

The compactor shuddered in front of the billboard. It asked another uncomfortable question.

DON'T YOU THINK ROXANNE DESERVES BETTER?

Construction workers leaning on shovels blocked her view. The foreman pointed at another pothole to be filled. The human shield was about to crack. Sebastian rolled down his window and stuck his head out.

"Hey," he bawled at the flagger. "It's our turn to get through."

Roxanne dropped her head and covered her eyes. "You're acting like a jerk."

"I'm late."

"Everybody is late."

The train of oncoming cars showed no end. The billboard issued a command.

STOP LYING TO ROXANNE.

"Come on," yelled Sebastian. He punched the horn; the blare made Roxanne jump. The flagger glared and thrust her stop sign forward.

"What the hell are you doing?" shouted Roxanne.

"The pain is back. I need antacid."

Sebastian took his foot off the brake, letting the car roll ahead a few feet.

"Stop this," ordered Roxanne. "You'll get a ticket."

The flagger pushed the talk button on her walkie-talkie, glowering at Sebastian during the entire conversation.

The quivering compacter flattened the last of the black, oily mixture.

Sebastian nudged the car forward. The flagger retreated a couple of steps.

"Back off," she screamed.

"Sebastian, you've gone from jerk to asshole," said Roxanne. "This is dangerous."

"It's like someone has a fist under my ribcage."

The last approaching car passed Sebastian's door. The flagger bowed and waved him through with a sweeping arm.

"You can proceed, Your Majesty," said Roxanne.

"Finally," said Sebastian. The Acura scooted away. "I'll stop into the drugstore for some Tums."

"See if they have anything to reflux your attitude while you're at it."

The shrill sound of a police siren interrupted Roxanne's rebuke. Two short wails accompanied flashing lights.

"And you think you're already late," said Roxanne, folding her arms.

Sebastian pulled in. The officer stepped out of her cruiser. She took off her sunglasses and tucked them into a pocket as Sebastian dropped the window.

"Ah, Mr. Hunter," she said. "Nice to see you again." Roxanne showed surprise.

"What's the problem, officer?"

"The problem is you didn't obey directions from the construction crew back there. Driver's licence, registration, and proof of insurance, please." Sebastian fished the documents out of his patent-leather case. The officer took them back to her cruiser.

Sebastian hummed to break the silence. He pointed at a man pushing a grocery cart overflowing with cases of beer bottles and blue bags stuffed with juice boxes and pop cans.

"Environmentalist of the Year," said Sebastian.

"Oh, really," said Roxanne.

The clatter of the grocery cart was the only relief from the silent treatment.

"What did she mean, 'Nice to see you again'?" asked Roxanne.

"She stopped me the night of Garrison's funeral because of the broken headlight."

"And that slipped your mind somehow?"

"Yes, it did. She saw I was sober and quickly let me go. It wasn't a big deal."

"And yet," said Detective Roxanne, placing a finger on her lips, "she remembered you."

"Maybe she's a *Here & Now* fan."

Roxanne looked over her shoulder. "Of course she is. Here she comes now with her autograph book." Roxanne threw herself back into the seat.

The officer opened a metal binder and handed Sebastian his documents and a ticket. "Stop means stop, Mr. Hunter. It doesn't mean threaten the flagger. By the way, fines are doubled in construction zones."

Sebastian breezed back into traffic. "At least this ticket is good for one thing."

"What's that?"

"It cured my heartburn."

●

Splat. Diagonal Ethan.

"Lame," muttered Sebastian.

Splat. Stand-on-his-head Ethan.

"Much better."

Splat. Face-plant Ethan. He plummeted to the floor.

"Save me, Sebastian, save me," said Sebastian in the frightened voice of a heroine tied to a railway track. "No one's going to save you," he said in villainous pitch.

Sebastian separated a stack of fridge magnets into two piles, bent one in each hand and performed a riffle shuffle worthy of a Las Vegas casino dealer. Ethan Tremblay's smarmy face festooned every magnet. The tagline rankled: Bringing the World to Your Neighbourhood.

The staff fridge was naked, apart from Sebastian's flying decoration. He lobbed another magnet. Ethan hit an edge, dropped and joined a pile of askew magnets on the floor. Sebastian kept tossing. List-to-starboard Ethan. Upright Ethan.

Ethan's debut as *Here & Now*'s new co-host was three days old. Three days of worming his way into the hearts of *Here & Now* viewers. Three days surrounded by toadies. Three days of bloated, tiresome war stories which, to Sebastian's eternal jealousy, were actually real war stories.

Sebastian heard guffaws from the newsroom. Time to enter the battlefield and start a firefight. Ethan sat on the edge of his desk holding court. Evan, Zoe, and Janice stood around mesmerized. Sebastian joined his doting colleagues.

"So here I was barrelling down the road towards Baghdad in an Abrams tank."

"Was that before or after they pulled down Saddam's statue?" asked Sebastian.

Ethan appeared stunned. Nobody ever interrupted him. Zoe's cough broke the inelegant silence.

"Before." His tone dripped annoyance.

"Didn't mean to break your rhythm. Go on."

"The air was rank. The crew hadn't washed in a week and the air conditioning was busted. They had the turret open, but the hum inside was like camel's breath," he said, screwing up his face.

Ethan knew how to spin a yarn. He paused for effect, added natural emphasis and was enthusiastic. And that voice, well, Ethan had great pipes.

"It had to be forty degrees inside the tank. The floor was slippery with sweat. The gunner turns to the commander and says, in this Louisiana drawl, 'Sir, my ass is sizzling. My momma loves baked buns, but I don't think this is what she had in mind.'"

His spellbound audience erupted into laughter. Sebastian couldn't help himself. He joined in. Even an enemy can be funny sometimes.

"The commander says, 'Boys, maybe we'll stop for a few minutes and make sure that Brasseaux's butt doesn't burst into flames.' Here we are, just half an hour from downtown Baghdad, Saddam has high-tailed it, there's nothing standing between us and history, and these treadheads want to kick back and drink Coke."

"What did you do?" implored Evan.

"I whipped out my credit card and said, 'Commander, you keep going and this credit card will buy this crew whatever it wants.'"

Sebastian decided to punch Ethan's flow again. "Where was *your* crew?"

"Following us in a Land Rover," snapped Ethan, his facial muscles taut. His story had flipped over into a ditch, wheels spinning. It took a moment to put four wheels back on the road and restart the engine.

"The commander was a cagey guy. He says, 'We're not checking into the Palestine Hotel. How about you pay for a night on the town when we all get home and you got yourself a deal.' 'Sold,' I shouted. 'Boys,' says the commander, 'let's get Tremblay to Firdos Square.' It cost me two thousand bucks, but I got to the square in time to see Saddam's statue being hauled down."

Sebastian continued his inquisition. "Other TV cameras were in the square. What's the value of a money shot if everybody has it?"

Ethan stood up. "Value?" he roared. "Value? I'll make this simple, Sebastian. It's iconic. It's an image that will outlive you and me. And I made sure CBC got it. Conquering armies tear down the symbols of the vanquished. You'd better remember that, if you ever get to a war zone."

"You know what they say: the first casualty of war is truth."

As Sebastian walked away he heard Ethan state, "He's got a mean streak and an ego that's bigger than mine."

•

Perfect conditions for a picnic lunch—blue sky and twenty-five degrees. Wind and humidity had taken the day off. Sebastian waved at Roxanne as he blazed up the trail around Long Pond. She sat on a park bench, tucked underneath a mountain ash on the edge of a grove. They wrapped arms around each other and kissed; a modest kiss, the sort people use when they don't want a public display of affection to be the talk of the town.

"How was your morning?" asked Roxanne.

"Fine, until Ethan started crowing about his time in Iraq. 'I won the war, I found Saddam Hussein.' The man is insufferable. Nobody is as good as he is. He takes the fun out of dysfunctional."

Roxanne stopped unzipping the cooler bag. "Sebastian, we need to talk."

"What about?"

"You."

"Don't you mean us?"

"No, I mean you. I'm really concerned."

"You shouldn't be." Sebastian reached for the cooler bag, but stopped in mid-stretch. "Did you hear that?" He turned his ear to the shadows in the woods.

"I heard a bird singing."

"No, not a bird, a camera shutter. Shush." Sebastian listened intensely while trying to appear unalarmed. He heard a bird trill, then the rapid-fire of a digital SLR camera, the sort newspaper photographers use to capture split-second movement.

"Someone is taking our picture," said Sebastian.

"I heard the clicks too."

Sebastian pondered the chances that the shutter noise belonged to his stalker. Not likely. Surely his stalker couldn't be that much of an oaf. But what if he was.

Carpe diem. The snitch wouldn't dare blurt out the truth to their faces. He was too much of a coward for that. Fight back.

"Let's casually walk toward the woods over there," said Sebastian.

"Don't get into a confrontation."

Sebastian and Roxanne held hands as they promenaded. A kayaker practiced rolls on the pond, righting her overturned boat seemingly with just a sweep of her paddle while hanging upside down. Sebastian intentionally paused to admire the demonstration before following the trail into the woods.

"You can come out now," said Sebastian to a thicket.

Bushes swayed and a branch cracked. A man wearing a Tilley hat parted the greenery. Binoculars hung around his neck, along with a camera and lens so big that Hollywood's paparazzi would lust after it.

"What were you doing in there?" asked Sebastian.

"Is there a problem?"

"The problem is my fiancée and I don't appreciate being spied on."

"Spied on!" said the man, his voice rising to reject the accusation. "I was bird watching."

"That's easy to say."

"Would a spy go around with a copy of *Birds of Canada*?" He pulled a book out of his knapsack and showed Sebastian the cover. Two puffins with rainbow bills and orange feet stood on the words Field Guide.

"A clever one might." Sebastian decided to call his bluff. "What exactly were you trying to see?"

"The red-eyed vireo," the birder shot back. "It's a songbird and I was enjoying a good look and listen before you interrupted me."

"I heard a camera shutter."

"That's what we do. We take pictures." He pressed a button on his camera and a bird with ruby-red eyes and white eyebrows appeared on the screen. "Its feathers don't ruffle as easily as yours."

"We're terribly sorry for disturbing you," said Roxanne, towing Sebastian away. She didn't uncouple until they reached the park bench.

"One day we're going to laugh at this," said Sebastian.

"Probably, but I'm not laughing now. In a way, I'm glad it happened. I know what's going on. I didn't want to believe it, but this episode proves it."

"I don't know what you're talking about."

"I didn't want to say this, Sebastian, but sometimes bluntness is required." Roxanne laid her hand on his. "You're not well."

"What!"

"I've been doing a little research and I think you're suffering from Post-Traumatic Stress Disorder."

Sebastian laughed. "Who told you that? Dr. Google?"

"Hear me out. Reputable websites say the death of a friend can trigger PTSD. Garrison died in front of you. Worse, you tried to save him and couldn't."

"PTSD is a bit of a stretch isn't it?"

"You're showing symptoms. You hear a camera and perceive danger. For no good reason. You can't mention Ethan Tremblay without launching into a tirade. The negativity is breathtaking. And the angry outbursts—swearing on the air, yelling at a flagger—that's not you. The pain in your chest, that's another sign. And most telling, you're having problems being…intimate. Ever since Garrison died, you've hardly touched me."

"Now just a second. This is…," Sebastian repressed the word ridiculous. *Play the PTSD card, idiot. It will absolve a multitude of sins.* "…a revelation. I had no idea. What are the other symptoms?"

"Feelings of mistrust."

"I don't trust anyone at work anymore."

"Flashbacks."

"I keep seeing poor Garrison slumping in his chair, over and over."

"Suicidal thoughts," she said with palpable anxiety. She bit a fingernail. Sebastian had never seen her do that before. He gently ran his hand down her face. She kissed the palm.

"Not at all. I swear. No thoughts about hurting myself. Definitely a case of two out of three ain't bad."

"You need help," she said. "Promise me you'll phone EAP this afternoon."

"I promise." He took her hand and pressed it to his lips. "Would you like me to massage your temples?"

Roxanne nodded and turned back on. Sebastian lowered her head into his lap. He brushed hair away from her closed eyes.

●

Janice collapsed on Sebastian's chest. She floated up and down with his breathing. They lay content. Janice even fell asleep for a few moments. She broke the harmony with a snort and spilled onto the empty side of the bed.

"That was the best 'therapy session' I've ever had," said Sebastian.

"What?"

"Nothing. It's a joke. I'm supposed to be somewhere else this evening confronting my fears."

Janice poured two glasses of Chianti Classico. "Stalker fears?"

"You could say that."

"Do you have any idea who it is?"

"I have suspects aplenty, but no concrete proof. I called the company that owns the billboard and pretended I was interested in doing a story. The guy laughed and hung up. I haven't seen the message since."

Sebastian sipped the wine. "I can't decide which is better—the sex or the 'medication.'"

Janice swatted his thigh with a backhanded slap.

"I'd really like the stalker to be Ethan Tremblay, but the timing's all wrong. It would make tomorrow even more pleasurable."

Janice turned on her side. Her eyes gleamed. "What's going to happen?"

"I've got him by his shot-off balls. It seems our Mr. Spend-time-with-my-family had a zipper problem in the Gaza Strip."

"No-o-o." Janice walked her fingers over Sebastian's chest. "Tell me more."

"I don't want to spoil the fun, but the tawdry details will squirt out."

"Where?"

"Who hates the CBC more than anyone? Who wakes up every morning thinking, How can I put the Communist Broadcasting Corporation on the rack today?"

Janice bounced upright. "Not Lily Chin. You told her?"

"Sometimes you have to sleep with the enemy."

"You're evil. I like that in a man." She raised her glass in tribute. "How did you find out?"

"The tattletales on the fourth floor of the Broadcast Centre. It's the worst kept secret in Toronto. Things got so tense that the Jewish Defence League was on the verge of making a public stink. They agreed not to if Tremblay left Jerusalem. CBC told him pack your bags or pack...your...bags."

"Remind me never to get on your bad side."

"This time tomorrow, Ethan Tremblay is going to be in a shit-storm."

●

Sebastian hit the refresh button on LILY LASHES OUT. Lily Chin was a *Toronto Sun* columnist. Her bio spoke of her take-no-prisoners attitude, her dogged drive to expose government stupidity, her relentless pursuit of the truth.

She's brassy, thought Sebastian, *a girl after my own heart.*

Lily Chin was the columnist most-hated and most-feared on the top floor of the CBC Broadcast Centre. The Mother Corp's embarrassments always leaked out in her column—from a drunken reporter's toe-sucking on an Air Canada flight, to an entrepreneurial cameraman who used CBC gear to film porn flicks. To Lily Chin, the CBC was left wing, anti-Israel, anti-business, and a waste of tax dollars. The sooner the government privatized it, the better.

After a couple of Scotches, Dozy Dan once called her The Snake.

Where are the fangs? Sebastian asked himself.

Chin's webpage updated. Sebastian gasped in delight. This was even better than he had hoped for. The headline on the video commentary was savage: *Reporter's Libido Stains CBC News.*

Sebastian clicked play. Lily motioned with her hand for the viewers to come closer.

Pssst. I have a secret. It's about CBC foreign correspondent Ethan Tremblay.

The monitor beside Lily used the same publicity photo as the fridge magnets.

Until last month, Ethan Tremblay lived and worked in Jerusalem, in the heart of the Holy Land. But the wisdom of King Solomon eluded him. So did the common sense of the Ten Commandments. Ethan Tremblay didn't know how to behave properly.

Tremblay made the mistake that's been getting men in trouble since biblical times—he let the little head do the thinking for the big head.

You won't find that phrase in the Bible, but the seventh commandment is pretty clear on the subject: Thou Shalt Not Commit Adultery.

The commandment appeared on the monitor.

There's good advice for staying out of trouble.

But Ethan Tremblay ignored it and had an affair with this woman.

The commandment dissolved into a photo of a woman holding an IV bag over a patient lying on a stretcher. She wore a white lab coat and a turquoise hijab. Her onyx eyes beguiled Sebastian. He felt jealous; Ethan had bedded a beautiful woman.

Dr. Haifa Saba treats the sick and wounded in the Gaza Strip. What commitment, what decency, except—Dr. Saba works for Hamas.

Hamas has declared a jihad against Israel—a holy war against the Jewish state. Since she works for Hamas, Dr. Saba supports the destruction of Israel. Since Ethan Tremblay knows Dr. Saba in the biblical sense, he must support the destruction of Israel too. What's next—holocaust denials?

Pictures of the reporter and the doctor blended together.

That's the kind of company Ethan Tremblay kept and your tax dollars helped him do it.

He spent your money to travel to Gaza. His reports were a ruse, a cover for a rendezvous with his girlfriend.

But it gets worse. The ninth commandment says Thou Shalt Not Bear False Witness Against Thy Neighbour.

Lily's spoken commandment was reinforced by a written version.

Ethan Tremblay put his doctor friend in his own CBC reports and let her denounce Israel.

Slow motion footage pilfered from *The National* complemented Lily's rant: Ethan in a flak jacket, Dr. Saba bandaging a child's arm. Perfect shots, thought Sebastian.

He let her say terrible things. He let her lie on the air.

All because he was sleeping with her.

The CBC's equivalent of the Ten Commandments gave Tremblay all the professional and moral guidance he needed.

It's called Journalistic Standards and Practices. You can read it online.

A blazing-red CBC logo filled the monitor.

I'll skip to the good stuff. It tells employees:

Don't put yourself in a conflict of interest.

Don't bring the CBC into disrepute.

Don't use CBC equipment for personal interests.

The phrases zoomed out from the webpage. Nice effect, thought Sebastian.

Ethan Tremblay broke several CBC commandments.

Sounds like firing offences to me. But I don't run the CBC.

The monitor showed a smiling Ethan on the *Here & Now* set.

Instead of sacking Ethan Tremblay, they made him a deal.

Leave town quietly and we'll give you a cushy job back in Canada.

The CBC did all of this to stop you from knowing about his tryst with a Palestinian doctor.

Lily tut-tutted several times.

Naughty, naughty. That's their secret. Tell everybody.

I'm Lily Chin.

"I do enjoy a good spanking," said Sebastian.

He pasted Lily Chin's web address into an email, typed Holy F*#k in the subject line and mailed it to Evan.

●

Ethan had a weakness for shortbread biscuits. He particularly enjoyed Walkers from Scotland as his midmorning snack. He always kept a tin with a Scottish piper on the lid sitting on his desk. War stories—he'd share those, ad nauseam, but shortbread, a reporter could lose a hand reaching for a finger.

Sebastian watched him savour the buttery flavour. Ethan pushed a crumb caught on his upper lip into his mouth. Even a particle was ambrosia.

"Ethan, could I see you for a minute," called Evan from his office door.

The bonny lad is in a wee bit of trouble.

Sebastian lined up his chair with his Paris snow globe. He could see straight into Evan's office. The window which ran the entire length of the door gave him a perfect view. Privacy was elusive in the newsroom.

Evan motioned for Ethan to take a seat. The boss showed none of his usual good nature. Only sternness flowed from his side of the desk. The more he spoke, the lower Ethan sank into his chair. Evan swung the computer monitor around. Ethan pinched his lower lip, a habit Sebastian had noticed whenever Ethan concentrated. He leaned forward as the Lily Lashes Out video played.

"Hi, Sebastian. I was wondering if I could ask a favour."

Sebastian's head jerked. One of the faceless, nameless interns stood by his cubicle. She shifted position just enough to thwart his espionage. Sebastian squelched his desire to scream.

"What do you want…?"

"Nikki," she said, filling in the blank.

"What do you want, Nikki?"

"My professor would like two reviews of my work."

Sebastian pushed the ball of his right foot into the carpet and wheeled his chair a few inches to the left. The angle was all wrong. He had a lovely view of Evan's bookcase.

"Nikki, could we do this—"

The intern cut him off. "She suggested like someone on The Desk do one review. I was thinking about asking Zoe, but like I don't want to insult Evan, he runs the shop after all, and then she suggested like getting a reporter to do the other review, I thought like, maybe you would do it...."

Sebastian tuned her out and stood up. He could see Evan's worried face, but Ethan's expressions were blocked by Nikki's head.

"What do you think?"

"About what?" asked Sebastian.

"Zoe or Evan?"

"For?"

"My work assessment."

"Go for Zoe. She's free right now. Grab her."

Nikki turned to confirm Zoe's idleness, allowing cloak-and-dagger snooping again. Ethan tapped his jaw with a fist.

"Perfect," said Nikki, returning to the blockade position.

I'm blind to the flogging.

Nikki dropped her eyes. "I have one other teensy favour to ask. I've always admired your reporting, like even before I started work here..."

"Nikki, what do you want?" demanded Sebastian.

She stepped back. "I, ah, I was hoping you would do the second assessment."

"Yes, yes. Go to your desk right now and send me the link."

"Oh thank you so much..."

"That fucking bitch," roared Ethan.

Fawning Nikki turned into horrified Nikki. She looked at the office in terror, then back at Sebastian.

"I'm sure he's not referring to you," said Sebastian. Nikki scurried away.

All typing stopped, all necks craned. Everyone in the newsroom was transfixed on the window of rage. Ethan jabbed his finger at the frozen image of the scornful Lily Chin. His voice boomed, "Fuck her, fuck her, fuck her."

The bridge of Ethan's nose scrunched into furrows. His capped teeth clenched. He snatched the Gemini off Evan's desk, his fingers warped around its golden throat. He drove the spiky statuette through the computer screen. Lily Chin was impaled; her face resembled a shattered windshield. Ethan rampaged out of Evan's office.

This called for a celebratory tune: "Werewolves of London." Sebastian put on his headphones.

Aaaooo! Werewolves of London.
Aaaooo!

●

The neighbourhood was the sort that reporters only visit, never live in. BMWs, backyard pools, Japanese rock gardens.

"We are definitely in the wrong business," said Janice.

"You can always marry rich," said Teddy. He stopped the van at the intersection. "Left or right?"

Janice checked her notes. "Left."

"I saw Ethan skulking around this morning," said Teddy. "He was headed to The Executioner's office."

"Really," exclaimed Janice. "We haven't laid eyes on him since he put Lily Chin's head on a pike."

"Will he survive?"

"Turn right. I think so."

"What makes you think that?"

"They can't fire him without firing the brass who made the deal. They'd have to admit they made a mistake. That's not going to happen."

"You're right," said Teddy. "He'd take them all down in flames."

"127. This is it."

The house was as smart-looking as a police officer's dress uniform: blue Cape Cod siding with white trim, a two-car garage and a large oak tree on a weed-free lawn. There was a minivan parked in the driveway and an orange bike with white streamers on the handle grips rested against the house.

"250,000 dollars a year certainly buys you a nice place," said Janice.

"The real-estate ad would say, 'Spectacular executive bungalow on mature lot,'" said Teddy, as he lifted the camera out of its padded travelling case.

Janice slung the pouch containing the microphones over her

shoulder. "Now this is travelling light. Bruce insists on taking something the size of a hockey bag. Sometimes I think there's a body in it."

"Not quite a body," said Teddy with a mischievous grin. He picked up the tripod.

"What do you mean?" asked Janice, also carrying the lighting kit.

"Bruce took out a bunch of stuff after your last bitch session."

"Go on." They headed up the walk.

"When he left the room, we buried a ten kilo weight in the bag."

"You bastards," said Janice laughing.

"Bruce hasn't found it yet. It's under a dozen cables."

Janice pressed the doorbell. She listened for the ding dong, a habit she acquired years before when a politician who "borrowed" government-owned paintings weaselled out of an interview by claiming his doorbell was broken.

"The best part was listening to Bruce boast to Sebastian about the new lightweight bag," continued Teddy. "The moment Sebastian picked it up he complained that it was just as heavy as ever."

"You're evil. I like that in a man."

"So I hear," said Teddy.

The door opened. "Hello, Chief," said Janice.

"Good day, Janice," said Paul Bennett. "My apologies for keeping you waiting. I had a moment of doubt, but my little girl squeezed my hand and said, 'Everything is going to be okay.' Come in."

"Chief, this is Ted. He's the cameraman." Bennett smiled as they shook hands.

"My wife and daughter are in the kitchen."

Janice spied a woman and girl at a table sorting through crayons. Mom stood up as the trio approached. "Marie, this is Janice and this is Ted."

"Nice to meet you," said Marie, initiating another round of handshakes.

The chief touched the girl's head. She wore a red beret covered in sequins. It was pulled down to her ears. "And this munchkin right here is our daughter, Clare." She ignored the adults and continued colouring.

"Hi Clare," said Janice. "I like your hat."

Clare sparkled like her sequins. "I like your hair. I used to have long hair too. Now I don't have any."

The chief coughed and turned away.

"I'm sure it will grow back and be as beautiful as ever," said Janice. She walked behind Clare and peeked over her shoulder. Clare coloured a dragon orange.

"Sometimes I wish I could breathe fire," said Janice.

"Do you like hotdogs?" asked Clare.

"I sure do. Wouldn't it be great to be like that dragon? Roasting hotdogs in seconds." Janice imitated a dragon's roar. Clare giggled.

"Why did you pick a dragon?"

"Because Daddy said a dragon lady was coming over."

"Clare," admonished Marie with the tone that mothers have whenever their children embarrass.

Janice laughed. "Your daddy's right. I *can* be a dragon lady, but not today."

"I'm going to pretend this dragon is you," said Clare. She looked at Janice's hair, picked up a yellow crayon and filled in the dragon's horns.

"Do you ever have horns?" asked Clare. Marie's jaw dropped.

Janice curled index fingers on the crown of her head. "They only come out at night." Clare cracked up.

"Where do you want to do this?" interrupted the Chief.

"You have a beautiful kitchen. What do you think, Teddy?"

"There's lots of natural light. And the family room is a nice background. Let's do it here."

"Janice, I have the photos you asked for." He opened the laptop on the breakfast nook.

Janice scanned the thumbnails. "That one," she said, touching the screen. "Blow that one up, please." The Chief double clicked the photo. Janice subtly looked at Teddy. He nodded.

"It's a beautiful shot," said Janice.

"It was taken about six months ago, before…" The chief's voice cracked.

The Clare on the screen showed off her gapped teeth; her blond hair tied in a ponytail. She saluted the camera with her father's police hat perched on her head.

●

The prurient and the political boiled together in the comments section of CBC's webpages. Sebastian was thrilled because all of it swirled around the exploits of the dethroned Ethan Tremblay. Sebastian finger-kicked the scroll button on his mouse.

Devine Law
He hates Jews. Fire him.

Fair Shake
He's a great reporter. Write on.

Bird Watcher
If Bill Clinton can sleep around and still be a president, Ethan Tremblay can sleep around and still be a reporter.

CBC Fan
He's a disgrace to his profession. And he has the morals of an alley cat.

Brainiac
What's in his head is more important than who's giving him head.

Kosher Dude
He's a schmuck.

Sebastian felt the urge to pee. Three coffees in a morning were definitely too many. There was an espresso with breakfast, a cup of dark roast from the canteen during the morning meeting and a latté from a downtown café after his shoot. Time to pay the piper.

He hopped up from his desk. The hallway to the left offered the more direct route to the washroom, but the chatty intern approached. This was no time for conversation, so Sebastian sprinted right. The route covered the same distance, but was more perilous. He would pass five edit suites. Delay could be lurking behind any and all doors.

Door number one. Safely navigated.

Door number two. Passage granted…no, passage revoked. An editor must have seen Sebastian's blur, opened the door and chased after him.

"Sebastian, are you playing golf on Saturday?"

"Can't think," said Sebastian. "I've got to whiz." He squeezed his sphincter muscles.

"Come on, yes or no. I need an answer. I'm doing up teams."

"No…Yes. Yes."

Sebastian raced past the three remaining edit suites into the home stretch. A hard right where the bathroom routes converged, then a sharp left past the photocopier brought him face to face with the male bathroom symbol.

He pushed through the outer door, the inner door, and spun towards the urinals. He froze.

"Ethan," said Sebastian, "you're back."

Ethan Tremblay glanced over his shoulder. "That one is free," he said, tilting his head at the urinal next to him, "unless you're waiting for mine."

"Welcome back," said Sebastian, sallying to the urinal. "I hope you don't mind if I don't shake your hand."

"Your hands are dirty enough as it is."

Sebastian ignored the poke. He couldn't think straight; he was bursting and fumbling with his zipper. *Damn these pants*, he thought, *were they designed for eunuchs?* He pulled up the waistband to straighten the fly. Zip—a highly underrated sound. He felt sweet relief.

"No one told us when you were coming back or if you were ever coming back," said Sebastian. "We were all wondering."

"Your concern is touching."

Sebastian stared at the wall. Ethan stared at an equally blank spot. Standard urinal etiquette—eyes straight ahead.

"A friend at the *Toronto Sun* told me that Lily Chin got her story from a leak inside the CBC," said Ethan.

"This is the only leak I know about," said Sebastian. He heard his urinal companion hit the plastic deodorizer.

Penis or prosthesis? What has Mr. Shot Off Balls got?

Don't look down. Don't look down. Look down.

Sebastian twisted his head a fraction and peeked below Ethan's belt. He raised his eyes and met Ethan's.

"Looking for something?" asked Ethan.

"I heard this cock-and-bull story about you. I'm simply trying to determine whether you have more cock than bull."

"And?"

"You have plenty of bull. As for cock, the legend is much, much bigger than the man."

"Sebastian, I should tell you to piss off. But I think it would be way more fun to piss on you." Ethan sidestepped and sprayed Sebastian's shoes.

Sebastian jumped back. "Jesus," he shouted.

"Sorry about that. I really need to improve my aim."

"Don't worry about it," snarled Sebastian, "I'm full of piss and vinegar." He arced urine at his antagonist. The stream ricocheted off the floor tiles in front of Ethan and despite his skipping maneuver, it splattered his shoes.

"Go piss up a rope," counterattacked Ethan. His salvo raked across Sebastian's pants.

Sebastian raised the artillery angle and scored direct hits on Ethan's shins.

The dueling flows crossed with symmetry so perfect they deserved a geometric designation. The Elliptical X was created during a CBC pissing match.

Ethan corralled the corporation's most gossiped-about genitalia back inside his pants and ducked out the door.

Sebastian holstered his weapon, pulled up his zipper with an angry tug and assessed the damage. His pants and Oxfords sported speckled patterns. He ripped off a paper towel and propped up a foot on the vanity. Pee dripped off the sole. He was just about to dab the brown suede when the bathroom door opened.

"Sebastian," said a startled Dan. "Polishing your shoes?"

"Not exactly." Sebastian lightly pressed his toes. "I had a little accident."

Dan moved in for closer inspection; the closer he got, the higher he raised his eyebrows.

"Your pants need a squeeze too."

"I got a hair caught across the tip," explained Sebastian.

"Ah, the perils of peeing standing up. Still, it beats the indignity of peeing sitting down." They both laughed. Dan gave Sebastian's shoulder a reassuring pat before veering off to the urinals.

Dan's stride locked. His front foot dangled in midair. It was as if he realized he were about to step on a landmine. The floor was awash. Dan's front foot retreated. There was no bridge over this troubled water. He lifted his pants legs and tiptoed back from the pool.

"I think I'll use the bathroom downstairs," said Dan.

"I had three coffees this morning," said Sebastian, hoping that would justify the deluge.

"Super-sized?" asked Dan.

"You know what they say, go big or go home."

Dan gave a half-hearted laugh.

"Drinks this evening?" asked Sebastian.

"I can't. I'm still cleaning up my own mess, so to speak."

Dan pulled a paper towel and took a giant step to the door. "Bye," he said, using the towel to shield his hand from any errant pee on the handle.

Sebastian finished squeezing the blotches and washed his hands, twice. He throttled his paper towels before pitching them into the bin.

He passed Evan's office on the way back to his desk. "Sebastian," called Evan. "There's news about Ethan."

"No need," said Sebastian. "Some prick in the can just told me all about it."

●

Sebastian made a beeline for The Desk. Evan leaned over Zoe's shoulder, pointing at something on her computer.

"Tell me it's not true," Sebastian bellowed to the producers.

"Yes it's true. Ethan is back in the anchor chair tonight," said Evan.

"As misguided as that is, that's not what I was talking about." Sebastian snatched a lineup off the counter and pummelled the top story with his finger. "Look at this slug—*Chief Speaks*. My story with Janice Stone's name attached to it. Incredible! Paul Bennett is finally ready to spill his guts, but I'm not assigned. Excuse my French, but what the fuck is going on?"

Evan released an exasperated breath. "Sebastian, does every perceived grievance have to be a typhoon?"

"I'm doing my bit for king and country here. Digging in the trenches, going over the top, trying to prove that the premier is a cokehead. Endless hours of pounding the phones. And when my back is turned, you give away my story. You hand it out like Halloween candy."

Sebastian mimed dropping a treat into a bag. "There you go little Janice." He rubbed an imaginary head. "You enjoy that. Never mind that it belongs to Sebastian."

He took a pen and scratched out Stone on the lineup, wrote Hunter next to *Chief Speaks* and circled his name several times. He waggled the revamped lineup under the producers' noses. "I own that story— paid for it with blood, sweat, and tears."

"Spare me the melodrama," said Evan.

"We're long past the point of a rational discussion. My story was pilfered, purloined, and pinched."

Sebastian's rant bewitched his colleagues. Even the Twitter addicts laid down their phones. His diatribes had a reputation for being quite entertaining, and no one wanted to miss a millisecond. Samantha Cormier watched from her desk. She threw the back of her hand up to her forehead and lounged in drama-queen fashion.

"Sebastian, nobody owns stories at the CBC," lectured Evan. "You had your shot and came up short. Apparently, he likes Janice more than he likes you. It was her, or nobody. And I chose her. I should have brought you into the loop sooner. You shouldn't find out by reading an outlook. For that, I apologize, but I'm not sorry for reassigning the story."

"I should have been asked," Sebastian fired back. "You don't steal another reporter's story."

"When I last looked there was no copyright on the story *Chief Speaks*. You work for the CBC; the CBC doesn't work for you. Sometimes we have to do things in the best interests of the newsroom, not one reporter. And as long as I run the newsroom, that's the way it's going to be."

"All hands on deck for the flogging, Mr. Christian," thundered Sebastian in a haughty Capt. Bligh impersonation. "By god, we will have discipline on this ship. Orders will be obeyed without question. Put Hunter in irons and take him below. He'll feel the lash during the newscast."

Zoe jumped from her chair. "The Oscar for Best Impersonation of an Aggrieved Reporter goes to…," she said in award-show hype while unfolding a piece of scrap paper, "Sebastian Hunter."

The newsroom exploded in applause. Zoe offered Sebastian her karate statuette. She won it during her university days and always kept it on her desk, just to remind reporters that she could kick the crap out of them if she wanted.

Sebastian waved off the award. "Just remember, Capt. Bligh's crew mutinied and set him adrift when they couldn't stand his bullying any longer."

He strode to his desk to wait for the debut of Janice's ill-gotten gains.

[seven]

Sebastian mused about life as a CBC reporter. *It's a lot like riding a Ferris wheel. One day you're on top of the world, the envy of all the philistines below. The next day you're dragged through their shit and you're looking up at their asses.*

He had done everything right and it still turned out wrong. He concocted Ethan Tremblay's downfall and positioned himself as the heir apparent to the crown. But the son of a bitch survived and usurped his ascendancy to the throne for a second time. To add insult to the larceny, Ethan would introduce Sebastian's paramour and her illicit story.

"Good evening. Our top story tonight—the chief breaks his silence."

Sebastian smacked the Bobblehead Ethan sitting on his desk, jolting it into spastic movement. Not the sort of fun the communications department had in mind when it came up with the promotional toy, but what did they know? The real Ethan turned to a different camera as the chief's mug shot appeared in a monitor.

"Three months ago, Police Chief Paul Bennett was arrested for drunk driving. He hasn't said a word about it since. That is until now. In an exclusive interview with our Janice Stone, Paul Bennett reveals how he went from a man who arrested drunk drivers to becoming one."

The mug shot changed to a live feed of Janice standing outside the chief's home.

"Here & Now's Janice Stone spent the morning with the Chief and his family, and she joins us now live. Janice."

"That back-stabbing slut," muttered Sebastian to the screen.

"Ethan, we all know Paul Bennett as a law and order cop. A man who loved catching the bad guys, especially drunk drivers. Tonight I'll show you a very different Paul Bennett. A vulnerable Paul Bennett. A man so distraught by a family crisis that he betrayed two oaths—to always obey the law and to never drink again."

Janice's report begins with a tight shot and soundup—a police uniform taken off a clothes rod. Paul Bennett hangs the uniform on a hook and strokes the shoulders with a lint brush.

He hasn't worn this uniform in months, but he still takes pride in its appearance.

The chief brushes the front of his uniform, glancing at the camera as he speaks.

"I know I'll never wear this uniform again. I don't deserve to wear it again, but this uniform is my life. I still can't quite believe I smeared what it stands for."

Today melts into yesterday. At-home chief dissolves into jailhouse chief—the infamous mug shot from the Orlando City Police.

"I disgraced myself, my family, and my uniform. I'm completely ashamed of what I did. I apologize to my fellow officers and the public. No one should drink and drive. I should have known that better than anyone."

Sebastian lunged at the screen. Apparently, the interview wasn't enough of a coup; Janice compounded the offence by scoring previously unseen video as well—surveillance tape from the Florida detention centre.

Chief Bennett is escorted to his cell, the door closes and the chief sits on a cot. He buries his head in his hands.

Paul Bennett spent ten hours behind bars. Long enough to sober up; not long enough to ease his pain.

"Up to that day I hadn't had a drink in twenty years. But that was the day I found out my little girl had leukemia."

Still photos float by: Clare blowing out the candles on her birthday cake, Clare screaming on the rollercoaster, Clare dancing with Mickey Mouse.

Clare had been weak leading up to the Florida trip. The doctors suspected cancer, but the Bennetts decided to go anyway. Clare was turning seven and seeing Mickey Mouse was her birthday gift.

"The doctor called me in Florida with the results of the bloodwork and bone-marrow tests. My little girl was in a fight for her life."

The chief's eyes well up.

"I imagined her dead. I was crushed. I saw a bar and started drinking. I hung off that bar until Clare called my cell and asked me to read her a bedtime story. That's when I got in the car. I missed that bedtime story. I'll never miss another."

The shot fades from the teary-eyed chief to file video of Sebastian chasing him at the Cops for Cancer event.

"Chief, why were you drinking that night?"

Sebastian heard boos and hisses from the far end of the newsroom.

"Must be the ghost of Garrison Hill," said Sebastian. The video dissolves back to present day.

"I was naïve to think that I could do one last good deed before the news broke about my arrest. I wanted to atone for my bad behaviour. That's why I went to the flag raising. It didn't quite work out the way I had hoped. I apologize for being a lightning rod."

That was Chief Paul Bennett's last day on the job. The last day anyone would salute him. Anyone, except his little girl.

The photo of Clare saluting and wearing her father's police hat is laid over her impish voice.

"When I grow up, I'm going to be a police officer, just like my daddy."

Her daddy is suspended with pay. A Florida judge will decide her daddy's punishment this fall.

The video changes to the chief's kitchen. Clare and her mother take chocolate chip cookies out of the oven.

Clare's cancer is in remission. The chemotherapy worked. Clare is out of danger.

The camera slowly zooms in as the chief speaks.

"We're so grateful for all that the doctors have done. They've saved Clare's life and in a way they've saved mine too. Now I just want to be a good father, a good husband, and a good police officer. A good police

officer always tells the truth, and doesn't hide from what he's done. He never walks away from his responsibility."

The camera catches Clare giving her father a cookie and a kiss. The chief scoops his daughter off the floor and hugs her. Clare squeals and laughs.

Janice Stone, CBC News.

Sebastian turned off the video. "A drunk driver *can* get good PR. Crime pays after all."

●

Sebastian had hoped to escape the newsroom before *Here & Now* was over, but phone calls delayed him. He was caught in Ethan's crosshairs.

"Well, if it isn't the bridesmaid," said Ethan. "Janice will be by in a few minutes to throw the bouquet. Maybe you'll get lucky and catch it. You might marry a scoop someday."

"Luck has nothing to do with good reporting," said Sebastian to Bobblehead Ethan. He turned to the real Ethan and did a double take. "Sorry about that. I didn't know which bobblehead was speaking."

"Janice has no trouble distinguishing reality from fantasy."

"This from a man caked in makeup."

Ethan ran an index finger down his cheek, coating the tip in foundation and concealer. He held it up to Sebastian.

"She doesn't need the glam. She's stunning just as she is. I used to think Janice's beauty was her strongest suit, but I was wrong. She's much smarter than I ever gave her credit for. What an impressive feat— getting Chief Bennett and his little girl. I nearly cried. Janice is doing your work for you."

Sebastian shoved the keyboard tray under his desk. "What would you know about work? You've been coasting since you arrived. You should install a hammock next to your desk."

"It takes a real journalist to find the human story. Journalism isn't all about being nasty. Where's the follow-up to the house going over the cliff? Whatever became of those hapless people? Maybe I should ask Janice to check."

"Speak of the devil," said Sebastian. Janice dropped her purse on her desk. "I'd love to listen to more of your hypocrisy, but my colleague and I have work to discuss."

Ethan lifted a tissue box off Sebastian's desk and tilted it towards him. "Crybabies should always have one handy."

Sebastian ignored him and grazed by. He pictured his shoulder smashing into Ethan's chest the way an NHL defenceman nails a player into the boards; a check hard enough to pulverize the glass and send Ethan head over heels into the spectators.

Ethan tossed the tissue box behind his back like a juggler. It flew past his shoulder and landed on Sebastian's desk.

"Janice, could I please see you in an edit suite?" asked Sebastian.

"Sure." Janice led him to Suite 1, the nearest one and coincidently the suite where she cut *Chief Speaks*.

The suite was soundproof and unless a busybody put an eye directly against the door's tiny window, there was no seeing inside. It housed a bank of monitors, an audio board, stereo speakers, a supersized flat-screen TV and even an old videotape player for archival stories. Reporters came here for finesse editing. And for private chats.

Sebastian was about to unleash his wrath when Janice cut him off at the breath.

"Don't say a word. First of all, I'm not apologizing. We'd all be dead waiting for Bennett to talk to you. And we'd all be dead waiting for you to say, 'Maybe somebody else should try.'"

"You should have asked me first," said Sebastian imperiously.

"We all knew you'd froth at the mouth if we did. It was easier not to. If Bennett had said no, there'd be no harm done."

"But there was harm done."

"Only to your ego. Not to your career. And certainly not to your appeal." Janice edged closer. "I would never do anything to hurt you."

"I feel like I was knifed in the back."

"I can rub that back," said Janice, moving in a solicitous manner. "And once I'm done with the back, I can rub the rest of you." Janice stroked Sebastian's cheek. He took her hand down.

"I need something else from you. I need to hear that you'll help me get rid of Ethan Tremblay."

"I don't like parachute anchors any more than you do," said Janice.

"He's still my enemy. I'm still your ally." Her lips glided to Sebastian's. "A deal sealed with a kiss."

Sebastian went to the door, locked it, and dimmed the lights.

"Now," he said, "about that backrub."

•

Sebastian believed that the best ad-lib is a written one. He went over his story again and again, tweaking the details—all hands had gathered for a post-show drink to celebrate Janice's scoop and the beating *Here & Now* had inflicted on the competition. If he had a believability meter, the needle would be bouncing into Believable.

"Honey, I'm home," said Sebastian, as he entered the house. He heard a drawer close in the bedroom. There were crumpled tissues on the coffee table. Roxanne entered the living room with puffy eyes.

"Are you alright?"

"You're late," said Roxanne. Sebastian apologized and recited his well-rehearsed perjury. Roxanne picked up the used tissues.

"Were you crying?"

"It was that story on your news tonight—Chief Bennett and his daughter. I cried like a baby. I just hate it when reporters manipulate my feelings like that. I hate it even more when it's Janice Stone doing the manipulating."

"Yes, she's very good at manipulation."

"Weren't you trying to get that interview?" asked Roxanne, opening the closet door.

"Yes, I did try. I know you think I'm heartless sometimes, but when I heard what that little girl had been through, I knew I had to do something. I owed it to Clare and her father to tell their side of this tragedy. There was just too much bad blood between the chief and me. I had to step aside. So I gave the story to Janice. It was the right thing to do."

"Stop or I'll cry again." Roxanne slipped on a summer jacket.

"Are you going somewhere?"

"Not me, we. We have pre-marriage counselling tonight."

"Right, of course," said Sebastian with all the sham enthusiasm he could rouse.

The drive to the therapist's office took ten minutes. Short of rear-ending the car in front of him, Sebastian couldn't think of an escape plan. No, he would have to endure forty-five minutes of excruciating questions and prodding to emote.

The therapist's door was ajar. Roxanne tapped twice.

"Come in," said a congenial Carrie Walker. "There's tea and coffee, if you'd like."

Sebastian and Roxanne both declined. They sat in the loveseat, while Carrie eased herself into a chair off to the side.

"We'll cover a lot of ground over the next six weeks, but the order is flexible," said Carrie. She leaned forward; Sebastian saw cleavage. The scoop neck blouse probably violated professional dress codes, but Sebastian wouldn't be filing any complaint. He was all for inappropriate clothing.

"I'll throw out a few topics and you can tell me where you'd like to start," said Carrie.

"That's a great idea," said Roxanne. She squeezed Sebastian's hand. He forced a smile.

"In-laws and family?" suggested Carrie.

"No," said Sebastian. He envisioned Dour Donna sitting between them. "Too early for tension."

"Conflict and communication?"

"Talking leads to arguments," said Sebastian. Roxanne rubbed her eyes.

"Children?"

"Another contentious topic," he said. "Something lighter, perhaps."

"Spirituality and religion?"

"We don't have any," said Sebastian.

"I see," said Carrie. "How about sex and intimacy?"

"Yes, finally a topic I can embrace."

"I'd thought we'd work up to that," said Roxanne, "but I guess we have to start somewhere."

"Does either of you have trust issues?" asked Carrie.

Sebastian shook his head. Roxanne looked down.

"Roxanne, is there something you'd like to say?"

"Sebastian is an incurable flirt."

"Not that again," groaned Sebastian. "I thought we settled that."

"I was asked; I answered truthfully."

"Roxanne, you're the only woman in my life. Now and forever."

"Roxanne," said Carrie, "what if that turned out not to be true? What if Sebastian were unfaithful?"

"My dearly beloved would pay, dearly." Sebastian was struck by her resolve. Roxanne had never before shown such firmness.

"And Sebastian, what if Roxanne betrayed her vow to forsake all others?"

He twisted on the loveseat to face Roxanne. "I would forgive her, if she wanted forgiveness. I would love her, if she still wanted love."

"You're definitely not candidates for the swingers' club," said Carrie.

"Wait a moment," said Sebastian. "Are you recruiting? Is this a test?" Roxanne gave him a swat on the shoulder.

Carrie laughed. "Can we talk about sex?" she asked. Sebastian and Roxanne nodded. "Are you comfortable with your sex lives?" Both nodded again.

"Are there certain things which are clearly off limits?"

Roxanne blushed and laughed. "Just one. No more body painting with wine. I couldn't get the stains out of the sheet." Sebastian's laughter mixed with Roxanne's. The jocular couple gave Carrie licence to join in.

"None of my business," said Carrie, waving her hands. Her breasts heaved. Sebastian visualized pouring wine between them.

•

Sebastian strolled through unfamiliar territory—the Shrine Club. He had never set foot in one before, or any service club for that matter. Fun he understood; philanthropy was a more difficult concept to grasp. Sebastian's philanthropy flared-up on Boxing Day, after much prodding from Roxanne, and was snuffed out by New Year's Eve, the embers extinguished by tax-deductible donations. He didn't care who received the money; Roxanne picked the charities.

Two portly Shriners lugged amplifiers to the stage.

"Have you ever thought about being a Shriner?" asked Teddy. It was no innocent question. He already knew the answer. The question was designed to goad Sebastian into an irreverent response.

"Do I look like the kind of man who would wear a fez?" said Sebastian.

"You'd look good in a tassel."

"A red cone hat and a Hugo Boss suit. Ple-e-e-se."

"Perfect for your stand-up." Teddy deliberately used an upbeat tone. All the better to irritate.

"If you don't stifle your contempt for my good fashion sense, then I'll be forced to strike back. Perhaps I'll declare a tripod-free day and you can shoot everything off the shoulder."

"Then I might be forced to declare a focus-free day. You'll be blurry. "

Sebastian picked up a white napkin and waved it.

"I'm glad we understand each other," said Teddy. "Next time we'll discuss the merits of wearing a Tilley hat on camera."

Teddy laid his camera down on the hardwood dance floor and picked a spot for his tripod. He spied a familiar face in the crowd gathered by the bar. "Isn't that Roxanne over there?"

"A fundraiser for a burned-out family of eight with no insurance, of course that's Roxanne. She's the worst kind of bleeding heart. She spends my money trying to better life for the unfortunate and the careless."

"You're a great humanitarian, Sebastian. A lover of mankind."

Sebastian spied Dean Head swinging his guitar case. "I've got to speak to the minister for a minute."

Dean Head was the province's finance minister: thirty-six, handsome, single and famous for dabbling in double entendres. His last budget speech generated cackles and desk-thumping from both sides of the house: Mr. Speaker, the government will grow jobs, stimulate the economy, swell the treasury, seed new industries, lay pavement, and penetrate foreign markets.

Dean Head also harboured naked ambition. Sebastian intended to lance it.

"What's a cabinet minister like you doing in a nice place like this?" asked Sebastian with a disarming smile.

Head laughed as he flipped open the hinges on his guitar case. He strummed his acoustic guitar and tuned it by ear. "The Clarks are my constituents. They were burned out of their house. They need help. If the member doesn't help, he doesn't deserve to be the member."

"Imagine how much help you could give them if you were premier."

"The job's not open. We already have a premier and I support her." Head plucked the A string several times.

"Sounds like a funeral toll. She has the lowest approval rating of any premier in the country. Your party is tanking because of it. The pollsters say you can't win the next election with her running the show."

"The only poll that counts is on election day and that's two years away."

Sebastian pointed at the open guitar case. "Look, an empty coffin, just waiting for a cabinet minister to fall into it."

"We have enough time to turn things around," said the still-breathing cabinet minister.

"Enough time if she were gone," suggested Sebastian. "The polls say people like you. You're the popular one. You could win the next election. She can't. If she doesn't go soon, you'll be in opposition purgatory for a decade."

Distant laughter blended with rattling beer bottles and glasses, while chairs scraped the floor. The discord masked their conversation, but Sebastian moved closer to make certain he wasn't overheard. "I hear there's a tape which shows the premier in a very embarrassing situation," he said in a concealed voice.

Head stopped torqueing a tuning peg. B was still flat, but he laid the guitar back in the case anyway.

"If I had that tape," continued Sebastian, "I could get rid of your problem in one minute, forty-five seconds."

"If such a tape exists, wouldn't the premier quietly leave to avoid a scandal?"

"She's in denial. She has a drug problem."

"That kind of language is slanderous," said Head.

"Not if it's true. I just need the proof."

"If such a tape exists, wouldn't her enemies leak it?"

"That's my fervent hope. The situation will get very messy, very quickly. Who knew about the tape? Who covered it up? Who didn't call the cops? Who didn't get the premier help? Who didn't do the right thing? A smart cabinet minister would be poised to seize power and turn his opponents into outcasts."

"You have a vivid imagination, Sebastian." Head wrapped his fingers around the guitar frets. "As the Emperor Caligula said, if only Rome had just one neck." He picked B string. "I should finish tuning."

"And I should go interview the Clarks about their misfortune."

Teddy raised a small light on a stand and aimed it at the stage.

"Let's grab the von Trapp family before *The Sound of Music* starts," said Sebastian.

The Clark children flocked around their parents. "I should have brought the wide-angled lens," joked Teddy.

Mr. and Mrs. Clark recounted the details of the terrible fire and thanked everyone for the outpouring of generosity. Sebastian caught Roxanne in the background talking to the finance minister, guitar hanging from his shoulder. They laughed as Head pointed at the TV crew.

The minister took the stage and bellied up to the microphone. "Welcome, everyone." Feedback screeched through the speakers. Head pulled back and waited until the squall faded away. "Must be an NDP sound system." The crowd laughed.

"It's great to see so many of you here supporting the Clark family. Neighbours helping neighbours. That's what this wonderful province is all about." Applause rippled through the room.

A couple of strums; a chord change; Head glanced at Roxanne and winked.

"I've always said money can't buy me. I was wrong. I can be bought for the right price." Head's descent into corruption was greeted with wahoos.

"That young lady over there will contribute one hundred dollars to the Clark Family Relief Fund if I play her favourite song."

Roxanne looked thrilled. Sebastian felt dread.

"First on the dance floor," said the minister, "Roxanne and Sebastian. Let's get 'em up here, folks." The crowd stomped and whistled.

"Teddy, if you record this, you will not die a man."

"This is worth losing an appendage for." Teddy clicked the record button.

The reporter turned reluctant dancer met Roxanne in front of the band.

"Even a CBC reporter can have a heart," cracked the minister. The crowd roared. Roxanne and Sebastian struck a ballroom dance pose.

"Roxanne," said Sebastian with a counterfeit smile, "we'll have lots to talk about at the next counselling session. I think we can jump straight to: Has your partner ever done anything to embarrass you?"

"Take a number, Sebastian. I'm at the head of that line. You only lead when we dance."

Sebastian stepped forward while Roxanne stepped back.

Gonna find my baby, gonna hold her tight,
Gonna grab some afternoon delight.

●

Sebastian followed the horseshoe shape of The Desk, bound for his own. "Morning, Zoe."

"It wasn't me," she said. That phrase always pierced his armour. It meant mockery was on the horizon.

The scorn sat in his chair in the guise of a yellow, diamond-shaped warning sign. A ballerina in silhouette sported a tutu; her arms extended above her head towards Dancer as she tiptoed above Zone.

"Can you show us how to plié," heckled Ethan. He bent his knees outward and unfurled an arm like a swan's neck. Sebastian heard snickers.

Ethan deserves a Riverdance high kick to the groin. And not just one. The entire troupe should deliver a buckled shoe to whatever gonads he has.

"I'm sure you already know everything you need to know about bending your knees," said Sebastian.

"Such rapier wit, but two left feet."

"At least they're on the floor and not in my mouth."

"You know, you'd be a natural on *Dancing with the Stars.* They love fading celebrities who make fools of themselves."

"We'll see who gets there first," said Sebastian.

"I'd love to continue, but my dance card is full." Ethan held up a stack of scripts. "I have a newscast to read."

Sebastian waited until Ethan left the newsroom before cornering Janice.

"Do it tonight. Just like we discussed. We'll wipe the smirk right off his face."

"Are you sure?" asked Janice. "We have time. I still have three nights of backfill after tonight."

"I can't stand the smug bastard anymore. It's time to take him down."

Janice gathered her scripts, checked her makeup with a pocket mirror and headed for the studio.

"Janice," said Sebastian. She stopped and looked back. "Have a good show, but a killer rehearsal."

"You're buying the champagne," said Janice. She gestured as if popping the cork and disappeared through the door.

Sebastian opened the TV software on his computer and chose channel 124—the internal feed from the studio. It was an eavesdropping portal. The Desk used it benignly, vetting pre-recorded interviews without the bother of actually being in the control room. Sebastian intended to expand its usefulness.

He watched Janice and Ethan wire up—the nightly ritual of attaching microphones and earpieces. The control room rapidly switched between four cameras, making sure the computer-encoded framing hadn't gone wonky.

"Where did Samantha go on her holidays?" asked Janice.

"Antigua," replied Ethan. He sat on the tail of his jacket to pull down the shoulders. "Did you see the video of Sebastian dancing with his fiancée?"

"Two seconds after I heard about it," said Janice. "Sebastian squirmed like a worm on a hook. It's a keeper for the Christmas blooper tape."

Ethan laughed.

Good girl; win his trust, thought Sebastian. He checked the time. 5:45. Just fifteen minutes to snare the game.

Channel 124 dipped to black. Rehearsal time. The monitor pulsated with *Here & Now*'s animation. To Sebastian, the drums in the theme were the drums of war. The headlines swished by; Ethan and Janice took turns reading.

Tonight—Animal cruelty. A dog dies in a hot car; the owner is charged.

Guilty verdict. A hockey star is convicted of sexual assault.

Closing time. A Band Council shuts down a bar it just opened.

Second thoughts. A transgender activist cancels a sex change.

No mistakes. A flawless run-through.

5:47. Thirteen minutes to showtime.

"These headlines are pedestrian," complained Janice.

"No oomph," agreed Ethan. "They certainly could use a goose."

"You're a quick wit," said Janice. "What would the Evil Ethan write for fun?"

"You don't give a guy much time."

"Come on. Make me laugh."

"Take the bait," pleaded Sebastian, one floor up.

"Hmmm," said Ethan. He scribbled madly on his script.

5:53.

"Hey Roddy," said Ethan on the control room intercom, "run the headlines again. Ms. Stone is demanding to be amused. I'll read them all."

Tonight—Man's baked friend. This dog is golden brown and light to the touch.

He shoots, he scores. The prison's hockey team trades up.

Indian givers. No hitting the bottle; the bar hits the road.

A girl can change her mind. A transgender activist sticks with the bird in the bush.

The camera briskly zoomed into Ethan and Janice. Janice raised a quizzical eyebrow. Ethan radiated smugness.

Good evening and welcome to Here & Now. I'm Ethan Tremblay. Our top story tonight—Hot dog. Fido is done like dinner.

Hubris has caused many implosions, thought Sebastian. What a wonderful human failing.

Channel 124 went black. Sebastian hit the stop button on his iPhone. His video ran thirty-six seconds. Thirty-six seconds of gold. Thirty-six seconds that would destroy Ethan Tremblay. Next stop— YouTube.

●

Ethan Tremblay's Politically Incorrect Headlines was a YouTube sensation. It had 125,684 views before Sebastian crawled into bed; by daybreak the number had tripled. Sebastian awoke to a radio newscast announcing that Ethan Tremblay was suspended and CBC had apologized for what it called grossly offensive and wholly inappropriate comments.

"What was he thinking?" asked Roxanne, as she dolloped yogurt on a dish of fresh raspberries. "Those were terrible things to say."

"That's the real Ethan Tremblay," said Sebastian, sipping on a coffee. "He says this stuff all the time around the newsroom, but there's never a camera. Last night he got caught."

"How did it get on YouTube?"

"He's made a lot of enemies since moving here."

Roxanne rested her spoon in her dish. "Sebastian, you didn't have anything to do with it, did you?"

"I don't like him, but I'm not stupid, Roxanne. I don't engage in career-limiting moves."

"I didn't think so. It's just… those PTSD webpages have me a little nervous. They talk about aggressive behaviour."

"Not me, Roxanne. My therapist is teaching me to how to relax." He rubbed the shoulder muscles so erotically touched by Janice's hands. "We're also trying exposure therapy. Every session makes me feel better about myself."

Sebastian downed his coffee and kissed Roxanne. "Got to run. I'm covering Question Period this morning."

Sebastian's car radio was always tuned to CBC. *The Morning Show* could barely finish interviewing one Ethan Tremblay denouncer before another was clamouring to get on the air.

"Joining us now in the studio is the executive director of Stop the Violence—Jennifer Allen. Ms. Allen, what was your reaction when you saw the video?"

"I was shaking with rage. Ethan Tremblay trivialized sexual assault. He used the most offensive locker-room humour imaginable. It's certainly not funny. It's degrading to women and inexcusable."

Sebastian drove by a billboard. Ethan Tremblay and Samantha Cormier photographed in happier times: BREAKING NEWS and ALL

THE RULES according to the ad. A spray-painted JERK in yellow, ragged letters covered Ethan's face.

"Finally, graffiti art I can appreciate," said Sebastian.

"On the phone is Bentley Smith of Dogs Are People Too. Mr. Smith, what did you think?"

"When it comes to correction, I don't believe in hitting. But I'd make an exception in this case. Someone should roll up a newspaper and whack Ethan Tremblay on the nose."

Sebastian's phone played a "Werewolves in London" ringtone. He turned down the radio.

"Hi Janice."

"You're missing a firestorm here. They're grabbing everybody's phone, every camera, checking every file to see who did the recording."

"I'm not worried."

"I got grilled by The Executioner this morning. The blood vessels in her forehead almost popped. I told her I was as appalled as she was. Said I had no idea Ethan would say such things."

"Did she buy it?"

"I think so."

"Sounds like she's being eaten alive," said Sebastian. "Ethan Tremblay will be eviscerated by the end of the day."

"Be careful. You're suspect number one. They're gunning for you."

"Someday they'll realize I did them a favour." Sebastian pulled into a parking space behind the legislature. "Talk to you later."

Sebastian walked through what the reporters called Rogues Gallery. Portraits of premiers past, all piously gazing down on the latest crop of earnest and sanctimonious politicians, all lusting after a painting of their own.

An elevator opened. Ambition walked out.

"Good day, minister."

"Hello, Sebastian," said Dean Head. The finance minister stopped, letting his cabinet colleagues file past the security desk into the House.

"You've got some nerve saying *we're* in trouble," kidded Head. "CBC is having a spot of bother of its own this morning."

"Yes, Ethan Tremblay is flaming out."

"We've got a statement about it today. Your bosses won't like it."

Sebastian quashed his desire to congratulate the minister. "No, I'm sure they won't," he said in his wounded, CBC-team-player tone. "Minister, have you given any thought to my request the other day?"

"If such a tape exists, I'm sure you'll be the first one to get it."

"What makes you say that?"

"Because you have a reputation for doing the most damage."

An electronic bell chimed, summoning the members.

"Duty calls," said the minister, slipping away.

Sebastian climbed the stairs to the press gallery offices.

"Ladies and gentlemen of the press, I am at your disposal," announced Sebastian, as he pulled open the solid oak door. He was swarmed by reporters; they scrummed him the way they scrummed the politicians below, questions flying from all angles.

"What the fuck happened last night?"

"Has Ethan been fired?"

"Was he drunk?"

"Did you have a hand in it?"

Sebastian's protestation of innocence was met with eye-rolling. He embellished Janice's information about the search for the culprit, turning the IT department into jackboot storm troopers.

"Admit strangers," droned the Speaker of the House over the PA system. Reporters and the public were "strangers"—a centuries-old British parliamentary term. Only the supercilious members had a right to be inside the chamber. The plebs entered by invitation only. Sebastian, the stranger, took a seat in the gallery reserved for journalists. The perch let him see both sides of the House. The premier's seat was empty.

"Statements by Ministers," said the Speaker. Dean Head stood amid desk-thumping. "The honourable finance minister and deputy premier."

"Mr. Speaker, we tend not to criticize the media on this side of the House. We believe in freedom of the press. But the profane headlines offered by *Here & Now*'s Ethan Tremblay cannot go unchallenged. Frankly, Mr. Speaker, one has to ask, Who do they think they are?"

"Shame," shouted some honourable members. "Shame."

Sebastian fired off his first tweet of the day: "*Rough day for CBC at the House. Govt. attacks Tremblay headlines.*"

Democracy is wonderful.

●

Sebastian caught sight of Percival Thompson entering The Executioner's office. Percival supervised the IT department, though today Sebastian considered it the SS department. He goose-stepped down the hallway, stopping his straight-legged kick just before crossing The Executioner's open door. He checked in with her assistant.

"Herr Hunter reporting as commanded," said Sebastian in staccato style with a thick German accent. He pointed to the office. "Vat is *he* doing here?" All those hours watching *Hogan's Heroes* reruns during his teens hadn't been wasted.

The assistant looked utterly confused. "I'm sorry. What did you say?"

"Never mind," said Sebastian in his regular tongue. "Alicia wanted to see me."

"Go on in."

Sebastian knocked and blew through the doorway. "Hello, Alicia. Percy." Percival leaned back in his chair, exposing his bulging midsection. He refused to answer to the name Percy.

"Take a seat, Sebastian," said Alicia. "I'm sure you know that we've had a security breach and I've asked Percival to investigate."

"Did you generate a ticket for that?"

"What?"

"It's just that whenever I need something from IT, I have to send them an email and it generates a ticket and they'll get around to it in due course. My computer could be crashing ten minutes before newscast time and I still can't speak to a human being down there. So I guess I'm wondering if proper procedures have been followed, or if there's a new procedure."

Alicia and Percival turned to each other in bewilderment. "Stop deflecting this investigation," said Alicia with a sullen face. "Hand over your phone, please."

Sebastian pulled his iPhone out of an inside jacket pocket and toggled between the two managers until Alicia motioned that he should hand it to the IT department's top man.

"What's the password?" asked the always officious Percival.

"Let me see if I have this right. You think I did something wrong and you want me to tighten the noose around my own neck."

Alicia slammed a hand on her desk. Percival jumped. "What's the damn password?" she yelled.

Sebastian was mute. Alicia breathed deeply.

"I'm sorry," said Alicia, "that was out of line. I shouldn't have sworn. Sebastian, that phone is CBC property and we require the password."

"One, two, three, four."

"You're joking," said Percival.

"It's not like I keep the nuclear launch codes in there."

"Don't make it easy for the Chinese hackers," lectured Percival.

"I blame Feist," said Sebastian.

More muddled glances on the other side of the table.

"The song—'1234,'" explained Sebastian. "Apple used it in a commercial. The earworm turned into a subliminal directive for my password."

"This is all irrelevant chatter," said Alicia. "Your computer and phone are off limits until we finish our investigation."

A muffled "Werewolves of London" ringtone seeped out of Sebastian's jacket.

"Excuse me," said Sebastian reaching into an inside pocket. He produced a second iPhone, his personal phone. He touched the Decline button. "Sorry about that. You were saying something about my phone being off limits."

Alicia frowned. "I need a direct answer—did you record the rehearsal headlines and post them on YouTube."

"No," said Sebastian without hesitating.

"Do you know anything about it at all?"

"No."

Seconds of silence passed. Sebastian knew the trick; he had used it many times himself. Nature abhors a vacuum. The interviewer offers quiet; the interviewee fills in the blanks. But not this time. Sebastian refused to speak the unspeakable.

"Are we finished?" he asked. "I have a story to get ready for the show. There was a unanimous, all-party resolution in the legislature today condemning the CBC. Funny how the man who caused this predicament isn't here, but I am."

"I'd better not find out that you lied to me, Sebastian," threatened Alicia.

"You're accusing me of lying?"

"No, but now is the time to come clean if you know anything."

"I've told you I had nothing to do with it. May I suggest you deal with the real troublemaker and not chase ghosts."

Percival's head snapped. "Ghosts, right."

Sebastian ambled out of the office. He listened to the radio broadcast piped into the hallway.

Now, the National Research Council time signal. The beginning of the long dash, following ten seconds of silence, indicates exactly..., "The moment Sebastian Hunter told them to shove it."

•

The woman strolled along the publicity photos hanging in the lobby. She paused by Ethan Tremblay. Happy and dashing, and the only Ethan Tremblay in the building at that moment. The real one had vanished into the airwaves.

Sebastian recognized her red hair. The same flaming hair which had tingled him in bed.

"Take a good look. I don't expect he'll be there much longer."

She spun around. "Sebastian." There was pleasure in her voice.

Sebastian stayed back, making a hug ungainly and impractical. "Hi Lindsay."

Lindsay closed the gap, but made no effort to wrap her arms around him. "Will you be hanging there next?"

"I'll either be hanging on picture hooks or swinging from a rope."

"Still making enemies, I see. Perhaps you could fill me in."

"The timing isn't good, Lindsay. I've got a real busy day. How about I text you when I see my way clear."

"I'm still waiting for the last text you promised."

Sebastian glanced at the receptionist. Joanie had surveillance skills the envy of the CIA. She licked an envelope and appeared not to be paying attention, but Sebastian was certain it was a hoax. He motioned for Lindsay to follow him away from the front desk.

"Lindsay, this is awkward," he said in a tempered voice. "I'm engaged. I'm getting married in the fall. My fiancée is the jealous type."

"Funny how you didn't think of that in Paradise Point."

"Roxanne and I were going through a difficult patch, but we've sorted things out since then." His voice was gentle, but his stance was cold.

Sebastian shut up with the sound of approaching footsteps. Janice walked through the lobby on her way to the canteen. She stripped Lindsay naked with a lateral leer. She left Sebastian to put the poor woman's clothes back on.

"I feel chilled," said Lindsay. "Does she always do that?"

Sebastian nodded. "She has a competitive streak."

"Remind me not to get too close."

Sebastian didn't like the sound of that. He needed to play his trump card—the contrite lover brush-off. It never failed.

"Lindsay, our time together was incredible. They were two of the happiest nights of my life." He touched his heart. "But somebody else occupies the space. We have to say goodbye."

"That's a wonderful fairy-tale ending. Except, I'm not ready to say goodbye."

Lindsay is a bunny boiler.

"We need to talk, Sebastian. And I'd rather not do it here."

"Let's go for a walk," he said with resignation.

Cars choked the road and conversation as they strolled toward the secluded river trail. Sebastian occasionally checked behind.

"Is there anything wrong?" asked Lindsay.

Sebastian wanted to say, *Wrong? What could possibly be wrong? I could be walking with an unhinged, spurned lover and followed by a moralizing stalker. Or maybe you're one and the same.*

Instead Sebastian said, "I have a kink in my neck."

Sebastian didn't relax until they veered off the sidewalk to compacted gravel and rollicking water.

A boy toddled towards them, his hand held by a stooped over mother.

"He's adorable," said Lindsay, her face radiant. "When they're that cute, you just want one of your own."

God, she's not here to boil a bunny. The rabbit has already died.

Sebastian stared at Lindsay's stomach. No baby bump. He analyzed her breasts. Plump, but not burgeoning. Still, it was only the first trimester.

"Kids don't like me," said Sebastian. "I'd be a terrible father."

"Don't be ridiculous. I know how tender you can be, how affectionate. You'll be a great dad."

Sebastian wiped his forehead. The toddler and his mother came abreast. The sweet, little boy kicked Sebastian in the shin without slowing his topsy-turvy step. "You're doing great, Jimmy," said the oblivious mom.

"Did you see that?" said a dumbfounded Sebastian.

"See what?"

"The little brat just kicked me."

"Come on. Kids don't go around kicking grown men."

"Well that one just did," protested Sebastian, pointing an accusatory finger at the tyke.

"Mine won't kick you."

Sebastian's heart sank with Lindsay's reassurance. "Have you told anyone?"

"Told anyone what?"

"That you're pregnant," said Sebastian.

Lindsay stalled and gave Sebastian an incredulous look. "What are you talking about?"

"When is the baby due?"

"There is no baby due. I'm not pregnant."

"You're not." said Sebastian, feeling a gush of relief. "But you said your kid wouldn't kick me."

"He won't, when I have one. But that won't be any time soon."

"Then what is this walk all about?"

"I expect we'll be seeing a lot more of each other. I've been accepted into journalism school. And when the applications open, I intend to apply for an internship in your newsroom. Help me get it." It sounded more like a demand than a request. "It's the least you can do."

"But you already have a career as an environmental researcher."

"You showed me Never Never Land. A place where everyone watches what you do and say. No one pays any attention to what I do or say. You can hold a nation's attention. You can change people's lives in minutes. It takes *me* years. And sometimes change never comes at all. I'm suffocating. I want what you have. I've seen a better career and I'm going to get it."

This woman is made of granite.

"Welcome to the club." He kissed her cheek.

Perhaps he had been too quick to dress her after Janice's undressing. He fantasized about both Lindsay and Janice clawing their way into his bed.

[eight]

Sebastian waved his passkey over the sensor, unlocking the side door. The security guard had tipped him off that Ethan was in the building.

"Evening," said the cleaner, pushing her cart outside the washrooms. Sebastian whisked by without a word.

Ethan laid a file box on his desk and opened a drawer. He took out his much-loved tin of Walkers shortbread and placed it inside the box as if it were delicate china. Sebastian crept through shadows; most of the ceiling lights were off. He half sat on a desk behind Ethan.

The warlords had the newsroom to themselves. The late-night news crew was out, probably covering a downtown house fire. A scanner on The Desk squawked. Paramedics radioed the emergency room over the wail of an ambulance siren.

"Patient has suffered smoke inhalation. ETA—three minutes."

Ethan grabbed the souvenir media passes hanging on his lamp: the Beijing Olympics, The White House, Pope John Paul II's funeral. He threw the whole bunch into the box. Ethan reached between mounds of documents to retrieve a photo of his wife and children. He wiped off the dust with a tissue before adding it to the wreckage.

He picked up Bobblehead Ethan, cocked his arm but held his fire. Bobblehead Ethan faced an undignified burial in a garbage can. He bobbed like a crazy man. Ethan gave a dispirited laugh and changed his aim. Bobblehead Ethan soared into a nest of media passes.

His business cards, the ones proudly declaring *Ethan Tremblay Host, Here & Now*, joined a pile of reporter notepads destined for the dumpster.

"What was it you said about conquering armies?" asked Sebastian. Ethan twitched. "They tear down the symbols of the vanquished." Ethan kept his back to Sebastian and continued his sorting. "Looks like you're doing it for me."

"If it isn't Sir Bastard Hunter. Come by to gloat, have you?"

"Gloating is unsportsmanlike, but you did berate me into remembering your sage observation if I ever got in a war zone."

"You can't fight a war on two fronts. You I could handle. But you and Janice," Ethan shook his head, "I surrender."

"You lasted twenty-four hours longer than I thought you would."

Ethan finally turned around to confront his harasser. "Damned with faint praise. Better men than you have done it before and lived to regret it."

Sebastian stood erect. "I don't scare easily. And I don't take kindly to threats."

"Enjoy your victory, Sebastian. I'm sure it won't be long before you and Janice start squabbling over the spoils. It will get ugly."

"At least it will be a fair fight between two people who deserve a chance at the brass ring. There won't be any interlopers."

"Here's something for you, Sebastian." Ethan held up a workbook with a spiral coil. "Respect in the Workplace," said Ethan, reading the cover.

"That's rich coming from you, don't you think."

Ethan flipped it into the trash.

"Where will you go?" asked Sebastian.

"I'm not sure. Another newsroom inside Holy Mother Corp, I imagine. Probably Toronto. They're not as good at backstabbing there."

"Ah, yes," said Sebastian, "CBC Toronto—where your friends stab you in the front."

Ethan met his rival's eyes. "Why did you do it?"

Sebastian closed to within cuffing distance. "For one, you rubbed me the wrong way, but that wasn't the main reason." Sebastian wanted him to beg.

"Inquiring minds want to know," said Ethan.

"You simply walked in the room," said Sebastian. "You took something I wanted. I decided to take it back."

"I guess you can't blame a shark for being a shark."

"I have a question for *you* now. How did you get tangled up with that doctor over in Gaza?"

"I got caught in a firefight between some Palestinians and an Israeli patrol. Bullets flew like sleet. One grazed me in a delicate spot and Haifa sewed me up." Ethan put the cover on his box. "You've seen her eyes. One thing led to another."

"Did you really get your balls shot off?"

Ethan picked up his box. "You'll go to your grave not knowing." He headed for the exit sign.

"You coward," yelled Sebastian. "You don't have the balls to tell me."

Sebastian heard receding laughter.

●

Sebastian couldn't stand it any longer.

"Strawberries love a sunny, well-drained site," said Dan. "And lots of compost."

Dozy Dan was killing him with boredom. He had to be stopped. Sebastian invented deliverance:

The bamboo blowgun poked through a wall of pointy leaves. The Mother-in-Law's Tongue offered ample camouflage. Sebastian heard a whoosh. A quivering dart dipped in curare punctured Dozy Dan's neck. The poison paralyzed him before his hand could even touch the quivering feathers. He collapsed face-first into his leek soup. The gurgling was mercifully short.

"I'm expecting a bumper crop," said Dan.

A wall panel slid open without a sound. A black-clad figure, his face covered except for his eyes, skittered into the dining room. He removed a throwing-star from his sleeve. The sharpened points resembled a snowflake. "Dozy Dan-san," cried the ninja, catching the dupe in mid-slurp. Sebastian saw a glint, heard a rush of air. The star embedded into Dozy Dan's forehead. His head cracked back; his eyes turned vacant. His spoon tumbled into his leek soup, splattering his shirt. The ninja bowed to Sebastian before disappearing back inside the wall.

"I can't wait to slather them in fresh cream," said Dan.

Sebastian reached under the dining-room table and pressed the eject button. There was a piercing boing. Dozy Dan catapulted over Sebastian's head, hurtling through the front window before he even had time to scream. Glass sprayed into the street. Sebastian heard a distant thud and a car alarm siren. The spring-loaded seat reset.

"We'll have plenty of berries for making jam," said Dan.

"I've got an idea," said Penelope. "We'll give people strawberry jam as wedding favours."

"Brilliant," said Roxanne.

"We'll tie cotton caps on the mason jars with twine bows," said Penelope. "And attach tags saying Spread the Love."

"It doesn't get any better than that," said Sebastian. "Donna, will you help spread the love?"

Donna surfaced from her quinoa salad. "I think there's been enough love spread in this family."

Penelope drained her wine glass. "Let's make a deal, Donna. Help with the jam and I'll take both of you shopping in Toronto. Girls' weekend away. Shop 'till we drop on Queen Street West."

"I can be bought," said Donna. "Just this once."

Penelope patted Sebastian's thigh. "You wouldn't mind losing Roxanne for a weekend, would you Sebastian?"

"Not at all. I'm sure I'll find something to do to stay out of trouble."

"A man is allowed to get into a little trouble during his last days as a bachelor," giggled Penelope. She squeezed Sebastian's thigh.

Prudish Penelope is no prude when she gets a few in. Try showing some inhibition, please.

"I'd toast the road trip if I had some wine," said Penelope.

Sebastian lifted the bottle out of the wine bucket. It was empty. "I'll get another. Care to join me, Dan? I've got a secret stash in the basement."

Dan followed Sebastian downstairs to a wine rack, next to the shelves holding the Christmas decorations and a bag of hockey equipment.

"Do you still play?" asked Dan.

"At least once a week during the winter. I love to score."

"I catch the occasional Leafs' game. CBC has a suite." Dan shook his head with the pathetic dejection of a broken-hearted fan. "The sacrifices I make for this corporation."

"I know exactly what you mean."

Sebastian pulled out a wine. "Laroche Chablis. Will Penelope like this?"

"Lately she likes anything that comes out of a bottle with a cork."

"Is everything okay?"

"She's stressed about the wedding. Mother of the bride nerves, I guess. You'd swear Roxanne was the first daughter ever to get married on short notice."

Murky voices from the dining room migrated to the basement.

"I think we're both in for a lot of 'Yes, dear,'" said Sebastian. They shared a collegial laugh.

"Being away so much doesn't help," said Dan.

"Do you ever get tired of the commute?"

"Yes, but I don't tire of the pay cheque."

"I can't wait for my own commute."

"Sebastian, I'm afraid I have some bad news. Toronto has changed its mind about your secondment."

"What?"

"I probably shouldn't be the one telling you, but since you brought it up. It's all because of this fuss over Ethan."

"What does that have to do with me?"

"He has friends at *The National*. They hold you responsible."

"Me!" said Sebastian. His indignation filled the basement. "What proof do they have?"

"None. Just Ethan's word. Did you actually ask him if he got his balls shot off?"

"What! He's the consummate liar."

"Regardless, they believe him and resources have been reallocated, as they say."

"Let me see if I have this right. Ethan embarrasses the CBC, causes a furious backlash, resigns from *Here & Now* in disgrace and I'm the one who gets punished."

"I'm sorry, but it's out of my hands. I can't interfere. Everyone would scream nepotism."

"Let them scream. His friends can hurt me, but my future father-in-law can't protect me. They're reneging on an offer. And they get to do it with impunity, it seems."

"When things cool down, I'll twist a few arms. In the meantime, isn't there an anchor job open? Skate where the puck is going to be, Sebastian."

Sebastian shoved the Laroche Chablis back in the rack. "Let's try this Ontario Chardonnay. It's got a great nose."

●

France, Spain, or Italy? Roxanne wasn't sure where to go first. The wine rack needed restocking, so she planned to buy in all three countries. To break the stalemate, she relied on her personal maxim: when in doubt, go to Italy.

Roxanne pushed her shopping cart through the South America aisle, completely ignoring the substantial offerings from Argentina and Chile. She and Sebastian freely admitted to being old-world snobs when it came to wine. Argentina and Chile might be nice places to visit, but you wouldn't want to drink there.

She sailed around the Horn, bound for continental Europe. Roxanne dropped anchor beside the shelf holding Chianti. She picked up a Ruffino Classico. A guilty smile broke out, her cheeks went ruby. She covered her mouth, but her petite fingers couldn't hide the upturned corners of her lips. Sebastian had thrilled her body by pouring Chianti over it and lapping it clean. A wild night in bed, fuelled by splashes of Tuscany's finest vintage.

As great as Ruffino was, Roxanne had a budget. Three bottles in the cart and no more.

"Excellent wine, isn't it."

The blush drained from Roxanne's face; the smile dissolved. She swore she heard a rattlesnake rattle along with the familiar voice.

"Janice," said Roxanne, as she took down the last bottle. "What a surprise." The word pleasant was temporarily excised from her vocabulary.

"You're smart to stock up now before the wedding bills arrive. I hear a wedding can cost 30,000 dollars. Have you and Sebastian considered eloping? 30,000 dollars would pay for an incredible holiday in Italy. Why drink Chianti here when you can drink it in a Tuscan villa."

"We haven't decided on a honeymoon yet," said Roxanne. Janice's cart penned her in. Retreat offered the only escape route. She would make a strategic withdrawal before the viper could strike, but until then, ambiguity was her best defence. "I'm sure it will be some place romantic."

"Yes, Sebastian is all about the romance."

Roxanne squeezed the cart's handlebar and forced a smile.

"Have you picked the date yet?" asked Janice.

"It'll be sometime after the fall ratings. Sebastian doesn't want it said that he left CBC in the lurch."

"A white gown against the autumn colours; you will look spectacular," said Janice, using the hype of a fashion commentator. "I know this amazing bridal boutique on Bloor Street called Mariée. Tell Jean Claude that I sent you and you'll get a discount."

"Actually, I'm sewing my dress."

Janice's cheeriness evaporated. If Roxanne had realized that bursting Janice's bubble would be such fun she would have done it long ago.

"Of course you are," said Janice. "I suppose you're designing it too."

"I'm modifying a pattern. Something I can twirl in. I think making my own dress will be far more rewarding than buying something off the rack."

"I can't wait to see it," said Janice.

Roxanne kept her distance. The snake was lying in wait.

"We keep fluctuating between an intimate wedding with only close friends and family, and something splashier. Guest list etiquette requires more diplomacy than a UN resolution."

"I'm sure you'll dazzle them, no matter how big the crowd. Don't spare the makeup. Fake eyelashes are glamourous. Every guy in the room will swoon."

"I only want one guy in the room to swoon."

"I think all the women will swoon over that engagement ring. I've never seen one like it." Roxanne spread her manicured fingers, showing off a white-gold ring with a pink, oval stone. "What is it?"

"Rose quartz. It was my grandmother's. Opa gave it to her before he set sail for Canada after the war. They didn't see each other again for two years. She came to Halifax after he got settled. They married and had fifty-five years together. This ring is love."

"How precious," said Janice, "and Sebastian saved a fortune." Roxanne winced. "Any other traditions, Mrs. Hunter?"

"Actually, I haven't decided if I'm going to be Mrs. Hunter. I may keep my own name."

"Ah, the great debate." said Janice. "What's in a name?"

"Just my identity."

"I should let you go. I'm sure you've got a million things to do. If I could just reach past you for a bottle of Ruffino."

"Oh, I'm terribly sorry." Roxanne wheeled her cart out of the way.

"You know," said Janice, holding the bottle, "I introduced Sebastian to this wine. We shared a couple of glasses. He said you'd love it."

"When was that?" asked Roxanne as she laid the bottles flat in the cart, making sure the labels faced up.

"It was after Garrison Hill's funeral. Sebastian gave me a lift home. I gave him a nightcap."

Roxanne felt fangs puncture her heart. Pain, terrible pain. She leaned on the cart to keep her balance.

"Next stop," said Janice, "Bed Bath and Beyond. I need a new fitted sheet."

Poison flowed from the venom sacs, the way liquid squeezes through a needle. Drops pooled in the wound. Roxanne had no antidote. It was a lethal dose.

"Bye." Janice slithered away.

Roxanne rooted around her purse for her to-do list. Buy Wine was the first item. Buy Fitted Sheet was the second.

The crushed list bounced off the Ruffino bottles. She abandoned the cart.

•

Flags flapped overhead. Sebastian pushed up his sleeve and checked the time. 6:10. The rendezvous was scheduled for six. He decided to give him five more minutes. He scanned the network of sidewalks leading to the university's administration building. Apart from a couple of hand-holding students, they were empty. Sebastian shifted his weight on the park bench. This one was certainly not designed for comfort.

A Cadillac SUV turned into the circular driveway and stopped by Sebastian. The tinted window dropped.

"Better late than never," said Sebastian. "I was having my doubts."

"So was I," said Chief Paul Bennett. "Get in."

"Yes, sir," said Sebastian with a lackadaisical salute.

Sebastian buckled his seatbelt. The SUV followed the loop out to Elizabeth Avenue. Bennett drove for a block, saying nothing.

"It's your dime, Chief. Why did you call?"

"Do I have your word that nothing will be repeated?"

"I don't waste my time with off-the-record conversations, but I always protect my sources. I'll verify the information with someone else before using it."

"I don't like your approach."

"Take it or leave it. For all I know, you could be setting me up. I won't be anybody's patsy."

The chief's eyes nervously bounced from one side of the road to the other. "I don't want my name attached to this. Agree or get out."

"You'll be Deep Throat."

"I have a package for you in the glove compartment." Sebastian popped the tiny door. Inside was an envelope with a bulge.

"Doesn't feel like anthrax."

"I wish," said Bennett. "No, it's something you've been after."

Sebastian ripped open the envelope and tipped it. A flash drive fell into his palm. He closed a fist around it.

"This is a very strange thing for the chief of police to do," said Sebastian.

"I would agree, except I'm not the chief of police anymore." Sebastian's eyes went wide. "I resigned yesterday. The minister of justice will make it official tomorrow."

Sebastian held the flash drive between his thumb and forefinger. "I've got a pretty good idea what's on this, do you?"

"I thought it better not to ask. I was assured that the data was obtained legally."

"And you trust the people who said this?"

"I have to. I'm going to be working with them."

Sebastian shook his head. "Chief...I'll have to get used to not calling you that...Mr. Bennett, you've sold your soul to the devil."

"I don't agree. Politics can be a noble profession...with the right people."

"Like you."

"Yes, like me. I believe in the rule of law and in helping people who need help."

"You're tainted. Why do they want *you*?"

"Your idea that I do an interview turned out to be brilliant." Sebastian grimaced. "Everywhere I go people shake my hand and wish me well. People can forgive. My associates did some polling and I'm not quite the leper you think I am. They want me to run for office. I can't be chief of police anymore, but I'm too young to retire. There are still things I want to accomplish."

"Am I speaking with a future minister of justice?"

"No promises have been made."

"Forgive my cynicism. The rubes may buy it, but I don't."

Bennett stopped at a crosswalk, letting two kids scoot across the road.

"What about your drunk driving charge?" asked Sebastian.

"I'm flying to Florida next week. I've made a plea bargain. I'm pleading guilty and will be fined 2000 dollars. No jail time."

"I can see the campaign slogan now—Vote Bennett for Good Judgment."

"You haven't lost any of your sulfuric wit." Bennett circled back to the university.

Sebastian tossed the flash drive end over end, catching it on the fall. "This doesn't make any sense. They could have just mailed the flash drive. Why get you to deliver it?"

"It's a test to see if I have the stomach for it."

"Being a flunky?"

"No, dealing with reporters like you."

"Don't be too sanctimonious," warned Sebastian, hiding the flash drive in his pocket. "You've got yourself involved in a coup, and there will be blood."

"I'm sure you'll cover it to the last drop." The SUV parked by the bench where the drive began. Sebastian opened his door and pulled out his phone.

"I should get to work. I hear the chief of police has resigned and is changing careers."

"Don't believe everything you hear," said Bennett. "Best get a second source."

Sebastian shut the door and the SUV rolled away.

•

Sebastian threw his car keys in the wicker basket on the hall table.

"Roxanne, I'm home." The absence of a response surprised him. Her text said, 'Come straight home. Special treat for dinner.'

His nose told him nothing was cooking in the kitchen. His eyes confirmed it: a food-free stove and no Roxanne. The living and dining rooms were empty too. He walked down the hallway towards the closed bedroom door.

"Roxanne?" Silence. Sebastian inspected the walls and floor. No sign of a struggle. He reached for the doorknob, bracing himself in case something unpleasant waited on the other side. His apprehension was a legacy of reporting on too many break and enters gone bad. Drug-crazed perps with no conscience, caring only about stealing enough money to feed the habit. Homeowners sometimes got hurt.

Sebastian opened the door a crack. A hinge creaked. Roxanne had nagged him about oiling it. He saw a flickering light on the wall and used a foot to nudge the door wide, fists at the ready. Roxanne's naked body lay on the bed, stomach down, her head nuzzled into her folded arms near the footboard. A pose so relaxing she could have been sunning herself on a beach.

Lit candles glowed on both night tables. A tray sat on the bed holding a chocolate fondue heated by a tea light and a muffin pan filled with fruit. Pineapple chunks, strawberries, and banana slices were piled in the cups. Sebastian uncocked his arms.

Roxanne slid her hands under her chin and opened her eyes.

"Welcome home."

"Why didn't you answer when I called out?" asked Sebastian with a tinge of annoyance. Severe vexation wouldn't be prudent, not with a nude woman on his bed.

Roxanne propped herself up on her elbows. Her pert breasts drooped. "I thought a little intrigue would lure you in here." She mimed reeling in a fish.

"I'm happy to be caught, but what's the occasion?"

"Blame the marriage counsellor. She asked about our sex lives. I could only think of one event that made me blush. A young woman should have more than that. Something to remember fondly when she's old. And her man should have that same glow. This is a night to create new memories."

Sebastian undid his tie and lobbed it on the bed. Roxanne wrapped an end around each hand and snapped it taut.

"I've got an idea," she said, "let's be risqué."

"Who are you and what have you done with Roxanne?"

"Remember your fantasy about being tied up?" she murmured.

"I distinctly remember that suggestion getting a cold reception." He took a wary step closer.

"Maybe I've been too much the prude."

"You come by it honestly."

"It's just trashy fun. Toss me another tie and your wish might come true."

"You don't have an ice pick underneath the bed, do you?" Sebastian made an exaggerated bend and playfully stretched his neck, trying to detect a honed point in the shadows.

"It's been done already," said Roxanne.

Sebastian whipped his least favourite tie off the rack and sent it sailing towards the damsel who offered distress. The rest of his clothes came off with frantic speed, piling up on the floor.

Roxanne slid the food tray to her side of the bed and the bare

Sebastian lay on his. He reached back over his head and grabbed the ornate scrolls of the metal headboard. Roxanne lashed each wrist to a decorative tube. She used a bowline knot, a knot she learned as a kid on her father's boat. An easily tied knot that cannot slip.

"Comfortable?" asked Roxanne.

"Comfortable and hungry," said Sebastian.

Roxanne stabbed a strawberry with a bamboo skewer. She dipped it in the molten chocolate, coating the bottom half of the berry, making it as luscious as any in *Gourmet* magazine. The strawberry fluttered to Sebastian's mouth. Roxanne teased him, refusing to lower the strawberry past his yearning lips. Sebastian lunged at the strawberry, pulling it off the skewer with his teeth.

"Delicious," said Sebastian. His compliment was rewarded with pieces of pineapple and banana dripping with chocolate seduction.

"You're not eating," said Sebastian. "You're going to need your strength."

"I wanted to make sure that you were looked after first." Roxanne churned a finger in the dark, rich swirl. She licked it clean. "Perfect." She picked up the pot.

Sebastian followed the fondue with wide-eyed trepidation as it glided round his body. Roxanne suspended the flight over his chest. She tipped the pot just enough for a dollop to fall.

Sebastian sucked in as the chocolate landed on a nipple. Roxanne's tongue flirted around his breast.

"Pour it," he begged.

"Are you ready for the flood?"

"Yes," he said in a hush.

The fondue pot circled his upper chest before swerving south and stalling over his erect penis.

"That might be a tad sensitive for a fondue," he said.

"You're absolutely right." Roxanne swung across his thighs, her legs straddling his. She sat, pegging him to the bed. Sebastian gasped.

"They say cold water causes shrinkage," said Roxanne, "I wonder what happens with hot chocolate."

Roxanne tilted the fondue like a melting pot in a steel mill. Sebastian's inflated eyes followed a cascade of melted chocolate. The waterfall coated his penis.

"Jesus Christ," he shrieked, while thrashing about. Roxanne rode out the bucking. The bull couldn't throw the rider. Sebastian's penis shrivelled.

"Are you trying to burn the family jewels?"

Roxanne shrugged. "I think we've just redefined the term hothead."

"You *are* trying to burn the family jewels. What's going on?"

"Well, pouring Chianti over your genitals is passé."

"What are you talking about?"

"I know about you and Janice."

"Know what about me and Janice?"

"Flirting is one thing. Fucking is another."

"You've got it all wrong. Untie me, Roxanne. Let's talk this out."

She poked his flaccid penis with a skewer. Sebastian tensed. "You let the little head do the thinking for the big head," she said. "If I remember correctly, Lily Chin said the same thing about Ethan Tremblay. You two have more in common than I like."

"Roxanne, this is crazy."

Roxanne hopped off Sebastian. She pulled a suitcase out of the closet and laid it by the bed.

"When did I ever cheat on you?" asked Sebastian.

"Between burying your colleague and cuddling with me."

"That's not true. Did Janice tell you that?"

"Actually, she did in her coy, reptilian way."

Roxanne groped underneath the bed. Sebastian strained against the ties. "Relax. I'm not after an icepick." She retrieved a phone and dialled a number.

"Hi Daddy." Sebastian felt as weak as his penis. "Would you do me a favour, please? Sebastian is tied up and needs a helping hand. I've got an appointment."

"No-o-o-o," implored Sebastian quietly.

"He has to move some stuff out of the house. It shouldn't take long."

Sebastian only heard bits of the reply, but caught the phrase "one hour."

"Thanks so much, Daddy. I really appreciate it and Sebastian will too. The door will be unlocked. Just come on in." She touched End Call.

"Roxanne, you can't let your father see me like this."

"You're right." Roxanne used a skewer to flick his limp penis from the right thigh to the left. "That looks more natural, for a lefty." She gripped the skewer like a dart and let it fly. It landed in the fondue. "Such a waste of good chocolate."

"Roxanne, we can work this out. Don't throw our relationship away."

"I'm not the one who did that. I simply brought it to a head, so to speak. I'm having a shower and then I'm going out. Don't be here when I get back. Or next time, it will be an icepick."

Roxanne turned her back and walked to the door. "He'll be boring, Roxanne," said Sebastian. His words bricked the doorway.

"Whoever you end up with, he'll be boring. Dull. Insipid. He won't make you laugh. He won't know how to make a bouillabaisse. He won't know anything about Warren Zevon. He won't stand in the Sistine Chapel and describe how Michelangelo painted the hand of God. He won't make you glad that you're with him."

"You think you're the only man who knows French cuisine. You're the only art critic. You're the only witty guy. I don't think so. The next man I'm with will be all of that and so much more. And he won't break my heart." She walked out of the bedroom with poise.

"Come back, Roxanne," he pleaded. Sebastian threw his head back on the pillow and tested both knots with a tug. He wasn't going anywhere. Roxanne appeared in the doorway. His heart raced.

"By the way, I've never liked Warren Zevon. We were both living a lie." Roxanne vanished.

"You bitch," he whispered.

●

Janice rapped on the apartment door for the second time.

"Hello."

No response. She knocked again, more loudly than before.

"Open up, Sebastian. I know you're in there. Your car is outside."

The door opened but came up solid against the security chain. "Go away," said a mousy voice. "Leave me alone."

"Let me in. I just want to make sure you're okay."

"You're hearing me," said Sebastian, "so you know I'm alive. Misery does not love company at the moment."

"I brought something to cheer you up." Janice passed a magazine through the crack.

The door closed. Janice heard the chain sliding out of the track. The open door revealed a sour Sebastian holding a Victoria's Secret catalogue.

"Very funny."

"It's a reminder there are plenty of fish in the sea. And some of them dress like that."

"I don't feel like fishing at the moment."

"You're worse off than I thought. This requires an intervention. Can I come in?"

Sebastian stepped back. Janice spied empty Chinese food tubs stacked on the kitchen counter and beer bottles by the garbage can. Sections of the *New York Times* lay strewn across the coffee table and one hung over a sofa arm.

"I love what you've done to the place."

"Did you say intervention or imposition?"

Janice brushed the stubble on his face, making a bristle sound.

"Did you break your razor?"

"I have no close-ups today. Shaving can wait."

"It looks quite good on you, actually. I could get used to a beard."

Sebastian pulled two beer out of the fridge and held them up. Janice shook her head so he put one back. The kitchen clock said 12:10.

"If I make it to noon before the first beer," said Sebastian, "I consider it an alcohol free day."

Janice laughed. Sebastian popped the cap off his Steam Whistle and took a swig.

"Why are you here, Janice?"

"To talk some sense into you. It's time for you to end your period of confinement."

"I'm not pregnant, I'm depressed."

"Stop whining. You're better off without her. She'd only hold you back. Endless family dinners, kids puking up on you, a house with a swing set, summers at the cottage, a career steeped in the mundane. Goodbye Beijing. Goodbye Jerusalem."

Sebastian pointed the longneck of his beer at Janice. "You're the reason she threw me out."

"Me! That's rich. Did you really think you could fuck anyone you wanted and Roxanne would say, 'That's okay, honey, a man has his needs.'"

"She wasn't supposed to find out."

"I guess some of your investigative skill rubbed off on her."

"I love her," pined Sebastian.

"It's amazing you can say that without the slightest embarrassment."

Sebastian slammed the bottle down on the kitchen counter. "I *do* love her."

"Stop pretending. This has more to do with rejection than love. A piece of you is wounded alright—your ego. Stop crying in your beer. She did you a favour. She didn't just throw you out; she threw you into a life raft. You would have drowned, taken down by the maelstrom of matrimony."

"Nothing comes without struggle and sacrifice. It was the perfect arrangement. And while you might not see its virtues, I certainly do. I'd like to get it back."

Sebastian's phone vibrated. He snatched it off the counter. Puzzlement tramped across his face.

"It's a text from Roxanne's mother. She wants to meet me."

"Don't go. It will not end well."

"I have to know what she wants."

"Save what's left of your dignity and tell her no."

"Penelope could be the emissary. Maybe Roxanne realizes that she went too far. Penelope might have an olive branch."

"Careful she doesn't slap your face with it," said Janice.

●

Sebastian leafed through a copy of *Around Town*. The irony wasn't lost on him. He hadn't been anywhere in days, much less around town. He was living the life of a hermit. No live bands, no artists' openings, no film festivals, no dating, and no sex. A more appropriate masthead would have been *Celibate & Cloistered*.

"Would you like to…oh, it's you," said the waitress, lowering her order pad.

"A latte, please."

"Let me guess, no Snoopy."

"If it's not too much trouble."

"I'm sure we can manage a fern."

Sebastian used the newspaper as a screen, hiding from the café hubbub. His eye stopped at the sex column: Carnal Counsellor.

> *Dear Carnal,*
>
> *My boyfriend cheated on me with several women. He's begging me to take him back. He's a louse of a person, but great in bed. What do you think?*
>
> *Having Second Thoughts*
>
> ####################
>
> *Dear Having Second Thoughts,*
>
> *The guy is pond scum. Forget him. There are men who are both great in bed and faithful. Hold out for one of those.*

"Hello, Sebastian."

Sebastian jerked the paper shut. Prudish Penelope hovered over him. Sebastian jumped to his feet, but was uncertain how to greet her. In times past, he would have kissed her cheek. Given the circumstances, it might appear too familiar. He considered a handshake. Too stand-offish for a woman he used to kiss. He opted for a simple gesture.

"Please, sit down," he said, pointing at the empty seat. Penelope laid an office envelope on the placemat as she pulled out the chair.

Sebastian heard a cup and saucer rattling. A shaky hand carried his coffee; the waitress had an exaggerated tremble. He imagined the cup wobbling off the saucer into his lap, so he laid the newspaper on his pants for protection. The caffeine calamity veered off at the last moment and touched down safely on the table.

"I'm so nervous," said the waitress. "It's not every day we get a TV celebrity in here." She took out her pad and pen with rock solid hands. "Would you like anything, Ma'am?"

"No, thank you. I won't be staying long." Penelope, ever discreet, waited until the waitress left. "No hot chocolate today?"

Sebastian brought his knees together. He hadn't expected cheekiness, but he remained stoic. "Penelope, I'd like to sort some things out."

"Me too."

"Roxanne has made a terrible mistake. She thinks I've cheated on her. I never have."

Penelope appeared unconvinced. Sebastian continued to tap dance. "This is all a simple misunderstanding."

The group at the next table burst into rowdy laugher as if they were in on the fraud.

"I can explain everything if she'd only see me, but she won't even answer my messages."

"This is exactly why I've come," said Penelope. "There certainly has been a misunderstanding."

Sebastian relaxed. *The cream puff on the menu wasn't the only one in the café.*

"The message is just not getting through," said Penelope.

The barista purged the steam wand on the espresso machine. A scalding hiss whistled through the café clatter.

Penelope leaned in. "I want to be perfectly clear."

The barista frothed milk in a steel pitcher. The whirlpool created a sucking sound.

"Leave… my… daughter… alone."

"What?"

The barista banged the pitcher on the counter three times. Milk bubbles popped. So did Sebastian's cockiness.

"Stop sending Roxanne messages. Cut all attempts at contact. Disappear from her life."

"I don't understand," said Sebastian. Prudish Penelope showed none of her usual persona—the doting matriarch who said things like, 'Sebastian, you're so funny,' 'Sebastian, you look handsome,' 'Sebastian, come sit by me.' He didn't recognize her.

"I had hoped you would go away quietly. But you ignored the warnings."

"What warnings?" huffed Sebastian.

Penelope untied the string on the envelope and folded the flap back.

She pulled out a piece of glass the size of a fingernail and laid it in front of Sebastian. He used his thumb and forefinger to hold it up to the sunlight streaming through the window. The clue was lost on him.

A second dive into the envelope produced a lipstick tube. Penelope removed the cap and turned the base. A scarlet bullet poked up. She placed the upright tube next to the glass fragment. Sebastian's eyes still flickered bafflement.

The envelope of tricks rustled as Penelope yanked out a photo and slid it across the table with her fingertips. He tilted the glossy print to get a better look. Sebastian and the eight by ten stared at each other. The photo said DOES ROXANNE KNOW ABOUT YOUR SECRET LOVE?

The barista yelled, "Our latte art special today is The Scream."

"You," said a flabbergasted Sebastian. "Why?"

"Because you cheated on my daughter."

"You're wrong, Penelope." Sebastian drew in a breath for more distortions, half-truths and outright fabrications.

"Stop the lies," barked Penelope. "I've been on to you since your fling with the redhead in Paradise Point. A friend in the bar tipped me off. I had a text before you and the harlot were out the door."

Sebastian stiffened. "That's your proof—a text from a gossip in a bar."

"I was inclined to give the benefit of the doubt, but then Roxanne just happened to mention seeing you hug a redhead in the CBC lobby. I decided you needed scrutiny."

Penelope pulled more photos out of the envelope and shook them at Sebastian. "At least the redhead had good taste in clothes, even if she couldn't keep them on. But Janice Stone, she dresses like the skank that she is."

Sebastian snatched the photos. He and Janice were in full lust outside her apartment—torrid embraces and deep kisses.

"You took these?"

"A private investigator. You must have been so grief stricken after Garrison's funeral that you lost your senses. What else could possibly explain tonguing Jezebel on her doorstep? What is it you reporters call this—the money shot?"

Sebastian touched the piece of glass. "You broke my headlight."

"Shocking isn't it, what some people will do for money," said Penelope.

"You put your daughter's name on a billboard."

"Yes, that was a bit rash. But one doesn't think straight when one's blood is boiling. You ignored the lipstick. I couldn't arrange a voice in a burning bush. A digital billboard seemed the next best thing. By the way, you get full marks for ingenuity, distracting Roxanne the way you did. Well done."

Penelope stacked the photos. "Roxanne hasn't seen the photos, but she will, if necessary. I'll give her the mettle to resist you. I'll hurt her to save her." Penelope turned away. "And I'll hurt her to save myself."

Sebastian looked confused. "Excuse me?"

"I was smitten with you, Sebastian. I tried to deny it. I tried to fight it. I couldn't. You didn't just break Roxanne's heart, you broke mine too."

Sebastian fell back. "The cougar and the cub loved me."

"I could stand aside for Roxanne, but not for the tarts. Those sluts destroyed our relationship."

"We never had a relationship," argued Sebastian.

"You're right, we didn't have sex," said Penelope. Sebastian shuddered. "But you touched my soul. I adore your wit, your intelligence, the way your hair curls, and God forgive me, those engorged chest muscles. You only had to be faithful to Roxanne in order for us to have spiritual love. But your libido got in the way. You couldn't keep it in your pants, could you? You ruined everything."

"Make things right with Roxanne and I promise to be a new man. It can be the way it was."

"How gullible do you think I am?"

"Make things right with Roxanne or I'll tell her what you told me, every salacious detail of your forbidden love."

"That's the Sebastian I've come to know and loathe. She'd never believe you and I'd deny it. Besides, you're forgetting about the photos. If you don't leave without a trace, these tawdry pictures will be delivered to every CBC email account in the country. I already have the addresses. There are *some* perks to being married to a CBC vice-president."

Penelope pushed her chair back and stepped away. Sebastian stayed sitting, his pretend chivalry exhausted.

"You can keep the photos," said Penelope. "I have plenty of copies."

●

Dumped. Humiliated. Blackmailed.

The abuse ends today.

Sebastian had been ordered to The Executioner's office. The summons came on official CBC stationery, signed by Alicia Gorski, Regional Director. Sebastian peered through a newsroom window. No gallows erected yet, but he'd swing at high noon. That is, if he let them. He threw the letter into the garbage can.

"What's going to happen?" asked Janice.

"They'll give me a fair trial and then they'll hang me. They want a scapegoat. They blame me for Ethan being run out of town."

"Don't you think they might be right about that," suggested Janice.

"Comme ci, comme ça."

Sebastian held up his iPhone. "I've been working on a commemorative scrapbook." He touched a scissors icon and then a photo of Ethan Tremblay on the *Here & Now* set. The photo peeled back and music started.

"There's a Warren Zevon tune for every occasion." Sebastian sang along.

Dry your eyes, my little friend,

Let me take you by the hand.

Photos of Ethan floated through the screen, along with headlines culled from newspapers and websites.

Laughing Ethan. *Here & Now Anchor Offends Everybody*

Apathetic Ethan. *Anti-Tremblay Alliance Demands Apology*

Irate Ethan. *Anchor pleads innocence: 'I've been set up.'*

Contrite Ethan. *CBC Host says 'I'm sorry.'*

Gloomy Ethan. *Signing Off: Tremblay Resigns*

"Photo manipulation can be such fun," said Sebastian.

Look around, my little friend.

Jubilation in the land.

"I'm not going down, Janice. They forget. I'm an excitable boy."

When Johnny strikes up the band.

Sebastian turned up the volume on the guitar solo and listened until the final notes died away. The time was 12:05.

"The Executioner hates tardiness," said Sebastian. "She should be sufficiently galled by now."

"Be evil," said Janice, with none of the usual frivolity. "I like that in a man."

Sebastian rehearsed his lines one last time. They would be his armour. The door to The Executioner's office was open. Alicia Gorski was flanked by Evan Forbes and Ruth Jazmin, the human resources manager. All three had their hands folded on Alicia's oak desk.

And to think I accused Roddy of being a trained monkey. See no evil, hear no evil, speak no evil.

A lonely chair waited for Sebastian. "Nice to see that it doesn't have wrist and ankle straps."

"Thank you for coming, Sebastian," said Alicia, "though maybe it's best to leave the absurdity outside. We could have gone on without you, but it's better that you're here. You're allowed union representation if you wish."

Sebastian waved off the suggestion.

"I'll recap the reasons for this disciplinary hearing. You made confidential matters public without authorization and you engaged in conduct contributing to workplace violence." Evan and Ruth nodded gravely.

"Proof," snorted Sebastian.

Alicia swung the monitor arm so Sebastian could see. "The IT department loves a challenge and you certainly gave it to them."

Sebastian watched the notorious YouTube video of Ethan's mock headlines.

"A girl can change her mind. A transgender activist sticks with the bird in the bush."

Ruth puckered her lips. Evan cleared his throat. Alicia's body constricted before she hit pause.

"IT ran the video through software capable of analyzing individual pixels," said Alicia. Sebastian leaned forward. "It could see dots on top of dots, and take away the dots we didn't want."

The screenshot dissolved to reveal a faint image. Hair, forehead, eyes, hands holding an iPhone. Sebastian's camera had caught his own reflection.

"That's incredible technology," said Sebastian. "Does CSI know about this?" Ruth threw up her hands.

"Sebastian, this is serious," snarled Alicia. "Do you have anything to say?"

"Anchors shouldn't say stupid things into a microphone."

"You would know that better than most," said Alicia.

"We're suspending you for a week without pay, starting today," said Ruth. "And you'll write a letter of apology to Ethan Tremblay. If you refuse, you'll be terminated."

Sebastian pulled an iPhone out of his pocket. His fingers strutted across the screen. "You might want to rethink that." He kept typing.

Alicia slapped her desk. "We're not negotiating here."

"I'll take the suspension, but as for the apology, and I mean this in the nicest possible way, Ethan Tremblay can go fuck himself."

Ruth leapt to her feet. "We're done here."

Sebastian finally lifted his eyes. "If you fire me, who will tell the loyal *Here & Now* viewers about the premier's cocaine addiction?"

Ruth sat down. Both she and Alicia turned to Evan. "What the hell are you talking about?" asked Evan.

"She's a coke head."

Evan the jurist transformed into Evan the executive producer. "You've said that before, but didn't have a scintilla of proof. I don't suppose you have a Rob Ford-like video, do you?"

"Actually I do. I have tape of her buying cocaine from a known drug dealer."

Evan beamed. "You have the money shot."

"We're not here to discuss the newscast," interrupted Alicia. "We're here to discuss Sebastian's discipline."

Sebastian laid his phone on Alicia's desk. Send filled the screen. His index finger hovered over the word like it was a detonation button.

"Wouldn't it be a shame," he said, "if the competition got this video. Can you imagine what Peter Mansbridge will say if he sees it on CTV and Global, and CBC has nothing? He'll be incensed. He'll be shouting, 'How did this happen? Who's responsible? Someone needs to be fired.'"

"This is blackmail," said Alicia.

"No, this is negotiation," said Sebastian. His finger quivered. "Start the suspension next week. Make it two weeks if you like. In the meantime, we have a good old-fashioned scandal to lead *Here & Now*. Every newsroom in the country will want this story. You can topple a premier today. Or you can topple me. Your choice."

The axis of no evil looked astounded. Alicia's head swivelled between her colleagues.

"Two weeks suspension, no grievance," insisted Alicia.

"I could use the holiday," said Sebastian.

"I don't like it, but I can live with it," said Ruth.

"Get your story lawyered," ordered Evan.

Sebastian took his finger away from the trigger and bolted for the newsroom.

Sebastian Hunter is not fading to black.

[acknowledgements]

Sebastian Hunter is an unscrupulous rake. He's not entirely my fault. I had help. *The Money Shot* was born in a novel-writing workshop. Colleagues Linda Abbott, Bridget Canning, Susan Flanagan, Lesleyanne Ryan, and instructor Paul Butler were particularly malevolent in their suggestions. Thank you.

My writing might never have found a wider audience if not for the Writers' Alliance of Newfoundland and Labrador. I was picked to be an apprentice in the 2014 Mentorship Program and was paired with Ed Riche. It was at this point my wife gave up all hope that I would use my power for good instead of evil. She feared Ed's wicked sense of humour and considerable talent would only encourage the worst in me. She was right.

I'm blessed with an inordinately high number of friends skilled in critiquing and proofreading. Ellen Alcock, Bruce Bourque, Ron Crocker, Marlene Dale, Sheila Fitzpatrick, Susan Follett, Fred Greening, Susan Howard, Marie Thompson, and Derek Yetman all saved me from myself countless times.

Thank you to the team at Breakwater Books. Editor James Langer made *The Money Shot* a better written book, while graphic designer Rhonda Molloy made it look sharp.

The characters in *The Money Shot* are fictional, but Bruce, Joan, Rod, and Ted really do exist. Chasing the money shot at CBC was easier because of you. Thanks for letting me use your names.

Lastly, you can't write a novel without a supportive partner, even one dreading the final product. Despite her misgivings, Deb left me alone to create a nasty Sebastian. The things wives do for their husbands.

Photo © Paul Daly

Glenn Deir is a former CBC television reporter who lives in St. John's. He used three decades worth of journalistic black humour to write *The Money Shot*. His memoir, *Sick Joke: Cancer, Japan and Back Again*, was short-listed for a Newfoundland and Labrador Book Award for non-fiction.